CHAPTER ONE

It was raining. Not the gentle spring rain that encouraged trees to bud and grass to turn from brownish-yellow to fresh green. This was a hard, cold rain accompanied by lightning, thunder and tornado force winds that blew the rain parallel to the ground. The driver side window was slightly open, the sharp, almost metallic smell from the thunder and lightning, with undertones of old asphalt and overtones of beaten down, wet grass slid in.

The aroma of the outside almost overcame the odor which impregnated the interior of the vehicle. It was a slight mouldy bouquet that crept up slowly. The scent of stale cigarette smoke, the hint of piss, mixed with the copper stink of blood and the stench of despair. Over all was the reek of the cheap perfume. The prostitutes used a lot in an attempt to disguise the foulness of being considered nothing more than tools used to quench lust and depravity.

There was no one else on the road, not surprising, given the foul weather plus it was two hours on the other side of midnight. They drove up Seventeenth Street, the light turned red for northbound Seventeenth Street at Christopher Columbus Blvd. N.W. The driver of the vehicle slowed and then stopped. No other cars, no headlights, no brake lights just the blurry, rain soaked, red of the stoplight.

"Kind of an oxy-moron us stopping here when we haven't seen another vehicle for hours." Harry Tungston, who was riding shotgun, pointed out to his rookie partner, who was driving.

"Well, it is a red light." Constable Xavier O'Malley said stiffly, as he felt a flush of embarrassment creeping up the back of his neck and start to leak onto his ears.

"Live a little kid, I promise this will not go on your probation report."

Xavier tried to shrug nonchalantly as he put the police half-wagon in gear and drove slowly through the red light. His vice like grip on the steering wheel of the van gave him away and elicited a low chuckle from his officer-coach.

"Don't worry I'm 'standing six' for you.

"Ah…standing what?"

"Standing six, its slang, coined by criminals, basically means being the look-out who warns the other bad-guy or guys that are involved in some type of criminal act that the police are coming. Then the bad-guys can flee before the police know what's going on."

Xavier, slowed the van, to listen to more of Harry's 'Pearl's of Wisdom.' Lucky, he thought, getting Harry as my second Officer-Coach. A legend when I was going through police collage, instructors were always telling 'Harry Tungston' stories. Funny, he's actually like that."

"Lets go down-town, see if we can find some action, anything is better than driving through red lights, empty streets and no calls. Maybe we will get some coffee for us and for some friends. Do you know much about informants and getting information Xavier?" Harry asked as he turned and looked at him.

"Just what I learned in police collage, which was pretty much nothing. We got told that dealing with informants was something we might get involved with when we were a lot more senior on the job. Instructors always seemed kinda nervous about the subject when it was brought up, which of course made some of us real curious."

"Well, I happen to like working my informants, and there are all sorts of ways of gathering intelligence, so call yourself senior and be ready to learn. You know what a prostitute is?"

"Hooker, whore, Ho; sure I do although my dear, sainted mother would faint dead away if she knew I know about those sinners that frequent the night. Mind you she has one son who is a priest, as pure as the driven snow, so she figured she could sacrifice one son to a 'worldly' profession. My mother knew she had no excuse to keep me from following in dad's footsteps and becoming a police officer. You gotta know that the Irish, according to my mother, have only three professions; priests, police officers and those who went over to the dark side; that being the Irish Gangs. Luckily she ran out of sons and ended up with a Priest and a Police Officer." Xavier said with an overdone Irish brogue.

Harry laughed and shook his head before answering, "Geez Xav, I always thought your mother's way of thinking went out with the potato famine and the 'Troubles'. Of course, ninety some odd years ago when the Police Force was in the early days of its formation, Scots, English and Irish or black Irish (he nudged Xavier and smiled as he looked at Xavier's blue-black hair), all of whom were Masons, were the only ones that were hired as police officers."

"Yes, my father started just at the end of that era, early seventies or there-abouts. He was only five foot eleven and the rest of the policemen called him 'shorty' because most of them were over six feet. I was only five years old at the time. Huh…funny when he died they even put that nickname on his tombstone, with mother's permission of course."

Geeze I haven't thought of dad's nickname or the funeral in a long time, Xavier thought with a sudden stab of sadness. The day they buried dad I think most of mother's joy and happiness got buried with him. His thoughts drifted further into old memories, old pain thinking of how little of the gentleness and none of the laughter remained just the strict, fanatical adherence to the Roman Catholic Faith and all the Latin mumbo-jumbo. Shit, I am supposed to go over on days off because Sebastian is home from the Vatican seminary for a visit. Maybe I could find a way to disappear on my days off? Gotta find some excuse. Something. Anything, to avoid going over to that plastic wrapped mausoleum, that my mother calls a house.

Harry's voice broke into Xavier's reverie.

"Xavier? Xav!"

"What? Oh sorry?" Xavier said.

"Wool gathering were you? Turn here and go east down Third Avenue; I want to see who is around the stroll tonight."

"Around? There won't be anybody out tonight." Xavier said.

"Really? Look without being too obvious. Always be aware of your surroundings. Never mind what's inside this Police vehicle; especially the computer. Too many have listened to the 'siren's song' that is the computer and never truly know where they are or what is happening around them. Some of those are the ones who get themselves promoted real fast, not mind you, because they know how to do police work. They just know how to make it looks like they are the ones doing the police work. You don't seem to be one of those types, thankfully; now tell me what you see outside."

"Well, we seem to be in the midst of a rain-storm of epic proportions, but I've counted three ladies of the evening. Two are tucked into the lee of the building on the south side of Third Street and there is a little one wearing a red, short jacket just inside the parkade on the north side. I haven't seen any of their pimps around though."

"Very good, partner. The two on the south side are Susie and Linda is the name of black one. Lenny, their pimp, is at home, keeping the home fire's burning and high on coke. Those two ladies know how much money they need to make to keep him happy. The pretty, little one in red is relatively new to the stroll and keeps to herself. She looks youngish but with some of 'The People' you just can't tell, doesn't talk much either. Other than her name we don't know much about her. I don't see her pimp, Big Willy, around tonight either. Lets drive over to the Mac's and get some coffees."

"What's her name?"

"Oh, uh Rose, Rosie something like that, I think."

Xavier parked the half-wagon and they both stretched as they stepped down, and then walked into the Mac's store. Xavier got two coffees for Harry and himself while Harry bought three other coffees plus packets of sugar and powdered cream.

Once they had the coffees they drove back around the block and parked on the north side of Third Avenue by the parkade. Harry gestured to the two prostitutes on the south side of the street while Xavier rolled down his window and called to the one on the north side. The two on the south side didn't need to be asked twice and hurried over and climbed into the half-wagon and sat on the bench seat behind the front seats. Rose hesitated, and then slowly walked over. All three were shivering from the cold rain and the bitter wind. Harry turned and gave them each a large coffee.

"Th…Th…Thanks Harry you're the best, any time you need some 'sugar' you come to me and I'll do ya for free. Black folk are not made for this cold or at least me and my black ass aren't." Linda shivered as she tried to wrap her short, tight, rabbit skin jacket tighter around her buxom breasts, which were barely contained by a tight, purple polyester shirt.

"Same here, Harry and I'll even do your pretty rookie for free too." Susie laughed as she squeezed onto the back seat, holding the large coffee wrapped in both hands and as close too her-self as she dared. While Rose climbed over both of them and settled the bench seat behind Xavier.

"Oh my darlings, your offers are tempting, and stir yearnings that I dare not yield too, for as you know my wife is a police officer as well. She carries a gun and does everything but dust me for prints when I get home." Harry said with a laugh that Susie and Linda joined in on. They both continued to giggle, and it was the sound of fresh teenage girls. They started to gossip with Harry and every once in a while Harry would say something that caused them to giggle again.

Xavier was glad he was sitting in the driver's seat and slightly twisted so his face was mostly in the shadow, they could see his smile but couldn't see his face flush at the 'pretty rookie' comment. He was a quiet participant as he watched Harry work his magic.

He is kind and these women see that, he thought. Harry gives them an 'out', he is not a john, their pimp nor is he busting them as a police officer. They sense his kindness and treat him like a friend that they chatter with. Their prattle is full of excellent intelligence though and Harry only really has to say a few funny things every once in a while. The only one who isn't talking is Rose sitting in the darkened corner behind me. Funny, there is something about her.

Rose had added nothing to the light-hearted conversation but sat there listening; she relaxed a little after she had watched Harry for a few minutes. A hint of a smile touched her lips as she turned and looked at Xavier.

Xavier had felt Rose's eyes on him and turned to her. He couldn't explain or even understand why all of a sudden he felt a warmth, a kind of internal, ancient sense recognition when their eyes met. Odd, it feels as if I've known her for a long time.

"Your partner is goodhearted, I have not seen those two ever sound that happy. Happy is a rare word or feeling down here." Rose said in a voice that slid under the louder conversation and reached only Xavier's ears.

"Yes he is and I am very lucky to have him as a partner."

As they drank the last dregs of their coffee they noted that the wind was abating somewhat. Time to get back to work, although the three in the back seat were loath to leave the warmth and laughter they had found for such a short time.

"Stay safe ladies." Harry said as he jumped out and gallantly slid the rear, side passenger door open for them.

"You to Harry. I don't understand half of what you say but it sure sounds nice." Susie said as the three of them got out and started to walk across the street.

Harry jumped back into the front passenger seat while Xavier put the half-wagon in gear. Both could smell the cheap perfume, wet rabbit skin and the vinyl smell of the thigh high 'ho' boots that Susie had been wearing.

"Pull over after we get out of the area and we'll talk."

Xavier nodded his head as he turned left onto Center Street, north-bound across the Lion's Gate bridge and up into north end of the city. He finally turned onto a quiet street, pulled over and stopped.

"So what did you think of our coffee stop?" Harry asked as he turned to look at Xavier.

"The biggest thing I learned was it's a lot easier and cheaper to treat people with respect. After those three women figured out that you weren't interested in busting them or having sex with them they relaxed and started to enjoy the coffee break. You really got them chatting or at least that's what they thought. There was some interesting intelligence mixed in with their small talk."

"Ah, yes, gossip-murder by language," Harry muttered before asking, "Such as?"

"About a robbery suspect whose weapon was a knife, he used the money for drugs, oh yeah and where the knife is stashed. Also about a pimp who laid a licking so severe on one of his girls that she nearly died. She is in hiding but so steaming mad at him for messing up her face that she might testify against him. I noticed that you gave Susie your number on a scrape of paper in case that hooker needs some help. Oh, and something about a missing girl but I didn't catch all of it."

Harry, who had been making notes of the conversation with Linda and Susie

while Xavier talked, nodded his head several times.

"You have good ears, Xavier, and have managed to distinguish between the wheat and the shaft, for the most part. And what should we do with this information?"

"Well, I know you've told me while information or intelligence gained from hookers is usually good, forget them testifying, too dangerous for them. They would disappear, not necessarily of their own volition.

Although most of that conversation was hearsay we can look at it as confirming other evidence we have or know. Such as the information about the hooker who got beat up, I don't think we will hear anymore about the incident, unless she calls us about some unrelated stuff. Maybe she'll call us about her pimp's drug-dealer for revenge, or some such. It was good that you gave her a number on a scrap of paper and not one of your cards. I've heard that hookers have been killed for less.

The suspect for the robbery and where the knife is stashed; we should be able to work something out with that since you have a name and where the weapon is. Have to go through the reports though and as for the missing girl, I seem to recall a juvie hooker that disappeared a while back."

"Very good, Xav. Now I have to discuss a few things with you before we carry on with this conversation. First off, I am not planning to do anymore Officer Coaching; I am burned out and tired of not being able to work my snitches. I am looking for a partner who works the way I do. You seem to fit the bill. There also seems to be enough of the Irish imagination left in you, so that some things that may seem strange to others, like tonight's coffee break with some 'Ladies of the Night' you seem to understand. Plus there is something about you that puts 'down and outers' even that little 'Ho', who is one of 'The People' seem comfortable around you and they don't trust anybody. The added bonus here is that you're junior so in a way I will still be training you."

"What? You want to work with me? Great! I mean yes. Shit yeah, this will be great and learn more about informants…" Xavier babbled a big grin creasing his face?

"Well then we are partners, hopefully until I retire," Harry returned with a smile.

CHAPTER TWO

Xavier and Harry did indeed work as partners for the next few years. At first they worked in uniform and Harry showed Xavier how an officer in an unmarked car will be spotted by the local citizens and criminals almost instantly, while they could drive around the area in a marked unit and not even be given a passing glance. Harry said it was because they were part of the background, they were expected to be there. He also pointed out that most bad guys weren't that bright, although there were exceptions, and some were just too lazy to get a real job.

In fact they were so much a part of the area they worked in that they actually caught one bad-guy breaking into a house. He had been half way through a window when the window slipped, wedging him in.

"Got locked out of your house, did ya?" Harry asked casually as he stood on the grass at one side of the outside of the window watching the backside and helplessly kicking legs of the bad-guy while Xavier stood on the other side holding his hand over his mouth so the stuck culprit couldn't hear his laughter.

"Why yeah, exactly what I did" the culprit wheezed, the heavy window and his intoxication starting to cut off his breathing.

"Well sir, you wouldn't mind telling us your address then?"

There was a pregnant pause, during which time Harry and Xavier smirked at each other.

"Ya know this here window is getting kinda heavy. Makes it sorta hard for a guy too think."

"Awe take a guess."

" 2011- ah-Nowell Rd.?"

Xavier and Harry burst out laughing as they helped the Culprit out of the window. The address there was actually was 6248 48 Ave NW.

"Not even close 'Buckwheat'," Xavier said between bursts of laughter as they searched and cuffed him.

"I know'd you cops have been following me but just can't keep up so ya missed a lot of stuff. Ya just got lucky tonight."

"If we've been following you as you say and missed what you've been doing; just to prove that, you should show us where else you broke into that we never caught you at." Xavier said.

"All right I just will" with that the culprit by the name of Jimmy Falks showed them the other twenty break and enters that he had committed in the last three weeks.

Harry and Xavier managed to keep straight faces until they had locked that particular bad-guy up. Jimmy Falks only found out about their deception, such as it was, when they stood up in court and explained the situation to the judge. The bad-guy was so incensed at their tricking him that he insisted the Harry and Xavier had somehow entrapped him.

The Judge had to explain several times that the only person who trapped him was himself when he got stuck in the window. Of course during the court case there had been several police officers sitting at the back of the courtroom, waiting for their cases to be heard, and some had to leave because they were snickering so hard that the judge had been forced to give them several stern looks.

Shortly after the conviction and lengthy jail time given to Jimmy Falks they were called into their District Inspector's office. Both of them were trying to figure out what they had done wrong. Most police officers deal in the truth, however, when interviewing suspects to whom lying is part of their very nature. Getting a confession from culprits may involve coloring the truth or out and out lying. In fact it may boil down to who tells the better, most believable story.

There were tales of some 'brilliant' detectives who had actually written a confession out that stated the culprit's partner in crime had done the criminal deed alone. The detective, who had written out the confession then when into an interview with the partner and shown him the phony confession, the partner was so incensed at the betrayal that he had rolled (confessed) not knowing that the confession was false because his buddy in crime was illiterate. There were many tricks of the trade as long as you didn't coerce the culprit. The police accepted the dichotomy for the most part, but it made them notoriously paranoid because they walk a very thin line, and sometimes they might slip a little, while catching the criminals. That didn't seem the case this time because the Inspector seemed down right jovial, either that or they had been caught big time for slipping over the line.

"I heard you two having been doing a great job at catching criminals, in fact I have some 'Atta-Boys' (praise noted in your permanent file paper indicating the actions taking and the resulting success, or transversely, an Awe Shit implying what a fuck up you are), "for you to read and sign." Xavier and Harry both gave an internal sigh of relief, as both thought of the times where there had been minor slippage onto the wrong side of the line, they signed the Atta-Boys without a twinge of guilt.

"Sit down, sit down, I have a proposal for you two." The District Inspector caught the worried look Harry and Xavier exchanged and sighed before saying "Don't worry it's nothing onerous and I think you two will be perfect for this job. There are few on this job that I trust completely you two happen to be on that list."

"Okay then, lets hear it, sir." Harry said as he gingerly sat on the edge of the chair while Xavier nodded subconsciously he sat down.

"As you know break and enters are up, in fact most crime is up, we just don't have the money to put the big teams with surveillance and snitches together." The Inspector continued.

"However others on the department and I have noticed that while in uniform and working your own zone you two have one of the highest rates for the arrest and conviction in the department. You also seemed to have developed quite of number of informants who have been paid well for their productivity."

Harry started to jump up from his chair to protest.

"Just settle down Harry, I don't know who your snitches are, don't want to know, and you don't hear me protesting about the money that goes to your snitches; that's what the money is there for. What

I'm proposing is that the two of you go plain clothes with unmarked cars we traded with the Horseman (R.C.M.P.) for. We also have some out-of-province license plates that we have been saving for just this type of operation. I, and the Superintendent in charge of informant management will back you. The Surveillance Unit and their teams will not be available for you're your use. Having said that I have complete confidence in your, shall we say, initiative. I will need a month end report from you two on criminal arrests, number of criminal charges with names of the accused, do you understand? You will have an office in the District Office, with your title being Warrant Squad supposedly only going after the really bad-guys with major warrants. If you need back up for an arrest or arrests you will advise me and I will pull in some uniforms who will go plain-clothes for the day under your supervision. Now what are your thoughts on this basically thankless job?"

"So what you are saying is we have 'carte blanche' to catch Bad-Guys?" Harry asked with a slow smile.

"Yyyeeesss, but please don't step over the line too much," the Inspector said.

"Don't worry Inspector I have a junior guy with me and I wouldn't do that…much," Harry responded.

"What do you think of all this Xavier?"

"I think I am looking at the best time I am ever going to have on this Job," Xavier said with a big grin.

"Ya know, I think your right Xav," Harry replied.

The newly appointed Specialty Warrants team ended up with nick-name Cagney & Lacy by the other uniforms. When Harry heard their new nickname he had dryly noted that the District building would have to be fumigated for Nitwits again.

Soon enough, everybody in the District lost their curiosity about the Warrant Team and moved on to the latest police gossip and police work. Some had their suspicions about the unmarked cars Xav and Harry were driving, and their odd working hours but they kept those suspicions to themselves. Only the District Inspector watched them but only because he was more concerned about them taking too many chances and not taking enough days off.

To Harry and Xavier it was like they had died and gone to heaven, or at least police heaven. They made sure they registered all their informants, except for one, with the Superintendent in control of Informants. They both kept excellent notes, a copy of which were filed in their respective homes away from the office; in case some goof within the police department wanted to make trouble for them or use their work to get promoted themselves.

Their regular notes and reports on those arrested, with property or dope recovered, along with the names of the accused including a few for bank-robberys, attempted murder and a vast number of culprits for break and enter. They were even clearing up break and enters in Banff, Strathmore and Brooks. Copies of all of those were also sent into the District Inspector with the month end report. The Inspector didn't seem to mind them going out of town now and then but out of Province was a big no no given that some Horsemen had no sense of humor when city police were treading on their turf.

The Superintendent gave them the money they needed for their informants and the request form were put in a special file. Harry and Xavier always made sure the informants signed a receipt, which was put in the file as well. Anything involving money they made double sure it was signed by at least four people.

Harry and Xavier were even given cash out of a special slush fund to buy some shoddy clothes from second hand stores, but for the most part they both wore their own old clothes and saved money on shaving and cutting their hair. The longer they were on the Warrant Team the shaggier they got; Xavier even got his ear pierced.

Very few of the other police officers knew or were interested in what Harry and Xavier were actually up to, except three senior guys and a couple policewomen Harry and Xavier both knew and trusted. Three Street District Sergeants were amongst the group and there were certain nights that those officers showed up in plain clothes and 'borrowed' unmarked vehicles from the surveillance unit. Members from the Surveillance would also be involved mainly because they had a plane. So if the ground units lost the 'Eye' generally the plane would have the 'Eye' in the sky that would give them directions back to where the accused were. They used one of the upstairs boardrooms and planned the night's activities.

All the men and women in the room had been trained in surveillance and tactical practices at one time or another. They were all handed files on the accused that were going to be taken down that night. The files included photo, criminal, drug and weapons history. Harry and Xavier would only call out the team when they were planning a large arrest of bikers, drug dealers and weapons dealers or combinations thereof. Everybody on that team knew exactly what their job was and the raids were done with the proper Search Warrants. A TAC team that just 'happened' to be in the area practicing night entries backed them up.

The 'Team' for the night of an Operational Plan spent two hours going over what was needed from each of them. Some covered windows and doors so none of the bad-guys escaped while the TAC team did a 'practice' entry on the doors.

It was funny, in an odd sort of a way, but bad-guys, in a panic to dodge the infamous TAC team, would look to the windows. Seeing only a 'women' guarding one of the windows would decide that that was way to go. Of course the bad-guys would reach the ground only to find that these were no shrinking violets but real women who could and would 'kick their respective Asses into next Tuesday' and enjoy doing it.

After each of these 'Black-Op Operations' they would have a de-briefing to discuss what went wrong and what went right. Either Harry or Xavier would bring in a case of beer for after the de-briefing. There was a lot of laughter and tall tales and adrenaline that went around the room along with bottles of beer till the team had settled down and the adrenilin slid back down to almost normal.

After each de-briefing those who had participated in the operation left with contented smiles on their faces and hoping the next Ops would be soon. The Black-Ops. team had all been warned when they each had been contacted initially that should anybody say anything too anybody outside of the team that they would be kicked off the team and banished to another District.

Most of the time Harry and Xavier worked alone, doing their own thing unless something really big came in and under certain circumstances they went to the Inspector.

One night Xavier was so excited he was pacing their office when Harry came in. One of their informants had phoned and told Xav about a serious bank-robbery that had occurred that day. During the robbery two tellers, and the bank manager had been seriously hurt. Xavier had received, within ten minutes of the robbery, snitch information about who the bank-robbers were, where they were staying, where the money was and what guns they had.

Harry and Xavier phoned the Inspector and he managed to be back in the office within ten minutes. The inspector set up 'eyes' (surveillance) on the hideout in a run-down motel room and called in the Staff-Sgt. of TAC team. The plan worked on what the police call the K.I.S.S. method (Keep It Simple Stupid). The more elaborate the plan, the more likely it to go awry.

Harry and Xavier were allowed to watch from a safe distance as the TAC team did the entry. Using the Ram as the key too blow open the door before throwing in Flash-Bangs and then tear-gas just as they made their entry.

When the TAC team finish blowing things up and arresting the bad-guys they gave Harry and Xavier the thumbs up. Xav and Harry grinned at each other, even though the small boy residing in their psyche, wanted to jump up and down they managed to maintain their decorum although they couldn't get the grins off their faces.

Many asked them why they didn't do it their usual way. Both replied that, given the seriousness of the offences and the suspects involved, to not advise the Inspector of what was going down would be like a slap in the Inspector's face. Besides it was such a serious offence that it was the Inspectors job to set up the operation, and inform the media when it was over. The last thing Xav and Harry needed was their respective mugs on T.V.

Harry taught Xavier about many other things as well, like how to stay out of certain police officer's way. Especially those who were bound and determined, by any means possible including stomping over other officers and lying, to get promoted. Xavier had seen this himself, how other had claimed 'certain' criminal investigations as theirs when their involvement had been minimal. Of course these mendacious individuals who had done little of the work but maintained that the glory was theirs. Those that knew the truth just shrugged their shoulders and carried on with the real police work because it was a waste of time to worry about the 'brayers of glory, when there were bad-guys out there to catch.

Time goes by too fast and where there is a beginning, there is always an ending.

Harry retired the same day Xavier got promoted to Detective. The party that celebrated those two momentous events was legendary for the number of police officers who attended, friends and enemies both. Long after Harry and Xavier had been poured into a 'blue and white Taxies' (Police Cars) and taken home, the party continued. It was not until, for the first time in the in the Gag and Puke's history, the bartender, who had worked there since its inception, finally had too kick out the the last of the hard drinking stragglers for being too drunk.

Even after being kicked out of the Cuff and Billy, a police after hours club more commonly known as The Gag and Puke, the party carried on. Once banished from their drinking place and still feeling the need for more beer, which some had stored in their cars in case of a beer emergency. A warming bonfire was started at the base of the ancient, large tree beside the club and the drinking continued.

Luckily, there were a few there who had not entirely drowned their wits in alcohol. It was one of those who suddenly realized there was a real danger of the the tree and club building burning down and called the fire department.

Needless to say the fire department was none to pleased to be called out in the wee hours of the morning by a bunch of sodden, drunken policemen who kept commenting on the firemen's skill or lack thereof. Several partiers had also stated that they could piss the fire out.

It took several minutes before wiser, less liquored police prevailed and those who were annoying the firemen were told to shut up and zip-up their respective pants.

And that was another part of the reason there were no guns allowed in the Gag and Puke because drunks with guns, even though they were police officers, was a frightening thought. There had also been many incidents where gunfire had been heard and a street-light had been blown out just above bad-guys who had happened to be walking by just outside the fenced police parking lot followed by drunken laughter.

The Police Chief, at the time, realized that it was a miracle nobody had been accidentally shot and banned those wearing gun and uniforms from drinking in the club. The cost of fixing streetlights went way down after that order went out.

But the club did serve very important purpose. When a police officer had been killed in the line of duty those who had been involved in the incident and those who had covered for the officers involved would come into the club to talk it out.

To talk about death and the one who had entered death's domain. Only the good and the funny parts of his or her life were remembered while the faux-pas' and mistakes were forgotten. The one they had lost and what had gone wrong and what had gone right. They told war stories about the deceased or injured and laughed and cried together. That helped lessen the rage and turn it into anger and then grief and feeling of brotherhood was strengthen. Some civilians would object to the 'us and them' but they didn't wear the uniform nor did the civilians understand the loss of someone who had been on the 'Job'.

CHAPTER THREE

Xavier saw Rose, after their first meeting, from time to time. There were intervals when he wouldn't see her for months, or a year or so. He would check the reports and run her name on the computer and find that she was doing time for aggravated assault, or even manslaughter.

When she had done her time Rose would eventually find her way down to the 'A' stroll area around Third Avenue south. Strange, he always seemed to sense when she was out of jail and back in the place where they first connected, the cusp, the start of the east end of her world around Third Avenue. He would head down that way and sure enough she was there. They would nod at each other then meet later at an isolated, pre-arranged spot.

Initially Harry came along on those meetings, Harry wouldn't say much just watch how the meeting was going. Rose began to trust Harry as much as she trusted Xavier. One of Harry's 'Pearl's of Wisdom' was never meet a female snitch alone, always have a partner with you or parked where he can see you. It reduced the claims of hanky-panky from bad snitches. Harry never said anything about Rose except that Xavier be very discreet about meeting with her because she was of 'The People' and there was a feel of other-worldliness about her, an old magic.

Xavier never registered Rose as an informant because she didn't trust the white race nor did she want her name written anywhere except as the accused on an arrest report. She did tell him about some of 'The People's' beliefs in the magic of Mother Earth and the Creator. Rose believed in the balance between all things even good and bad, how she felt despair for the whites, who had lost their understanding of mysticism and with it the balance within themselves.

Yet she trusted him because she said he had a very old soul and somehow he had an aura of magic surrounding him. She sensed a bond with him. Cash held no interest, all she seemed too want was for Xavier to watch out for her people, 'The People' who had been lost to the temptations of the dark underbelly of the city and some creatures who had hurt her friends.

He would take the names and generally those named had warrants for their arrest or he would do some digging. Usually the information Rose gave to him plus his own investigation gave him enough to arrest them. Either way they ended up in jail. He came to enjoy his few meetings with Rose, once they got the information business out of the way they would sit and talk as friends.

Xavier admired her quick wit and rare laugh. Rose had told him once that she believed that a long ago they had been one, the male and female parts of a whole person. At first he a laughed gently at the thought, but the longer he was around her the more it made sense in an odd sort of way. Xavier trusted Rose as he trusted few others.

Rose began to tell him bits and pieces of her life and the history of her people before the white race-humans came to the shores of the Americas. How the Creator had infused The People with a type of magic to care for the land, the animals and how to leave the land unscarred and pure in its beauty. She told him of how some of The People retained more of the mystical forces and became Shamans, Medicine men or women and some few women even became Spider-woman. She had hesitated and seemed to study him before naming the last name aloud.

"It sounds to me like you are not so much afraid but wary of this Spiderwoman from long ago?" Xavier said.

"Of long ago? Xavier the magic still exists and so do those who I have named especially the Spiderwoman. The one who holds that title now is growing ancient by your standards, several centuries I think."

"The time for her to fade into a new Spiderwoman and pass on her power's is coming soon, perhaps this century." Rose replied with a sigh.

Xavier had given her a look that was slightly skeptical.

Rose felt anger flare within her at his look of disbelief as she asked, "So you do not believe me and think I talk of wishful fantasy?"

"No, no Rose it's not that, it's just that we to have many stories of ancient times with sorcery and witchcraft in them."

"You do not understand, Xavier. What I have told you is in the here and now. I know the whites like to think they cowed The People long ago and tried to remake us in their image. But only the outside edge crumbled while center, the hard core of The People has remained and carried on."

Xavier had looked at her and thought of what his race had done to destroy or at the very least assimilate The People into the white race. He also knew that they had been treated like poor, backward cousins who couldn't even raise their own children.

The longer he had known Rose and some of her friends the more he realized that his thinking, in fact, the white race's thinking was wrong. 'The People' were proud, intelligent humans that his race had tried to destroy. He did feel a kinship with Rose that he couldn't explain but when she told him of her belief it made sense. Xavier felt the truth of what she had told him and he gradually accepted it.

Even the part about his being a mystic somehow bonded to her made a weird kind of sense because when he did interviews with bad-guys they always confessed. Even the hardened criminals who had been interviewed by FBI profilers in the past and said nothing would listen to his questions with, initially, crossed arms (a sigh of defiance and obstruction) and at the end of his quiet, easygoing interview they would confess. His partner in the interview would have to mentally shake himself almost as if he had almost fallen asleep. While the bad-guy was sitting there completely relaxed, it was only when he was put back in a cell that the accused realized he had just told the pigs everything including ratting out a few of his buddies.

Both Xavier and whatever partner he had at the time would go over the video and audio-tapes and there wasn't anything untoward in the interviews; just Xavier asking questions about the offence. Granted his style of interviewing and the questions he asked could be at times seemed odd: asking about relatives and otherwise what seemed unrelated questions about the offence were, in the end, perfectly legit. They were proper interviews with no coerion or violence.

CHAPTER FOUR

The last time he'd seen Rose, she had seemed worried and distracted. She kept asking him what time it was, that more than anything than else made him uneasy. She had never, ever asked him about time before. She had always seemed to have her own internal 'Rose Clock' that worked on a slightly different time-space continuum.

"It's good to see you Rose. It's been too long. What's wrong? I have never seen you this worried and agitated? Usually you are calm, quiet and the passing of time or at least time in the white sense hasn't seemed to cause you worry."

"Maybe in the past, when I thought I had nothing time held no meaning. Every once in a while a wisp of 'Before' drifts through my mind, parts of it stays while the rest disappears except for thoughts of the Spiderwoman," Rose whispered. Then she straightened and her voice took on more of its normal tone as she met his eyes.

"I was with a friend last night that had managed to get his hands on some real black tar opium." Rose held up her hand as Xavier frowned and opened his mouth to say something. "I trust you, Xavier, because you have never judged what I do to get by, this is not the time to start. Xavier nodded reluctantly as he settled back into the driver's seat of the vehicle to listen.

"As I was saying, we both smoked the opium and began to 'chase the Dragon'. At first it was like all the other times. A sense of floating and rightness, this was my proper place within the world of the Dragon where a thousand ideas float by, all of them about a better world. You think you will remember them, especially the one you have caught with both hands and your heart. It seems like the peace at the very brink of death. Suddenly, something was there that shouldn't have been! It, I think, was a malevolent Spirit at first. It was destroying my dragon dream! Calling me Spiderwomen and tearing my dreams apart yelling at me to beware! The time was coming for me to leave this city. It, the spirit or whatever, yelled and then it whispered in my ear that the

'Soul-Slayer' has broken apart the bonds 'The Creator' had put upon on it. It would come disguised as a scared and scabbed white man covered in the dirt of what the white race has done. He searches out those who are weak in spirit or soul. The Soul-Slayer will gather close those who have relinquished their soul to him. He will use the white's weaknesses against them, drug users especially since it weakens their souls so quickly, the more souls he destroys the stronger he becomes. He is the other part, the brother of the Reaper and carries a Scythe of his own! The spirit hidden within the opium dreams called me a Spiderwomen in waiting!"

"A Soul-Slayer?" What?" Xavier asked a worried look on his face.

Rose studied his face her eyes locked with his. Xavier felt as if her eyes were probing into his very being-testing to see if he had the ability to understand. Then she pulled her eyes away and stared out the van window staring into the darkness beyond.

The silence stretched and pulled out between them and it seemed like an elastic eternity before time sprang back and Rose finally spoke. Her quiet voice seemed large after the silence.

"It is time I told you of some more things that are part of the magic of 'The People' especially of one Being or Spirit who was turned from a Wizard, who the Creator had granted great mystical powers too help those who had lost their way because their mind and souls were weak. This Wizard was called Soul-Saver and for millennia he used his power to help those among us who were weak in mind and soul. With great gentleness he would help them to find their way back to us. That is until one fateful day when he was tricked by a red sprite, who lived on the hatred in others. Soul Saver thought he was leaning in to touch the mind of a distraught human and instead tasted the black foulness of a particularly malignant being.

The Soul-Saver had always done his work by probing the mind and through it the soul of the lost one without ever directly touching the soul. Finally to be tricked and drawn in too taste a soul, especially one so foul had driven him mad with the strange, acid sweetness of the soul, like opium or heroin the addiction was almost immediate.

It turned him from helping those whose souls been lost into a monster twisted into something so evil that he craved the souls of any that came close enough be they foul or fair. Not to save but to slay because he felt the power of owning the Id-soul, and his power grew. The Creator and the rest of us saw him actively hunting 'The People' whether they were ill or not and stealing their souls, sucking them dry.

The Soul-Saver had become a Soul-Slayer and must be put down or put away so he could harm no other. It took a great deal of power from the Creator with the assistance of the Universal Turtle, Shamans, Medicine men and women, and Spiderwoman but finally the Soul-Slayer was banished to a place in the Beyond. Special spells and wards held him there, until recently that is.

Somehow over the millennia he has figured out an opposing incantation that broke apart the wards that bonded him. It didn't help that throughout the millennia we had become less diligent in guarding him and eventually even forgotten about him. All except that is the Spiderwoman, who only remembered while going through an ancient book of spells. She rushed to Beyond only to find his prison blown apart and he was gone.

The Universal Turtle sensed from a place beyond a Black Hole in the universe that the symmetry of earth had become somehow unbalanced. He started to work his way through the cosmos, along the Milky-way, dead-dying, giant red suns with their attending planets and just forming suns with stars, meteors and Black Holes of the universe that he tended and headed towards earth.

This Soul-Slayer is coming. He-It is very close, or has just arrived. I feel him; he revels in cruelty, wallows in wickedness and takes great joy in the death of souls, spirit or essence whatever you call that within you that makes you, You.

His sign is also the Scythe but it is the Soul-Slayers Scythe. The spirits keeps whispering in my ear, beware-beware. He comes too gather the shriveled souls of the evil ones that have already been offered to him. Then he will collect the souls of the weak. The Soul-Slayer smears the grime, the dirt of the lost, crippled souls upon his body like a shield that attracts the carcass flies. The shield protects him against the incantations of the good. It is his amour, or so he thinks, against those that would truly see him for what he is. He will secure his army in the east end of the city where only the hopeless and the homeless hide. The dark under-belly of the city will be his palace, for none but the police care or notice, he thinks. The People are lost and he can do as he wishes. Xavier I am in the 'Becoming' part of being the new Spiderwoman rising!" Rose said while observing his reaction.

Xavier had been initially just listening to what she said but the more she talked the more he turned towards her and what he saw in her face, as she spoke those words; her face normally a smooth, toasted, light brown was ashen gray. Her sloe, shaped, ancient eyes that had seen so much, were wide with fear, as she looked back into the darkness of the night. Part of the attraction he had always felt for her was that they seemed too totally understand each other. They could complete each other's thoughts. It was not sexual, more like they had been twins or one in another life and somehow found each other again having retained the similar, if not exact, way of thinking. But now her words were like heavy chucks of ice that struck him, bruising his thoughts and beliefs sending icy spasms climbing up his spine, like death was playing piano on his backbone with heavy cold hands. Xavier reached up and tried to rub that feeling away. His neck was cold and clammy.

"What the hell!" He fell quiet as he tried to digest her words.

"You are-I think-a part of me, my Familiar. You understand Familiar? It means you know me, you are part of me as I am part of you. You are part of my weapon against Soul Slayer that no one knows of even I don't know how or why. It just is."

Silence…neither spoke until the crackle of the radio broke the unbearable muteness. Xavier picked up the mike and his voice almost cracked as he answered in to low voice.

"2890, Detective O'Malley?" Dispatch asked using his call sign.

"Yes, go ahead."

"Can you meet 2892?"

"Tell them the usual spot in half an hour."

"Ten four."

"Xavier, maybe you have been the balance while I have been tested. Something or someone will force me into an action that goes against your laws. I sense that I will be gone for a while…watch for the sign of the up-side down Scythe."

"Wait, I need more, who is the Universal Turtle!"

"I have no more to give you other than for you to listen to your inner voice." Rose said with a soft sigh. She got out of his vehicle before he could stop her. She disappeared leaving him alone with only the scent of crisp, snow covered fir trees to remind him that she had been there at all. She was gone and he didn't see her for a long time. He checked his sources and found out she was doing time for an aggravated assault.

Xavier read the report, in which the police had indicated it was probably self-defense. He realized that a good or even a mediocre lawyer should have been able to get her off on self-defense. That was when he started reading all the previous reports and court documents that described Rose's life living and working on the hard, unforgiving streets of the city. Survival was a constant battle some of which most police understood and tried to help but they were there to enforce the laws not be social workers.

He made a horrible discovery as he read further. Most of the charges against her could have, should have been dismissed or thrown out on the bases of self-defense. He talked to some lawyers that tried to defend her and found out that she was her own worst enemy. Rose like some of The People, refused to say anything in their own defense. She would answer questions; in a monotone voice either 'yes' or 'no' and refused to elaborate. The whole time she was being interviewed Rose would have her head lowered and would refuse to look at anybody.

He had encountered these phenomena with The People before and he thought perhaps it was simply a matter of a different culture, different race. They would not look anybody in the eyes as that was considered rude in their culture, particularly with white race who were considered very rude. Unfortunately that was, and is, one of the corner stones of white society, looking somebody straight in the eye when you tell the truth. White people tended to elaborate on everything while The People simply said 'yes' or 'no'. This made interviewing them a nightmare.

He couldn't visit her in jail. Too many knew he was a cop, it was too dangerous for her so he had to leave her to do the time. All he could do was keep watch and listen to his inner voice as he waited for her to return to the world.

CHAPTER FIVE

The ground, faintly brushed with snow, was frozen rock-hard in undulating rows of winter fallow. Bitter winds whipped and whirled as they danced across the frigid fields under the endless night sky toying with the dark figure that half-ran, half-stumbled across the rough terrain.

"FFuuuccckkk! It's Ccoolldd!" Joel, screamed! The raging wind tore his words apart as soon as they left his lips. He hunched his scrawny shoulders even closer to his thin body and pulled the hood of his sweatshirt down over his head as far as it would go. Ahead, just slightly to the right, was the huge old barn. He had seen its silhouette against the gray, racing clouds while walking along the south edge of Highway One. Looking back, seeing the headlights on the highway, he was amazed at how far a distance he had managed to come.

Those headlights look so small from here, like a moving, flickering, continuous line of life. Were the people in those vehicles happy? Were they sad? Were they angry? Well at least they were driving, still in the world, they had somewhere to go, someone to see. I am leaving the world; I have no one nor anywhere to go just this old, vacant barn, he thought to himself as he continued to wallow in self-pity, sadness, despair, betrayal and love lost.

Of course in his 'me world' he had tampered so much with the truth that his memories had little to do with reality or the lives destroyed because of him.

Joel's whiney, chill-covered cry was only for his plight, not the pain he had caused others. He cried into the wind again but the wind blew it back as if it wanted no part of him.

He finally made it to the east side of the barn and began feeling along the rough wood as he stumbled around a corner, feeling for the outline of a door. There, there it was! He had found a small side door that initially refused to open.

After shouldering, then kicking it, the door, with a screech that matched the wind, reluctantly opened and Joel fell into cold, dusty silence. Laying there trying to catch the breath that the wind and physical effort had torn away he could feel a dull ache in his shoulder.

"Shit, I am not heavy enough to start shouldering doors," he said with a giggle that trembled on the edge of self pity and weak tears. The sound of his voice being swallowed by the large quiet freaked him out. Oh man, it's so dark in here like 'can't see my hand in front of my face' dark he thought. His ears adjusted from the howling wind to the quiet. That was when he realized that he was not the only creature in the barn. He could hear the squeaking and rustling of mice, bats casting out the tiny chirps that were part of their radar and some type of barn owl hooting. In an odd way those sounds comforted him. He wasn't alone even if it was just varmints. Most would call me a varmint.

Alone, in a deserted barn, with that one thought he came the closest he would ever come to realizing who and what he was.

Introspection had never been Joel's strong suit and his first honest thought didn't linger long in his brain that was only geared to taking care of Joel above all else. He was exhausted and needed some sleep. He felt around until he found a corner, probably part of a stall, with lots of old straw in it. Curling up in the corner he fell into a restless sleep where bad dreams were his only company.

Cold eating away at sleep, plus a full bladder finally forced Joel to get up in the morning. There was enough dim light for him to walk down to the other side of the barn to take care of business. On the way back to the stall he looked around in the dull grey light but could see nothing of interest. Once back where he had slept he sat down and took inventory. He had water but not too much, perhaps enough to wash down the pills bought with last of the cash, last of very ill gotten gains.

He sat quietly on the straw bale and thought; I could just light a match, poof-a flaming pyre, kinda like a Viking going down on his flaming ship. Hold on, wait a sec, seems to me the Viking was already dead so the flames couldn't hurt him. I'll stick to the original plan; suck back a bunch of pills, then float away, peaceful like.

He got the pill bottle out of his jacket pocket, rolling it around, staring at the little round container as he contemplated his next move, I could just keep going west where he wouldn't find me-naw he would find me and then the pain, the pain-he promised, but if I do what is expected; an easy death, a quick, gentle suicide; strange word that. Hari Kari now there's a word, or two words, need to man up for that though-need a real sharp blade to disembowel your-self. One-Eyed Jack's face flashed through Joel's mind.

Shit, gotta get this done! He looked down at the pill bottle, shook it and listened to the rattle of the pills inside then looked at it again as he it held in his soft, callus free hand. Hands used to defraud and, write phony cheques, prey on the trusting, the elderly. He had even victimized his own family. But now he had gone too far, way to many people were looking for him especially One-Eyed Jack. Better to go this way.

Childproof the lid said, more like adult proof Joel thought as he struggled with the lid. It finally popped open; half the pills flew out and landed on the floor. Joel desperately scrabbled to get the pills before they disappeared between the floorboards. Too late to get all, he managed to get some. Those recovered and those still in the bottle he promptly tossed into his mouth so he wouldn't lose anymore. He swished some water around in his mouth then swallowed the water mixed with pills while he continued to scan the floor for more of the elusive blue pills but to no avail.

Gradually Joel felt grogginess taking hold, pulling him deeper. Wait!!! Did I take enough to kill me or just give me a pleasant sleep? Have to be sure...

Stumbling around the barn as his brain started to shut down. Wait-there-there something laying-his brain was starting to slur his thoughts. An old stretched out-torn cloth, T-Shirt maybe. Stepping up, almost falling, on the corner of an old dried-out hay bale. Fumbling, he managed to tie part of the cloth around a beam just above, and then tied the other end around his neck just as his knees gave out and he dropped off his unsteady perch. He felt something tighten around his neck, his survival instinct took hold and he made a feeble attempt to bring his arms up but he was too drugged. Joel jerked twice then died.

The city had a raw, dry winter that year. Not much snow, just a bitterly, cold, hard wind that sucked the moisture from everything, including the corpse swinging in the barn.

CHAPTER SIX

It was a hot May Day when the District Sergeant received a phone call, on his mobile phone, from dispatch about the call that had just popped up on his computer. Dispatch told him that the 10-32 (code for sudden death) was suspicious according too panicked civilians. They had been taking photographs around and inside an old barn on the west side of the city when they had seen a body hanging inside.

The District Sergeant met the civilians on the highway near the barn. They kept stating that the body looked suspicious to them. They had never seen a corpse before but watched a lot of the C.S.I. programs.

Oh perfect the Sargeant though, he had no doubt that they had found something, maybe a corpse. He was annoyed with all these 'CSI' detectives that watch shows of that ilk and thought it made them a police officer. Civilians could be a pain in the ass at times, he thought, he gave a minute shake of his head as he turned to look out at the barns in the middle of a large dusty field.

He was about to make the trek across the field when a car crew pulled up. Both officers were junior. He told them to get statements from the civilians before they came out to the barn. The last thing he heard was one of the civilians talking to the two police officers about the 'poor bastard just hanging there'.

The Sergeant, who, in fact, was a newly promoted Detective, cursed under his breath about the promise he had made to Millie, the District Sergeant that he was filling in for. She was on a much-needed vacation. No doubt Millie would get a good laugh about this when she returned and heard the story about how Xavier O'Malley had trudged through a field in a uniform. Oh well, he would probably laugh along with her. He shrugged as he began the difficult walk across the soft, furrowed, field to the distant barn. He got to the barn ahead of the two officers and started sniffing the air, no smell, so not freshly dead. He found a small, partially, opened door and stepped in. The light inside the barn was dim and he stopped till his eyes adjusted. It was just as well he did for had he taken two more steps he would have been dancing with the corpse. Startled, he let out a gasp as he stepped back to take a better look at it.

A perfectly mummified corpse, even the Egyptians couldn't do better, although they removed the innards, brain and used special wrappings, he thought. This mummy was dressed in jeans, sweatshirt under a leather jacket, there was a ball-cap lying directly under the body along with a pair of sneakers. As the corpse had shriveled during mummification, the sneakers fell off.

The skin on the skull was light colored, the hair on top of the skull blonde, so Caucasian and given the clothes probably male. The perfectly dried out epidermis looked like the buttery, smooth, tanned leather that the fashion industry used for expensive purses.

Xavier reached up and lightly touched the forehead of the corpse with his forefinger. It was firm and smooth just as he thought. A thought wandered across his mind...HHhmm maybe I shouldn't have done that without gloves on and then he shrugged to himself.

Xavier pulled out his flashlight, turned it on and made a closer examination of the corpse. The eyes of the body were sunk in and dried out to such an extent that they looked like little black marbles that were still attached inside the socket with what looked like little pieces of leather. He knew that those pieces were what were left of the nerve bundles. The face, as the moisture had been sucked out of the skin, had tightened and pulled back so there was a grotesque, lipless, toothy smile on the countenance. The nose had collapsed inward. The neck bowed and stretched from the pressure of the homemade noose.

The arms, hands and legs had all stretched out because of the way the body had been positioned at the time of death. It looked, at first glance, like a poorly hung scarecrow, he thought as his eyes drifted to the surrounding area. He noted that the victim had used a low support beam in a stall to wrap some type of cloth around, then knot it about his neck. He must have been standing nearly on his tiptoes on the corner of an old hay-bale when he wrapped the cloth around his neck and then stepped or fell off hanging himself, he thought.

It was only then that he noticed an orange tinted, pill bottle lying on the floor to one side of the corpse. He made a mental note of where the little bottle was lying in relation to the body, when he bent to pick it up he also saw a small pill partially hidden beneath some hay. The pill was a distinctive blue and familiar. Morphine. The old saying came to mind, 'rocked gently, painlessly, in the God Morpheous' large arms until he would wake no more.' This guy must have really wanted to make sure he did the job on himself so he hung himself as well.

Xavier bent and picked up the pill bottle, turning it around in his fingers till he noticed the paper inside. He pulled the paper out; it was blank except for the rough drawing of the Soul-Slayer's Scythe.

He felt like he had been shot in the heart, the small piece of paper drifted out of his suddenly senseless hand. He stood there, unable to move except for his skin crawling with apprehension and dread as he remembered Rose's words. His heart began beating again but it felt like all the blood had been pumped out of it, nothing was left but a dried out muscle that kept on spastically pumping.

"Holy Shit…Karen! Karen, come here…our first body! It's a hanging, right, Sergeant? Almost doesn't look real, does it? Sergeant…you ok? Karen, about time you got here…look at this! Sergeant did you drop this?" Constable Sarah Conner babbled as she held out the scrape of paper.

Xavier at first didn't hear the voice, but gradually, like a mosquito flying around his head at night, the annoying sound pulled him out of the shock and kick-started his brain.

"I'm fine and I'll take that paper thanks. Once your partner has regained her wind, I'll tell you both what we have here," Xavier said in a near normal voice as he took the piece of paper.

Xavier spent the next half-hour showing and explaining to the two young police officers about mummification and hangings, suicide and corpses. He also explained what he expected in their report about this incident.

"In all likelihood this is a suicide, but we will wait till an autopsy has been done, just to be sure. Now which of you two constables can explain to me why it will be a relatively easy job for 'Alberta Body Removal' guys to get this body on a stretcher then haul it back to the morgue van?"

Both Constables looked at him puzzled. Suddenly Karen smiled and said, "Because this corpse is all dried out, that's why."

"Very good. Now you need to wait for the Medical Examiner and the body removal guys to show up so you might as well start your report now. Call me when you're clear and I'll buy you two coffee."

Xavier left the two of them standing by the partially open side door doing their notes. He started the long walk back across the dusty field to his District Sergeant van. He smiled faintly at the thought of the two eager, young police officers he had just left, before his attention turned to darker matters. He felt a pang of guilt twist through him. Xavier had not exactly forgotten Rose's words, they had however, been shoved into the back of his subconscious by day-to-day living and working. I wonder if that was truly a suicide? There was nothing in the barn or on the body to suggest otherwise but the pill bottle was old, scratched and the piece of paper was dirty looked like it was torn from something else. Those morphine pills were not prescribed by any doctor, no doubt they were prescribed by a drug-dealer, probably enough for someone, our corpse maybe, to overdose. Could be the dealer suggested that suicide would be best.

As Xavier trudged back through the large field he thought about that last conversation with Rose and all the things he had learned in his new position as sargeant in charge of the Gang unit; although he had to admit that it had been most fortuitous that he was subbing for a friend today otherwise he would have never found the evidence that helped back up Rose's tale. Interesting though, how 'all the stars had lined up for him to be working this very day' he felt an icy chill climb up his back.

Shit, I would like to talk to Rose about this. She would understand about the corpse, maybe even know who it was and how he had met up with this Soul-Slayer. There are things that she would know, but at least I can start keeping closer watch. Maybe being assigned to this new unit will make it easier to poke around.

Because of Xavier's ability to handle and direct informants, plus his skill at setting up Operational Plans that were usually successful, he had been assigned to the newly formed Integrated Gang Unit. The Police department had decided that the unit should be formed after there were several shootouts between opposing Asian gang members. There were a staggering number of shots fired by gang members that missed their targets entirely. Unfortunately during one drive-by shooting, a civilian happened to be in the wrong place at the wrong time and was killed by one of the indiscriminate shots. This of course caused a hue and cry from the media and through them the good citizens of the City demanding that the police take action. The police, who had taken the situation very seriously from the start, also realized that until a few innocent civilians had been killed, nothing would be done.

The police knew what would happen, and had already set up a smaller unit so it was a simple matter too flesh it out. The Intelligence unit and the Homicide unit at the direction of the Police Chief and other senior department heads already had the core of pre-selected personel who were talented and motivated in various fields of investigation who already had some operational plans worked out. Once they aquired all the man-power they needed, they could hit the ground running.

The newly christened Integrated Guns and Gang Unit was ready to go in a matter of days with a mandate to identify gangs, gang members their positions within the structure of the gangs and prosecute them. It wasn't that they were cynics, okay they were, it was just that they understood that the politicians considered them a necessary evil. The police had had to fight for money, equipment and respect ever since they were formed.

A lot of police officers had a silent snicker at the fact that the Asian gangs, in particular, for all their black-market, high-powered handguns couldn't hit the side of a barn. Some jokers in the department acerbically quipped that the whole hand-eye coordination problems some Asians had in relation to driving might also have something to do with their ability to shoot straight. The joke that was making the rounds at the time was 'How could you tell an Asian gang-banger? By the number of bullet holes in the sides of his car, so even if he didn't get killed at least the shooter killed the victim's shiny new car.

Xavier knew the biggest problem they had with the Asian gang-bangers was that the police couldn't seem to get informants working inside the gangs. There were some under cover officers that had been working on the Asian gangs and what their effect was on the citizens, who happened to be Asian. Xavier was told that in a lot of cases there was so much intimidation going on in that particular community that those citizens were afraid to say anything. They also didn't trust the police here because they were scared that they were as corrupt as the police were where they had come from. Of course the Asian Gangs considered suburbia their turf and because they were mostly involved in the high-end drug trade they could afford the nice, shiny, fast new cars and the best guns, automatic weapons and such from the thriving black market.

With the other gangs in the city the Guns and Gang Unit had managed to get informants and in fact had inserted undercover police officers within certain gangs. Of course the best solution was to get your own people inside gathering the information. Xavier knew that with the Asians they would have to rely on surveillance, wire and other mechanical devices.

Just as the Gang Unit was being set up there was another shooting and in that one a particularly vicious Asian gang managed to shoot dead two members of the opposing gang. Granted as with all the other shoot-outs or drive-bys there were a large number of casings strewn about but this time several of the bullets had managed to find their mark.

Xavier and his team, through surveillance and other means, put together a comprehensive dossier of who's -who in the Asian gangs. The files included those with lengthy records and immigrants status. In some ways it was not unlike how Al Capone ended up in jail, not for all the murders he had committed but for income tax evasion except in the case of Asian gangs it was immigration.

With the Asian gangs the top gang members were being deported, not for the murders they had committed or for the lengthy criminal records they had but because they had not followed the proper procedures and paperwork for immigration. Plus some had arrived on Canadian shores as students with student visa's and then had deliberately fallen through the cracks and now the Guns and Gang Unit in co-operation with immigration were finding them. Their student visas had expired, in some cases years before. Delighted Immigration officers were shipping them back to their country of origin as quickly as they could.

Xavier and the other team members grew to know most, if not all, of the gangs in the city including their old standby the Biker Gangs. As a result of the intelligence gathered by his team, including surveillance photos and addresses, members of the Gang Unit were in high demand by both homicide and drug units to identify possible gang members and in some cases dead bodies.

Xavier, mostly because of his position in the gang unit, managed to keep watch on the downtown eastside. What he saw alarmed him.

CHAPTER SEVEN

Like all other big cities, this city had the downtown east end that contained the usual number of run down fleabag hotels where rooms were rented by the hour. The bars in these establishments were meeting places for small time drug-dealers, whores, pimps and thieves, they were like flies swarming around a still warm corpse.

The Cecil Hotel stood in the center of all the illegal activity. There seemed to be a 'Cecil' in most cities. This abattoir of a hotel drew the most flies; the lowest of the low lingered there. The broken sidewalk surrounding it had been splashed with blood too many times to count.

But there had always been kind of a status quo in the east end, a balance of sorts, where if you were ripped off by your drug-dealer you handled it and the drug-dealer didn't show his face again until he had better dope. There were stabbings and the odd shootings but the uniformed police officers that worked in the area knew pretty much everybody down there. So they would put out the word and pretty soon the bad-guy would show up or someone would make a quick phone call and the bad-guy would be found hiding under a bed or in a closet.

It always amazed Xavier that some of those clowns actually thought that they couldn't be seen if they hid in a closet with some clothes over their head.

He had checked with other teams and uniformed officers and they all agreed that the 'Ostrich Theory' (if they can't see you, you can't see them) was prevalent amongst bad-guys, especially those who were doing meth, ice, crack or crank, all of which caused deep, dark paranoia. The paranoia was too such extent that they would develop cleaning fetishes and clean with a mop in one hand and a handgun in the other.

To Xavier it seemed like the entire east end was now high on crack or crank. He didn't remember a time when it had been this tense. Used to be he would recognize some low-life or snitch and he could have a reasonably pleasant conversation with him or her, see how things were doing. Now people lowered their eyes and scurried away. He had seen Susie, her face bruised black and blue, the course humor that she used to have had been knocked out of her.

He talked to her briefly; she was nervous and paranoid about her new pimp named Jack who had taken over from her old pimp. Xavier had asked if she had seen Linda, the black hooker, lately? Susie got real quiet for a moment, he could see torment creasing her face before she whispered to him that Linda had talked back to their new pimp and had mysteriously disappeared. Xavier didn't keep her to long, he could feel the fear radiating from her. She gave him a morose, final glance before she scurried away. Xavier saw that Susie had lost weight as well and from the look of the sores on the skin of her face she was doing crack. Sadness overcame him as he thought of the plump, giggly Susie he had first met when he was still a rookie working with Harry.

Xavier didn't believe in coincidence but lately things were getting really strange. A few days after he talked to Susie he got a call from the Homicide Unit. They needed him or one of his team to meet a Homicide Detective at the west side of the river by the Bird Sanctuary to see if they could identify a female body. His guts tightened, no it couldn't be, probably some junkie female that overdosed. He made his way down to the Bird Sanctuary turned in at an open gate and followed a dirt road to where he saw the police car, M.E.'s (Medical Examiner) vehicle and to add more of a sense of the macabre to the scene, the big 'Alberta Body Removal' van parked. It would seem everybody was awaiting his arrival.

Shit, don't let this be her. Don't let this be-her he thought as he walked over to where all the Homicide detectives and other officials needed to verify a death were standing over what looked to be a shallow grave. They look like a group of vultures standing over a kill.

He steeled himself for what he was about to see and then looked down at what everybody was looking at…the body was in advanced stages of decomposition …never mind that, I have to look at the face. Just look! He thought as he finally looked at the face. Oh shit! Fuck!

It's Linda.

Her skin, which had been rich, dark mahogany, was now dark gray with a slight under tone of putrid green. He could still see some of the distinctive features of her face although it looked like she had been beaten. There was the circular scar on her left cheek where her mother burned her with a cigarette, right under that someone had used a knife and carved a small scythe. It was hard to see because the skin had started to spread apart during decomposition, the edges were beginning to soften. Her throat had been slashed from ear to ear, a large gaping wound which corpse flies seemed to be using as a landing zone. Maggots were wriggling around on the rabbit skin jacket that Linda had worn since he had first known her. Although her right hand was swollen with purification he could see a little flash of gold. She must still be wearing the small gold band on her pinky finger. Linda had told him once that her sister had given it to her. Thank God Rose is in the slammer and reasonably safe he thought.

"Looks to be a hooker I knew from the stroll, name was Linda-Linda Johnson. Her father turned her out when she was only thirteen. I have had occasion to talk to her from time to time and I think she had a little boy that her mother has custody of," Xavier said.

"Just another Hooker, when we move her she'll stink up our van," one of Body Removal aides complained.

Xavier whirled on the one who had made the statement, "she wasn't just a hooker, SHE was a human being who had some excellent qualities including a great sense of humor. Linda, the 'she' you spoke of, was forced into some wrong choices along the way. No one deserves to die like this, beaten, having her throat slashed then dumped into an unmarked, shallow grave."

There was a pregnant pause where some at the scene felt embarrassment for Xavier and some fought to keep their anger from flaring up over a smelly carcass that they would have to transport to the Coroners Office.

Xavier broke the silence by saying, "I may have a suspect for you

Ted, I just have to check out a few things and then I will get back to you," he said to Ted Chalker, the Homicide Detective, who was handling the case.

"Thanks Xavier. Lucky we have you gang guys to help with this kind of stuff. It sounds like you knew her Xavier?"

"Yes I did know her, she was a good sort, and every once in a while passed me some information that was useful."

"Hazardous occupation."

"Yes, but I'll tell you I have never see it so tense down here. It seems like the balance has shifted somehow, snitches see me and go the other way. The nickname 'One Eyed Jack or Jack' is the only whisper I have heard, a very scared whisper. We've been trying to locate 'Jack' because since he has been around 'crank' and 'crack' have really blossomed into the drug of choice, so far no luck. Usually I would already have him in custody by now, but everyone down here has become so skittish and paranoid since this 'One Eyed Jack' and these drugs have arrived, unfortuately he is still in the wind."

"Xavier make sure you have someone covering your back when you find this guy, I have heard the rumors as well. We have had a couple of homicides where there were whispers about a 'Jack' so far he has been very illusive. I have talked to some real tough 'down and outers' who have said that those who disagree with him or cross him tend to disappear or show up dead. He has a cadre of freaks, you know the type, and they'll do anything for drugs or just for the vicious thrill of the kill."

"Ted I have never knew you have so much imagination. Yes I have heard those rumor as well, I just haven't been able to find him."

They left the conversation there and watched the Alberta Body Removal guys scooped up the copse of Linda, put her in a body bag and zip it up quickly before more of the scent of her death escaped.

"Ted make sure Ident takes photos of the body but particularly of the face."

"Already done Xav, they will also be taking more before the autopsy."

Susie obviously had been beaten and too scared to talk. Now Linda is dead, Rose was right. Now I need to find this 'Jack' and find out what the hell is going on, Xavier thought as he watched them slide the wrapped body into the back of the body removal van.

CHAPTER EIGHT

A mucous missile just missed his ear and landed on shoulder of his leather jacket. The projectile was compliments of a large biker, who had yet to learn the niceties of a co-operative, friendly arrest, Reese must be on 'roids' (steroids) again, Xavier thought with an inward sigh.

"You son of a bitch Reese! Gawd dam-mitt, someone get me a spit-mask, NOW!" Xav yelled before, finally, with the help of two uniformed officers, he completed flipping the biker over on his stomach. Reese could spit on the floor all he wanted until they got a mask on him. The two officers continued to practice various, painful holds on the biker, by the name of Gary Reese, while Xavier cleaned and sanitized his jacket where the mucous missile had landed.

Finally when he deemed his jacket sanitized he looked down at the biker.

"Had enough, Gary?"

Gary reluctantly nodded his head within the spit-mask.

"Fuck Gary, you and I are getting to old for this shit. You gotta know when you spit you're gonna get hurt" Xavier said as he stood to one side watching and trying too judge if Gary was going to try anymore stupid moves.

I suddenly feel old, he thought, when I look at these eager young police officers, ready to jump in should this goof of a Biker gets docent (crazy) again. I can almost feel the adrenalin pulsating through their bodies as they hope this biker even twitches in the wrong way. Just like the police dogs wanting to get a bite of the bad-guy they had just tracked down. Dogs had even 'Sac'ed (briskly nudging the bad-guy's balls) a guy to get him to move or twitch, that would give them reason to bite. For me the adrenalin still comes, making me feel like I can do anything, but it takes longer for the rush because the adrenalin and my body carry the memory of the pain that comes after the excitement is over. Xavier smiled at his own thoughts as he watched to make sure Gary didn't try to kick.

She had been watching him since she had stepped off the prisoner's elevator. Smiling to her-self when she heard Xavier warning the guy he was struggling with. For all that he could appear easy going, she knew that beneath that exterior he had the heart of a warrior and though lean, he had the strength to back up any warning. She could see him waiting and watching the big guy on the floor ready to react one way or the other. Yet, to those around him, except her, he seemed relaxed and calm. She sensed his watchfulness and behind it the sadness and sorrow. He feels my thoughts! And then she was looking into his gray eyes.

Xavier had subconsciously heard the prisoner elevator doors open, as he had been fighting with Gary, and sensed somebody on the periphery. Suddenly he felt an urge-no-an impulse, as if something was yanking at his head up to look up…What the fuck…he felt his head jerking up until his eyes locked with the deep, velvet brown eyes of Rose.

Rose looked at him and anyone else watching her would have noticed nothing different from her usual stoic expression. Xavier saw the slight lifting at each corner of her generous mouth and the smallest flash of acknowledgement in her eyes. He took his cue from her and did nothing untoward that would attract attention…it's a good thing nobody can see how my insides have knotted up, he thought.

"Alright lets get this goof processed guys" the nigh shift 'Arrest Processing S/Sgt' Hank Taylor growled.

"Had enough Gary or do you want to go a few more rounds?" Xavier asked in a quiet, dispassionate, voice. With steely determination he had forced himself to focus on the task at hand as he spoke to Gary.

Gary nodded that he had enough and Xavier could almost see the fight sliding out of Gary's body. It took the two uniformed police officers and Xavier to assist the big biker getting to his feet. They then walked him over to the Prisoner Processing area. They searched him again, taking his cowboy boots and some cash from him, all of which was filed under Gary's name until he was released at which time it would be returned to him.

Once he had been processed, Xavier walked Gary back to the Paramedic's office. Damn this is taking forever, he thought. The paramedic checked Gary's heart, blood pressure and what kind of drugs he had taken. The paramedic nodded, without surprise as he noted the usual signs of 'roid' overuse...the chipmunk cheeks, short, bulging neck and from the arresting officer, in this case detective O'Malley, the bikers initial behavior. Xavier informed the paramedic that the suspect exhibited all the signs of 'roid rage' including starting to remove his clothes because his brain, due to his overuse of steroids, was unable to control his inner body temperature and as a result he had begun to heat up from the core outward; kind of a prolonged 'hot flash'. Luckily the biker still had his pants on when they 'scrummed' him. A maneuver where several police officers jump on the raging suspect too overwhelm and bring down a large subject, similar to a pride of lions bringing down a Cape Buffalo. Of course the suspect like the Buffalo continued to fight. With the suspect it was because of 'roid rage' or other drug or mentally induced behaviors. Xavier had said that trying to hold on to the biker had been like trying to get a grip on a greased pig because the accused had been sweating so much.

The Paramedic nodded at the classic signs and had Gary placed in cell seven, the medical cell closest to the paramedic's office so he could be physically checked every few minutes. That way the paramedic could watch for any more of the danger signs from a possible steroids overdose.

Finally, Xavier thought, as he tried to walk casually back to the Arrest Processing area. He knew the Prison Guard that was escorting Rose up to the counter. He waved Hank Taylor off and indicated that he would handle the processing out of this particular female prisoner. Hank nodded with relief and started to get his stuff ready so he could go home and the dayshift staff sergeant could take over.

"Hey Dave, you looking for a sergeant or staff sergeant to go over and explain those parole documents to that hooker, I'm your man."

"You're a Detective aren't you Xav?"

"Same rank as a Sergeant, besides I want to talk to her bout her ex-pimp" Xavier returned.

Dave looked over at the staff sergeant, who nodded okay, as he finished getting his stuff together.

"Ok, saves me time," Dave said with a shrug as he handed off the parole papers to Xavier.

"You might as well take those cuffs off her and take them with you, save you a trip. I don't think she will be running off anywhere."

Dave smirked at the quip and thought, I don't give a shit if he flushes that little whore down the shitter long as I can get out of here and back up to Spy Hill Remand before the evening rush hour. After he got the Remand handcuffs back he turned and left.

Rose had stood quietly as the prison guard removed the cuffs. As he walked off she sighed, and almost imperceptibly relaxed. Her long blue-black hair, hanging along each side of her face, served as effective shields so Xavier could not clearly see her features from the side.

Not that she had ever really let her thoughts be mirrored on her face except, of course, for the night she had told him about the Reaper. What was it that Harry was always quoting when they were together? Oh yeah, from Shakespeare I think 'A book where men may read strange matters,' he thought.

"Follow me please. I can explain these parole papers to you. We'll go into one of the interview rooms. It's easier if we are both sitting down," he said as he directed her to an interview room that was reasonably clean, although all the rooms, even though cleaned with bleach, retained the faint, acrid smell of piss, puke and blood.

Each of the three interview rooms, used to be called interrogation rooms, but given that the word interrogation was now considered Politically InCorrect, the rooms were now called Interview Rooms.

The name of the rooms had been changed, but the spirit of the rooms remained. Of course certain words were never mentioned in front of Defense Lawyers, who were just looking for ways to show what brutes the police were. Each room had a metal table with metal stools on two sides in it, these were welded to the wall just in case some accused became enraged at what he was being charged with and felt like throwing something.

"Rose take a seat, there is a camera up in the corner by the ceiling so I have to go through the motions of serving these papers on you. There is no recording equipment so we can say what we want with relative privacy" Xavier said as he took the seat opposite her.

She nodded watching as he slid the parole papers over to her and with a pen appeared to be directing her attention to various parts of the paper. She put her left hand on a corner of the papers, her head slightly bent so her hair prevented the camera from revealing her expression on the monitors in Arrest Processing behind the counter.

"I'm glad you're finally out of prison but in a way it was maybe good that you were locked away. Safer. A lot has happened since you have been inside. Most of my news is not good, I am sorry to say," he said as he really looked at her and thought, she has turned from pretty into handsome. There is too much sadness in her face to let the beauty shine through. Her skin is still the color of underdone toast but there are a few more lines around her eyes. She still carries herself with a kind of fluid grace that belied what her life had been.

"I've heard some things, people come and go while you're in prison, they tell of news of outside world," Rose said with a shrug.

"I don't know what you have heard but I will tell you what I know," Xavier replied.

"Tell me."

Xavier needed no more urging than that and began to tell Rose what had transpired since the last time he'd seen her. He started with the strange suicide west of the city, in the old barn and the first sign of the Reaper he had found there. From there he went on to tell her about how the east end of downtown and the stroll where she used to worked had changed. He was watching from the outside so he probably had missed the start and more importantly when the Reaper or 'Jack' had begun to exert his influence. Finally he told her what it was like now. The feeling of absolute fear and paranoia that hung over the east end like a black pall, and how it affected the people they both knew including Susie. It was then he told about Linda and how in death, the 'Soul-Slayer Reaper,' had marked her. He explained how the Gang unit, which he was in, Drug and Homicide Units were searching for 'One Eyed Jack'.

Xavier had not told anybody about the 'Reaper' angle simply because he understood how the police officer mind worked. He knew they would have looked at him surreptitiously, awkwardly. They would humor him as they slowly, discreetly pulled away from him because he obviously had lost his mind if he believed in such a bizarre tale of crap. They would have done nothing, avoiding his madness because it might be catching. His superiors would have done nothing, except have the police shrink look at him, then have him directing traffic in the back ally or some such mundane job. The police only dealt in police reality that included the 'Reaper's Scythe' which to them was not the mark of a terrible Spirit. It was simply the mark of a serial killer who was using an upside down 'J' therefore 'Jack' made sense. They also understood and knew that someone was flooding the area with Crank and Crack and from what little they had heard from their respective snitches the culprit was likely this 'One-Eyed-Jack'. Unfortunately this particular bad-guy had proved elusive, to date.

Rose had been watching him as he told all that had happened in her absence. She had the chance to look at him closely as he talked, and was startled by his physical appearance. His hair, which had been a thick thatch of straight black hair, strands of which tended to stick out here and there, was now more silver than black and it was longer.

Xavier's complexion used to have a healthy, almost ruddy tone to it. Now he was pale. He has traveled where there are only shadows, she thought. The pallor emphasized the lean angles of his face and made him look much older than he was. He looked exhausted, like he had seen too much and sleep was a stranger. His mouth, which had always seemed made to smile now had a slight twist of cynicism. The eyes, though, had not dulled and still retained that sparkle of intelligence and empathy mixed with a touch of humor as he met her gaze.

"Ah age, it changes all of us. Yet there are favored, remembered, cherished parts that seem to never change to those who are closest to us those are what we see in each other. It is only those who have never truly known us except by our exterior that we present to the outside world that see us age."

"I see you have gotten as bad as Harry at quoting things. How is he by the way?"

"Harry never changes, except his hair is whiter and he is racked at times with arthritis. He has become quite adapt at telling the weather, or so he says. I am glad he hasn't been involved in any of this. I wish I wasn't involved in this, just another police officer doing his job."

"But you are involved, including the spirits and worse yet you understand it don't you" Rose asked?

"Yes, but I still don't understand why I sometimes see things that mean nothing, almost. It is like I'm on the very edge of something. And Soul-Slayer, or at least the thought of him fills me with dread."

"I too feel I am on the very edge, but is it of the abyss; or understanding? I had much time to think while I was in jail, the Spirits have been whispering to me. Don't look at me that way Xavier, it is easier for me because I am of The People and The Creator is allowing more memories to come back to me."

"I'm sorry, it was just seeing the body of Linda."

"Yes, I saw it too through your eyes and I shed tears for her. Our Spirits, yours and mine, are being woven back together; we were once one, which is why we seem to see, feel and understand the same, particularly when we are in close vicinity.

I also saw the suicide in the barn. It sounds like a white kid named Joel. Never knew his last name, but you could tell from the way he talked, his clothes and his attitude that he was from wealth and felt entitled. It was like he was taking a walk on the wild side and if you couldn't do anything for him you were invisible. I saw him once give cash to one drunk to beat up another down-and-outer that was past out. He looked where I was standing, put his finger to his lips and smiled."

"He was a weird one, perhaps a sickness lay on his soul. He was like one of them old televisions where the rabbit ears don't work proper so you put tin foil on'em. But even then, images don't exactly stick together so sometimes you get two faint images of the same thing like the good side and the bad side never connected as a whole person. Understand, Xav?" Rose asked with puzzled, unsure look on her face.

Xavier paused for a minute, played with his pen then gave a small almost imperceptible nod of his head. "I think at some point Joel might have been perhaps like the rest of us, maybe a little richer. There are good, rich people out there. Somehow though, he might have got too much stuff and to little love and attention. Maybe that started a tear in his psyche or soul, our sense of self, what we are. Joel experienced very little and was given everything without having to work for it, that was the first little tear. Or Joel simply had no conscious, and simply did things to please himself and his ego. Then he got mixed up with the Soul-Slayer and drugs. The drugs weaken even further what was already unsteady and weak or just not there. That is how the Soul-Slayer destroyed him."

Rose's face cleared, "yes that make sense. That is why Soul-Slayer simply had him kill himself because Joel had already lost his soul."

"Did Joel buy a lot of coke and crack?" Xavier asked.

"At first yeah, but then he broke the rule of all dealers," Rose responded.

"Started using the product himself?"

"Yeah, just too arrogant. I heard the Soul-Slayer was involved with him. Then Joel just disappeared. No one asked about him, no one seemed to care. With his blonde hair, nice clothes and expensive, leather jacket that little shit-head didn't belong down here. Or, then maybe he did. He was just dressed wrong for the dance," Rose snickered to herself and shook her head.

Xavier watched her as she read and then signed the papers and wondered what she was thinking.

She signed the parole papers with illiterate indifference, her mind wandering, thinking; fuck, even with Xavier explaining, then watching me sign the papers, like I can read. Sign them! Sign them! Gotta blow this joint. Huh, funny one, cause I am gonna suck in the smoke from a joint soon as I get out. Just sign'em, sign and be gone, gone, gone. The band Chilliwack, always did like them, she thought. My last day, my last night of freedom with my friends, last time to be wild and crazy as her stomach twisted into slick knot of excitement at doing the wrong thing. She felt disapproval bubbling up, she pushed it back down into her subconscious. Tomorrow I will think on this feeling. Not now.

"So where do we go from here?" Xavier asked breaking into her thoughts.

"Our paths go different ways. You follow the police path. That is where you will do the 'Soul-Slayer' the most harm. He does not know you are aware of his existence and thinks you are simply another stupid cop. Let him think that while you watch, wait and learn about him. I must go to the mountains where the Spiderwoman waits for me. I am bonded to her even stronger than the bond to you. My time in this world as 'Rose' is almost done. Perhaps she will help me find the proper magic to bind this Soul-Slayer and destroy him. You and I though will come together again for we are the different sides of one."

There was nothing more to be said. Xavier quickly went over the paperwork with her and she signed it. He gave her part of the paper work and as he did they shared a long look, it was one of understanding. Xavier escorted her from the building and watched her walk east down Seventh Avenue S.E.

CHAPTER NINE

Discharged into the downtown area the first thing she did was head for a booze-can only two blocks from the police headquarters. There weren't many pimps and hookers hanging out which was unusual and those that were there looked tight and uneasy. Her friends bought her some drinks, a couple of lines of coke and some 'oxy' for old time sake. She relaxed in the back of the bar. The mixture of drugs and booze were furtive friends of hers which, when combined, made her feel like she was flying 'round the top of her world.' They also got her in the mood to earn some money the usual way.

While sitting in the Booze-Can, Rose got told that her old pimp, Big Willy, had left town in a hurry to deal with some 'Ho' problems in Vancouver. Several young, low-level pimps sidled up to her, told her they could protect her and handle her financial matters while her pimp was out of town.

In other words she thought, I do all the work, going down on some butt-ugly, shit-head in the front seat of a battered, old car, which stank of rotten fish. Or even worse 'doing round the world' in the back seat of what always seemed like the same car. That damn country song 'Looking for Love in all The Wrong Places', rolling, rolling through my head. Scrawny, skinny, boys trying to act like big time pimps, can't wipe their own assholes, never mind protecting mine.

Rose, who had always loved theme parks with all the gaudy, colorful rides, thought that her life had become like a poorly maintained carousel – Lions, horses and elephants locked into a circle with their manes whipped by a wind only they felt. Colors now faded into milky nothingness, with only a bare hint of past glories. Time was coming soon to take life's ride by her-self and become what she was meant to be.

She decided to ply her wares at the Cecil Hotel, a place held together by cracked, decrepit, old bones, while misery wall-papered the rotting rooms. Human cockroaches were attracted to such places; they skittered here and there in the dark corners, selling drugs and sex.

The old hotel seemed impervious to, or perhaps, it gained strength from all the unhappiness and hopelessness, the smell of which, wafted through the old hallways, and probably had helped to keep the moldy walls standing.

Rose sat at a small booth in a dark corner of the bar, drank some more drafts, a double rum and coke and discreetly injected part of a 'speedball'. Then she waited for the additional liquor and drugs to mix and find their way through her brain and body. As Rose sat there she pondered the information the bartender, a friend of hers, had told her.

Wendell, one of my dearest friends, such a drag queen and funny as hell even after all this time. He warned me to get out of town quick cause they got warrants out for me already, then asks me if I want to make some quick money. Wendell looked worried though, said be safe? Maybe the 'john' is weird bout women of The People or something. Well I can take care of myself, always have, always will. Just gotta find a ride and a bit more money then head out to the west of the city, west of the Bow River, west into the mountains. West to where I can smell fir trees that still cradled the snow on their boughs, so crisp, and clean. I can feel the mountains pulling at-no calling me as if someone waits for me Rose thought woozily.

Sure enough, just as she finished those few thoughts, there was a sudden, warm surge within her body and pulsating stars before her eyes. For a brief moment she felt an odd kind of disappointment with herself, for doing drugs. There came a brief, green smell of the clean mountain air. I will be up in the mountains soon enough, but I still need some money and a ride. At least being stoned made things easier. It had been a long time since she had felt this fine-- very high and stoned enough to suck some down and outer.

A biker, wearing Hell's Angel's colors, long beard, baldheaded and tattooed all over with a large beer-belly looked her way. She smiled coyly in his direction, pushed herself up and staggered to his table without falling and sat down – a major accomplishment – given how high she was starting to soar as she thought Christ I should rewrite that song, I ain't got air beneath my wings, I got fucking crack! Rose laughed so hard at that she nearly pissed off the Biker (never a good thing to do). After a brief discussion about price, her head disappeared beneath the table. You could tell from the Biker's red face and fixed, blank eyes that he was getting his money's worth.

Once she was done, Rose wiped her mouth with some napkins and gulped down some beer to wash away the wet, sticky, dead fish taste of 'Sparky the sperm'. With their business completed, she pushed the Biker from the dimly lit booth as he finished zipping up his pants.

During the rest of the evening while she plied her trade, Rose heard other snippets about this white guy who wanted to party with a hooker from The People. Towards morning she could feel herself sliding into a crash and burn. Her head was aching and her jaws were starting to lock. Time to do a final trick.

She looked at the 'john' who seemed to want her services and thought, shit I bet this poor boy don't even have two fives to keep each other company in the pockets of those old, baggy, work pants.

"So what are you looking for," Rose asked, as she looked him up and down?

"Uh, you know, a blow job. How much it gonna be," he meekly asked?

"Twenty, you got twenty," she asked? Then watched him shake his bowed head as one foot scuffed the worn carpet.

A sudden idea popped into her head. "You got a ride, a car and five?"

He nodded, and the slow smile of a slow brain spread across his face.

"Here is how this is going to work: I'll give you a blow-job for five dollars and you drive me in your car to the west side of the city by the Bow River. Deal?"

He nodded.

"What's your name, anyway?"

"Names Joe, and yes, lady, got me a van and five dollars," Joe's mouth stretched into an even bigger gin.

Rose returned the grin as she thought; things coming together, ride, money, more money from the john by the river-maybe booze, drugs.

One trick more, then to the Rez. The mountains – wish I could speak People lingo…wish I was smarter…wishing…wish…wanting – waste of fucking time. That cartoon Popeye…

"I is what I is," She whispered and shrugged.

Joe and Rose stumbled out to Joe's dirty, rusted-out, van, which Joe had hidden amongst some tall, ratty bushes behind the Cecil. Once inside Rose gave him a half-hearted blow-job which seemed to make him happy. Then they both fell into a drunken, drugged, exhausted sleep.

***

"Hey, lady you wanna go to the river now? Sun is shinning, it's afternoon maybe," Joe was saying as he shook her shoulder, while holding his five dollars in the other hand.

"Wha…What? Where are we? Oh, yeah, Joe,right? Holy shit! Have we slept this long," Joe nodded and smiled. She saw the money in his hand.

"Great. Let's go Joe. Have you ever had an honest to gawd blowjob?" Rose asked as she sipped some stale water from a water bottle she had found in the back of the van. From the puzzled look on his face, Rose guessed that counting the one she had already given him, he had maybe two in his life. As they drove out of the downtown area, Rose felt a surge of sympathy for this innocent. He seemed in some unexplainable way more People than white. She guessed he would always be on the sidelines because of who he was. Rose gave him the very best blowjob he would ever have.

CHAPTER TEN

The day was clear and warm, the sky a late summer baked blue. The hours were drifting through the afternoon towards twilight, which was still a time away. There was just the faintest touch of pinkish gold staining the underside of the odd, white fluffy cloud that floated above the mountains to the west. The air smelled of just mowed grass and late summer freedom emphasized by the distant almost desperate laughter of children. There was a velvet sheen to the grass, tree leaves and sky that made their colors richer, deeper while the shadows were more intense and textured. Sunlight played with the droplets of water released from sprinklers turning them into millions of prisms reflecting a multitude of colors.

A dirty, white, panel van with black smoke boiling out the rear rusted tail pipe pulled onto the gravel on the north side of the highway, just east of the bridge that crossed the Bow River breaking the bucolic scene in half. The passenger door opened and a slim, small, woman of The People with long, shiny black hair climbed out. She was wiping a dirty tissue across her mouth. The woman grimaced as she threw the tissue to the ground, then she turned and looked back into the van.

"Thanks for the ride Joe."

"No problem, Rose. Thanks for the blow-job." Joe put the van in gear and left her in a cloud of dust and small gravel.

Rose watched him drive off, and although she smiled, she felt the heat from her blood boiling. But that was the way it was every time she had done some 'Ho' sex with a white-man. Big white man, little dick, I gotta admit though, that Joe seemed innocent, kinder than most white men, probably 'cause he's a retard.

She ran across the highway, plunged down a gentle, grass covered embankment on the south side of the road and east of the bridge. Just for a moment, she felt free unfettered by the bitter chains of adulthood. She was a young girl again, before her virtue and innocence had been ripped from her. When anything seemed possible.

She slowed to a walk when she reached the bottom of the hill, she could still hear the distant laughter of children. Strolling along a path that for a time eased along the riverbank. She heard the pleasant sound of the water flowing over the rocks, and sometimes the water seemed to rippled in protest as large boulders, half-submerged logs or sandbars attempted too impede its course.

There were a variety of old, tall trees to the left, their thick branches reached out and intertwined with branches of other ancient trees forming a high, mottled green ceiling almost like she wasn't at the edge of the city in the river park but in an old growth forest. The further she walked along the path, the fainter came the sound of the river, and the closer together the trees became. Similar to the descriptions told by elders of huge, ancient forests. She sat down amongst the large, exposed roots of an aged willow with her back against the rough trunk. The leaves above, and around her trembled each time a slight breeze ran its fingers through their leaves.

Rose took in great gulps of the sweet air, even lifting her arms from her sides, in the hopes of enlarging her lungs to inhale more of the fragrance. After this last stint in prison, she had thought her sense of smell was seared away forever. She had just been released from prison yesterday and aside from the happiness at seeing her Spirit brother Xavier, she was weary and worried. The activities of the last twenty-eight hours had drained her and she felt a vague, uneasy disappointment with herself for falling back into her old ways. So easy, too easy to go back to what she had known since her mother had stolen her from the Rez when she was twelve.

She wished for the umpteenth time that she were a young girl again. But wishing never got me nothing except frustration and pain, she thought. Forgotten memories of her childhood had been coming back to her all day, first a trickle then in a flood.

First came her early childhood and her mother, a woman yearning for the bright lights of the city, dumping her with George Bear-Claw, a Medicine man strong and proud. She had only been two at the time.

George had gladly welcomed her into his large, loving family on the Rez in the foothills rising up to the Spirit Mist Mountains and there she had thrived.

As she sat beneath the willow tree she let the memories of her past flow over her accepting them and letting them become the part of her that had been missing for a long time.

She remembered being happy as part of George's family. Happiness and love were not just words but actual feelings that her body now absorbed like water quenching the terrible thirst of wandering in a desert of empty gray words that had meant nothing for so long.

The doors to her remembrance of things past had swung wide open now and she sat there watching with her mind's eye a campfire with several elders sitting around it. Her adoptive father George, who was the most powerful Medicine man of the northern tribe of The People, was sitting amongst the elders. On the right side of his head Golden Eagle feathers entwined in his long dark hair. The necklace he always wore was strung with sky blue beads on either side of an amulet that held his magic. The amulet glowed with a kind of mystic energy in the firelight.

Beside George sat a pretty child with long blue, black hair that was unbound. That's me at twelve she thought with a smile. The recollections were the movie of her life and she sat there and let them flow into her. She heard a song within that part and began unconsciously to hum it. Then she remembered the aroma of birch wood burning in the bonfire. There was also the smell of old, well cared for buckskin and the scent of fresh, cold fallen snow that made her feel like she was up in the high mountains.

She sat there in wonder as her memories awoke from their long slumber revealing the otherworldly looking woman standing by the flickering firelight. The woman had long silver hair that had been tightly braided and then wrapped twice around her slender neck and pinned with a beaded hair ornament. George had stood as the woman approached. She had takend a few more step until she was standing beside him. Although George was well over six feet the woman did not have to look up at him. Her garb had been an ancient buckskin sheath with porcupine quills covering both sleeves, they made a pleasant clicking sound each time she moved her arms. There were small dream catchers on the shoulders of the sheath, with beaded webs covering the breast areas with a type of fine, gossamer silver thread connecting the beaded webs. In the middle of the chest area was sewn a silver spider, and on the skirt was a large woven web.

Rose felt the old awe and wonder as she realized whom, as a child, she had been staring up at.

It was the Spiderwoman, a woman of great supernatural power granted to her by the Creator. She knew the secrets of their world and the universe. The Spiderwoman was looking at her through a veil of delicate spider webs with a kind smile on her handsome face as she asked George, "So this be Rose?"

George in his position as Medicine man for the northern People had nodded proudly.

Rose thought of how in her own child's voice she had declared, "You are a Spiderwoman."

She recollected how the Spiderwoman had agreed with her but then stated, "You too will be a Spiderwoman but first life will test you. You will have many hard times or thorns so I decree that your secret People name will be Rose Many thorns. Most, if not all of the thorns must be endured or vanquished before I can teach you the Way and Wisdom of the Web."

"You will survive or die alone and unknowing but if you survive, and I think you will, you will always feel the pull of the western mountains. Until, like a salmon, knowing it must spawn will return to the stream where it was born no matter what barriers might be before it. Like the salmon you will feel the strong urge to return to the mountains and I will be waiting for you with the knowledge that you crave. For now you will forget this night and what has been said here until the time be right. There is one more thing, despite the rage you will feel for the white race there is one who you will see from time to time. Your lives are woven together whether for good or ill I cannot tell, but it is for good I think."

"You will now forget me and the words I have spoken until the time is right, you will know and feel when. Then you will come to me in the Mountains of the Sprirt Mists." As the Spiderwoman spoke those last words she lifted her arms and moved them over Rose's head once, then she stepped beyond the firelight and was gone.

Now the dam in her mind had burst completely opened and that happy time living with George's family and talking to the Spiderwoman took their place within the library of her memories superceding all that was negative. Rose let her mind run lightly over the event that had come after. Such as her drugged out mother kidnapping her. Then selling her to a pimp that ran a 'kiddie trick pad' in the city so she could pay for drugs. The police, finally, busted the 'trick pad' and placed Rose in a foster home rather than taking her back to the Rez.

Recollections ricocheting through the years she had spent in various crowded foster homes, some child care workers were good, some abusive and some who had cared too much for too long until they had burned out and only saw things through weary, indifferent eyes.

She had run away several times until finally the foster care system had given up and she was on her own at sixteen, illiterate with no job skills except those that involved lying on her back or sucking real hard. The faces of the pimps and the johns flashed by, their white faces glowing with the sexual itch they wanted her to scratch. All the drugs bought, sold and sampled in order to hide within the artificial, calm indifference while satisfying the perverse appetites of clients. The violent acts she had been forced into in order to protect her People who lived on the streets of the city and herself. She smiled briefly as she thought of the only White she had cared for, the one named, ironically, after Saint Xavier who had, in a time long ago, burnt many of The People at the stake for alleged worship of demons.

Xavier, a white cop, the only one who could make her laugh, the one who always tried to protect her and knew that most of her stints in prison were wrong. But the most important of all he believed her about the Soul-slayer and the danger the Soul-slayer presented to both The People and the White Race. Xavier had seen the effect the Soul-slayer had had on those that managed to survive in the hard scrabble society of the east end of the city and those who had died by the Soul-slayer's hand. He had done all that while she was in prison.

Prison the last reminisces for the library of her mind; the heavy gray fog that never changed. The smell was part of the fog, always singeing nose hair with the odor of desperation and hopelessness. Every which way she turned, the reek followed her-sweat, puke, and at times, the metallic smell of blood. The underlying stench of badly cured concrete, pissy, shitty and moldy with just a hint of bleach.

To Rose, the guards were nothing more than silhouettes with no defining features who spoke in rough red voices. She never had never looked at them and had kept her head down. The smell, the constant foulness of prison had over-ridden almost all, until now, that is. This golden moment when her life now made sense seemed to have broken the back of prison memories, prison stink, prison fog.

Rose had never gone out of her way to make friends in prison. Some of the prisoners were of the White Race and blended into the fog. The fog people never wanted to have anything to do with The People. The People were wary of Rose. It was almost as if they sensed she was of The People but more-much more? She had always been aware that The People were unsure of how to behave or be around her and it puzzled her as much as it did them.

Now she understood why she always tried to protect them almost like they were her children in the mystical way that a Spiderwoman is the Magical Mother of The People. She had always yearned for a family to take care of and all along she had a huge family and never knew it.

She sat beneath the old willow seeing in her mind's eye all the thorns that she had broken or overcome. Rose finally understood her place in the universe and for the first time since she was twelve she felt whole and right.

CHAPTER ELEVEN

Through out the time Rose had been sitting beneath the willow tree regaining all that her life had been and would be there had been a nagging thought at the back of her mind. The 'john' she was supposed to meet. The arrangement she had made before her life had gone through this change- this understanding-awareness of the whole of what she was.

Somewhere in these woods there was a 'john' looking for her and from what she could remember from the night before she had been warned that he was dangerous. It was at that point that the golden moments she had been having tarnished a wee bit.

Destiny! I should have been able to choose my own path she thought. She stomped along anger making her blind to where she walked. But the more she walked the more she comprehended why she had to be left to figure out life, the hard parts of being, the time of learning how too survive in the worst situations. Even the friendship with a White cop and their closeness started to make sense. The bad situations she had been in and worked her way out of had all been part of the lessons on being a Spiderwoman. She half expected to hear the existing Spiderwoman giving her advice, guiding her but there was nothing. Apparently she was going to have to get herself out of this situation alone.

She had been so involved with her internal monologue she could have walked off a cliff without noticing.

Rose stopped suddenly, her survival instinct kicking in like an internal emergency brake. She looked around and was startled to see that it was late afternoon. Purple shadows were starting to darken the lower parts of some of the trees like a silently creeping mist. Their tops were still painted with the pinkish gold of late twilight but the night was quickly eating away at the last dregs of day. Night would soon hold sway even here at the edge of the city.

She could see a faint trail and she followed it until she observed a dilapidated, old blue tent off to the side of the trail. As she got close she heard a faint rumble that sounded vaguely familiar. The closer she got the louder the snorting-grumble became, in an odd way it was comforting, a sound she had heard before that had no danger clinging to it. The sound was similar to a big ol' bear tucked away hibernating in a cave while the winter raged outside.

Then it came to her that her father George Bear-Claw's wife, Clara, had always complained that she didn't know whose snoring was worst George's or his nephew Jimmy Antelope's? It would have been wonderful if it had have been George for she could have used his advise. But she knew it wasn't George. She had run into George a few times when he came into the city for supplies. His face had always twisted into sadness when he saw her and he begged her to come back to the Rez. Rose had always felt annoyance at the pity she thought she heard in Georges voice and her pride had swollen blinding her to the fact that he only spoke to her out of love.

Still it would be almost as good to see Jimmy, they had been close when they were young. She gingerly lifted the flap that lay over the tent doorway and leaned in. The smell of mouthwash hit her like a punch in the nose and in her haste to step back she nearly fell over.

Rose started to gag as the pungent scent flushed out unwanted memories. Back flashes to when she was young, living on the streets and it was icy cold. She didn't have money enough for the company that alcohol or drugs brought. But she had just enough change for two bottles of the blue mouthwash. The hard way too get drunk, the blue colored mouthwash was especially toxic, like drinking arsenic mixed with paint thinner its stench only partially hidden by the cloying, sweetish odor.

Towards the end of the month, prior to the pogey cheques coming in, most down-and-outers were out of money. That was when the sales of mouthwash soared in the inner city pharmacies. Vanilla, real vanilla, had been stupendously popular in the east end pharmacies and grocery stores until they changed the ingredients and now it was only of interest to people who actually baked. But mouthwash went flying off the selves, because along with the usual dental and medicinal ingredients, mouthwash had a base of alcohol. The combination was toxic to the body.

Mouthwash hangovers were said to be as bad as death by a thousand cuts, and in fact some in the throes of a full-blown mouthwash hangover longed for death. Every once in awhile a body of some down-and-outer would be found floating serenely in the river with a strange smile on his or her purpled lips. Of those who watched the body being pulled from the river one or 'taother' would nod sagely turn to whoever was beside them, "That's old Mary (or Sam, or Jim). Last time I saw 'em they was drinkin that blue shit. Yes siree that's what kilt 'em."

Rose thought of the one time she had done it, so broke couldn't afford to pay attention, never mind food. Fuck food I needed alcohol, drugs. Mouthwash, quickest way to end the longing for while, but the agony of the return felt like the Reaper was pounding your head with his scythe. The thought of how she had drunk two bottles of that shit!

Mouthwash hangover! Thought I was dying-puking my guts out with such force that it felt like my guts had turned inside out inside my body 'til all that was left was the dry heaves and the cruel hope that the Reaper would sympathize with my condition and invite me into his world. Rose vividly recalled that one time and had sworn she would not touch that shit again. And she had stuck to that promise because every time she saw a certain shaped bottle or blue colored liquid she would feel sick, bile starting to rise up in her throat.

"Jimmy, is that you?" She moved back towards the tent opening and, holding her breath, tried to get a better look inside the dark interior.

There was a sudden snort, then the groan of someone in terrible pain.

"Whadda ya wann?" a gravelly voice responded.

Jimmy's voice-he was drinking that shit again!

"Ya wanna go party?" Rose asked sarcastically. She reluctantly ducked and stepped into the tent. Jimmy seemed to be floating in a pond of blue vomit. The area around his mouth was crusted in white, the rest of his face was blue stained like he had been dead a few days. Rose felt a twinge of fear, and then an immense anger boiled up from her stomach and rolled out her tongue.

"You fucking idiot! If ya hadda wanted or needed something I woulda helped ya! But nnnooo ya go out on your own and drink that shit! Ya know the doctors had said your liver was so fucked up that that if ya took anymore yous could die! Ya know I love ya even from when we was little kids, I would do anything for ya!"

"Rose! Rose! Stop shouting! I can hear ya! Jimmy pleaded as he tried to plug his ears with his hands. Then Jimmy, in a whisper, said "Rose you was in jail and you know they won't let anybody with a criminal record inta see ya."

Rose, who was still having trouble controlling her temper said, "Well ya coulda written."

Jimmy burst out laughing, even though the action made it feel like his brain was falling out, whispered back, "Well if I hadda learned how to write and you hadda learned how to read I guess ya woulda had a point there."

Rose stopped short just as she was about to enter into another loud speech and there was a blessed silence in the tent, or so Jimmy thought.

Rose eyes widened as she put her hand over her mouth and giggled softly. Jimmy was suddenly reminded of when they were young and had pulled some stupid stunt Rose would always start giggling and they'd be found out. He smiled at her and she met his smile half way.

"Oh Jimmy, your right on that point only. I can't afford to lose my best friend and cousin, I just can't. Beside I think things might start going better now and I will always need you! You're my best and only cousin. What would I do without ya? " Rose said in a tearstained voice.

Jimmy studied her face, what he saw there was a faint glow and he understood as he reached out with a trembling hand and touched her cheek. Suddenly he felt better almost like he was going to stay in life and even wanted to survive.

"You know! You have figured it out about the Spiderwoman!"

Rose just looked at him and smiled in acknowledgement and acceptance. There were no need for words, she hugged him tightly and then told him that there was someone wandering the woods looking for her services as Rose and she had to get rid of him.

"I'll go with you, you might need some help."

"No Jimmy this is something from the old life, the final thing, this last thorn and I must deal with it. You get some sleep and we will talk in the morning," Rose said before she turned and bent to step out of the tent.

CHAPTER TWELVE

Rose searched for the trail she had been on before she had found Jimmy's tent and thought to herself, I truly have lost some of my abilities as one of the People when I can't even find a simple trail in a white man's park. After much searching she managed to find the faint path she had been on when she had been side tracked by the old tent. It was relatively easy to follow as the full moon above cast a pale light on the forest. The path descended a slight slope before it flattened out and she came upon what must have been one of the partygoers. He was a male that looked almost too light skinned to be one of the People but perhaps he was a half-n-half. He was slumped sideways on a large stump gripping a half full bottle of cheap whiskey as if it was a key to paradise. He seemed to be having a hard time focusing on her and life in general. There were also several empty beer cans scattered around and the grass had been flattened.

She stood there for a few minutes debating with herself about whether to stay there or continue to look around for the White guy to let him know she wasn't interested. Abruptly the evening birds stopped singing and the forest became silent. Rose sensed something was wrong.

'Something evil this way comes' she had heard that phrase some-where before. It often popped into her brain just before something bad been about to happen. The phrase was lighting up the front of her brain like a neon-sign-flashing-flashing warning. There was some-thing, no someone malignant close by. The only way she could think of describing the feeling was like the sensation she had had when she had been very young and a seemingly, kindly looking old man had offered her candy then tried too convinced her that it would be safe to come to his house to warm up. Her senses had screamed a warning just as the old man had reached out to grab her.

He just missed grabbing her and she ran and ran until she could run no more then turned back to see how far away he was. He was still back at the spot where they had met and just for a moment his face transformed into a mask of evil with red fiery eyes, bulbous forehead with curved horns upon it. He had smiled at her his teeth like broken gravestones, even from where she had run too, his breath was massively grotesque, like something long dead. Then she heard him talking to her only it was like a whisper in her head. "I'll see you again little girl, you are mine too destroy!" She had turned and run again until she had a stitch in her side, her legs were shaking before she had stopped and looked back. Nothing-Nothing the old man-demon was gone. Ever since then she trusted her senses about dangerous things even though she came to think that that had been a nightmare, she never forgot the lesson. This was the same feeling.

She could feel her knife strapped to her leg under her jeans and just above her sneaker, I have a knife; a branch-a sturdy branch I need one, she thought her eyes searched the forest floor. Wait there's one; she bent to pick it up.

Of a sudden adrenaline surged through her entire being. Rose's thinking became crystal clear, her body prepared for fight or flight. A sudden chill running up her spine on the warm night dimpled her skin as all the thoughts flashed through her mind all at once.

Fuck! Fuck! Panic began too edge around her thoughts, someone close, watching. Then a calm voice whispering in her head-think-calm-survive, you can use your instincts-it doesn't know how strong you are.

"Hello, pretty flower. You come too party with old Franz?" a gentle older voice ripped through the silence. It came from somewhere behind her. Rose jumped, let out a little gasp and whirled around to see who had snuck up on her. She could hear the thick, smooth as icing tone ladled on the surface of the voice of a jolly older man, but the beneath the kindly intonation he couldn't quite hide the razor sharp, hard tones of rage.

Franz looked like an old mountain man whose visible skin had been cooked to a deep brown by constant exposure to the weather. He had an odd, stiff legged gait, like his knees had been fused so they couldn't bend. His face was deeply wrinkled, especially around the eyes, nose, and forehead. He had a thick beard and his moustache was scrawny and extended over his mouth, he constantly played-fondled with the moustache with one of his tough, huge logger hands. He was doing that now with his left hand as he watched her and she couldn't tell if he was frowning or smiling because his hand was playing with moustache and hiding his mouth. Even though his skin was brown Rose could see he was of the White Race. Franz's eyes were the palest blue with infinitesimal dots for pupils so there was an almost no difference between the whites and iris of his eyes and as a result they stood out like bright lights surrounded by dark brown skin. If the eyes are the windows to the soul, Franz had no soul for his light eyes held nothing except bright death and now she knew what it was like to be a deer caught in headlights.

"What is your name, my little princess," Franz asked?

Rose saw an almost purple-red color creep up through his beard and onto his deeply tanned cheeks, as he looked her over. It was summer so all she had on was a thin tank top, and tight jeans. Suddenly she felt naked and she had to force herself not to bring both hands up to cover her breasts.

Rose's mind began too race around like a squirrel caught in a cage. Shit, Shit, Shit! He is crazy – dangerous now, when he seems to not have had very much to drink. I could get bad hurt. If I can just get the fuck outta here before he turns mean I might survive! Gotta think, been in trouble before…gotta think!

"Rose" a quiet voice whispered in her mind. "He is not all he appears, a Wer-spirit has taken over his body. Only a serene, tranquil demeanor that belies your thoughts and actions can defeat him, you must let him think you're just a stupid woman." Rose heard and the quiet voice helping her to understand. She managed too control the adrenalin racing through her body taking several deep breaths helped to calm her.

"Betcha ya dance as pretty as you is." Franz said in his icing smooth voice as he stepped right up against her grabbed her one hand with his one hand while he wrapped his other arm around her. She could feel his hot, huge hand gripping her back as he hummed some tune. That smell, the smell from her childhood, the odor of long time dead seemed to seep from him and started to numb her determination.

She began dancing with him. At first, he didn't say much and the smile upon his face seemed forced like he was trying to keep her calm, Rose smiled back tentatively. Then he pulled a small whiskey bottle out of is jacket and took a large swig out of the bottle before offering her some. She took a sip, but that seemed to anger him, so she took another sip, I have to keep a sober head she thought.

Just like every other fucking john she thought; the more he drank, the more his cruel dangerous side came out. He squeezed her arms and pulled her hard against him, laughing when her face contorted with pain. He stopped any pretense of dancing and stood watching her as she took a step back. His big, meaty hands clenching and unclenching like pistons warming up an engine.

Fuck! Can't get my legs move! I know when a guy clenches and unclenches his hands like Franz is doing it is part of the rage that is building inside him. That's when things are gonna get rough – Gotta Calm Down – think; I aint no sheep to be led to the slaughter.

Franz, with amazing speed, grabbed Rose by the shoulders and began to shake her, all the while ranting, screaming about how much he hated women, especially that bitch that birthed him.

"She distracted my father from loving me, made my father draw away from me. That bitch used sex to lure my father away; I will make all bitches pay! Besides no one cares if another one of the People disappears. How wonderfully satisfying it is to feel the softness of their throats, as I press harder," he hissed. "Is your throat soft?" He whispered as his hands slid from her shoulders up to her neck and at first almost massaged her throat before his massive hands began too tighten.

"I've always found that the women of The People have throat skin so much more tender, far finer than a white whore's. I wonder why?"

Franz panted, pulling her against him as he started to strangle her, tighter and tighter his large hands squeezed and she could feel him getting more excited by the hard, growing lump in his pants as began to press his entire body into her.

Rose struggled harder, arms and legs flailing as her brain started to shut down from lack of oxygen, watching him lick the scrawny, chewed hair that his covered lips might be the last thing she saw in this life. NO! NO! Not now, not when I am so close! With the last of the air she forced her brain into fight mode and managed to bring her arms up. Hands turned into claws to rip his face open and blind him. Franz saw the claws coming for his face and instinctively he let go of her and jumped back. He swung his fist at Rose striking her on the side of her head. Rose dropped to the ground like a rock and lay still. Franz laughed then spit on her still body and walked away, no doubt to get some liquid courage and a place to bury her.

Rose jumped up once she sensed he was out of the immediate area. The idea of heading for the hills had seemed like a good plan. But as she rubbed her throbbing throat she thought she likely she didn't have time to head for the hills and she knew she couldn't withstand another attack. Time to take the attack to him, that fucker tried to kill me, no way I am going to run, I aint ever run from a White, she thought!

She ducked down in the tall grass, listening as she looked around. Nothing moving. Her head was still ringing from the punch to the head, and a massive headache rode roughshod across her forehead. She duck-walked through the underbrush as she looked for the other guy who she had seen earlier sitting on a log drinking. Maybe he could help her.

When she found him, he was slouched even further down on the log, having a twenty-six ounce nap: with the bottle of whiskey, now almost empty, clutched in his arms.

Every god-damn-male I have dealt with tonight has been drunk, she thought with deep anger. Gotta keep moving or that asshole will kill me. Rose rifled through the passed-out drunk's pockets-nothing!

At least she had a knife. Then she saw the axe lying behind the log. She grabbed it then remained crouched as she ran to a nearby stand of bushes by the trunk of a large tree.

She hunkered down behind the bushes, trying to calm both her heart and her breathing so she could hear if anyone approached. Rose didn't have long to wait before she heard crashing and cursing from somewhere close. Then Franz stepped out of the bushes to her right. She stayed down watching him. He had a large hunting knife in his right hand as he looked around and his brows grew together as he frowned at not seeing her prone form.

He slowly approached where the light-skinned male lay in alcoholic oblivion. Franz bent over the unconscious form, maybe thinking, he wasn't as drunk as he appeared. Rose moved quietly closer. Franz leaned in even further and raised his hunting knife a manic smile forming on his face he muttered "Yeah helped the bitch, now your gonna die fer it! He had raised the knife even further and then started too bring it down in a killing blow.

Rose leaped towards him axe raised. When she was almost on him she swung the axe in a graceful arc with all the strength she had. The axe hit him once on the back of the head, just above where the spine and the skull join. He went down like a pole axed steer and lay still beside the passed out half-n-half.

Franz still clutched the knife in one hand while his other hand trembled and twitched twice and then was still while blood spurted up passed where the axe was embedded and landed on the head of the lifeless form that had been Franz. She was surprised at how little blood there was, usually head wounds bled and bled. Maybe the axe had acted like a kinda dam blocking the rest of the blood.

Rose decided that she should try to get the axe out of the back of Franz's head but it refused to move. Oh Man-Oh Fuck! The shock of what she had just done was starting to sink in and with it hysteria was starting to over-ride good sense. Wild giggles began to force their way out of her mouth. She stared at the big body with the axe sticking out of the back of his head. Ok, first I hafta get the axe out of his head she thought. After several tries the axe hadn't even wiggled or budged. Gotta get my shit together, gotta get the axe out!

Finally, she put her misgivings about standing on a dead body aside and stood on the back by the upper spine of the deceased Franz. With more leverage she worked the axe back and forth, back and forth. Finally it started to move. The sound of the steel axe head grinding against the skull bone was sickening, while the feel of the broken brain beneath the bone was like plums that had gone over weeks before. Suddenly, the axe burst loose with a final sucking sound. Rose tumbled forward over Franz's leaking head, landing in a bunch of pinecones and burst out laughing.

"What the hell?" Why did I have to get the axe out, she thought? Oh yeah, evidence…got to hide the axe cause it has my bloody fingerprints all over it, Jesus, Rose!

"Gotta get my shit together! It's not like I haven't killed before." She whispered in a ragged tone feeling like she had just run a marathon. Gotta take care of myself; no one else will she thought as she tried too claw back the raising hysteria that was clouding her ability to think. She got up deliberately avoiding the body went to check the dead guy's tent.

"Nothing much here, I'll have to have a better look at it in the morning when I'm not so tired. Oh wait a sec, what's this?" she muttered as she saw a blanket and a bottle of booze in the corner.

She grabbed the full twenty-six-ounce bottle of vodka along with an old blanket she found in the corner of the tent. She laid the blanket over the body and kicked the bloody axe under some scrub by the body. She would dispose of it properly in the morning but she would dispose of the vodka tonight, she desperately needed several large drinks to drown out the sound of the axe working against bone. She then walked towards where she thought Jimmy's tent was. She managed to find the tent by following her nose until the faint scent of mouthwash ruined the fragrance of the woods.

Once she found the tent she walked a distance away and settle beneath an old Fir tree so the only odor was the smell of tree sap. Rose opened the bottle of vodka and took several large swigs before she gathered some old pine needles into a mound. She took one more swig before settling on the mound and falling asleep almost immediately.

CHAPTER THIRTEEN

Morning came too quick.

Jimmy tentatively climbed out of his mouthwash soaked tent. The fragrance of the woods and the birds singing in the bright early morning light was just too much for his raw senses and stomach causing him to puke blue vomit for what seemed like the last part of his lifetime, but it was actually only a few minutes. He felt a little bit better after unloading a part of his misery and decided to go down to the river to cleanup. That too might also ease the pain still bouncing around throughout his body and brain when he moved or thought too fast. Of course standing still was much easier, but standing still could only last so long or there would be a whole lot of mouthwash drinkers turning into statues.

That thought almost made him smile as he forced himself to move, step after painful step. He imagined all the frozen mouthwash drinkers some under bridges, some lurking in back alleys standing frozen in whatever pose they were in when the mouthwash took hold. The image struck him as so funny that he started to laugh and that immediately caused such a sharp pain in his head that he nearly passed out. Jimmy was a mangled mess and anybody looking at him would think he was having a stroke with one side of his face frozen in a half smile while the other side was drooping down and his foot slightly raised.

Jimmy finally managed too make it down to the river although he teetered on the edge of falling on several occasions. The cold of the river water numbed some of the pain so he dunked his whole head into the river and got the wildest brain freeze he'd every had. When the brain freeze had passed he washed his hands and neck then drank some of the water, which cleased his senses even more as the icy water surging through his rotten teeth added another dimension to his pain.

As he finished his morning absolutions he thought of the bearded white guy he had seen as he had been stumbling down to the river. The white guy had been slipping and sliding as he was coming back up from the river. Even though the white guy had been holding his hand over the back of his head Jimmy could see a lot of blood dripping down from under his hand. Just what was it Rose had said to him last night? He couldn't remember.

Jimmy made it back up to the tent just as Rose was waking up in her place under a fir tree.

"Hey, Jimmy, still feeling blue?" Rose asked with a smile.

"Naw I'm ok, except my head feels like it is full of rusty old nails that are rattling round in there, what a hangover. Say, that fella you said you was gonna to party with, looked in even worse shape than me," Jimmy returned. Suddenly wished he had not opened his mouth, nor been the cause of Rose's sudden frozen look. Her mouth had turned down and seemed to have locked there.

"I need too finish the job," Rose whispered as she turned and headed to the river. She returned a half hour later her face, hair and hands were wet. She kept wringing her hands, almost as if to make sure something was gone from them. (If Xavier had been with her the first words out of his mouth would have been "Out, out damn spot! What have you been up to, Lady Macbeth?) Of course Jimmy had no idea who or what Shakespeare was but he had a petty good idea, just like Xavier would have, just what Rose had gone too make sure of.

"Jimmy I gotta ask you something," Rose said with a tight smile as she sat beside him on the old log he was perched on.

"I thought you might," he returned.

"Jimmy, I want you to forget about last night and today. Do you think you can do that?"

"You know me. I can't remember things from this hour to the next," Jimmy responded.

She spoke briefly to Jimmy about him seeing her last night and it probably would be best to forget the entire goings on of last night and this morning. Rose felt the urgent pull of her returned recollections. Go west-Go west, the voice in her head urged.

"Jimmy I have to go," she said gently.

"The Spiderwoman has called you," Jimmy said as tears started to leak from his eyes.

He remembers, she thought as she put her arm around his shoulder and gave him a gentle squeeze.

"Don't worry it's only rarely that I remember those days when thing's were so good, like now. Mostly I remember nothin' cause the alcohol and mouthwash hide the good and dull the pain of my days now," Jimmy said with a sigh.

"It doesn't have to be that way Jimmy, go back to the Rez stay away from the White's poison and you'll be okay. You and I can laugh together again from time to time."

"Maybe I will, I miss George and I do miss the Rez but I don't know if I wouldn't miss the poison more, but I jist might try." Jimmy responded with a sad attempt at a smile.

Rose squeezed his shoulder, she suspected that he would see the inside of mouthwash bottle before he ever got it together enough to go back to the Rez but she would talk to George anyway. She hated to leave Jimmy in this state but there was nothing she could do for him right now.

Time now for her to be turning and walking away; back towards the highway that would lead her west towards the mountains, her step steady and quick as she walked back through the trees that had been so welcoming last night. Rose climbed back up the embankment and crossed the highway to the side that ran to the west.

As she started hitchhiking west along the Trans-Canada Highway, mulling over what had happened in the last two days while watching for cars.

Havta do whatever is necessary to get by. I needed money, drugs and a ride. Hafta get outa the city. 'The Belly of the Beast.' She didn't know where she had heard that saying but it described the city, the beast. This latest death, it was self-defense, but the Whites had the power and might call it murder. Maybe that's the reason we are bonded, and why I feel like he is my Familiar because I need his help and because in some ways he understood her more than most. Her Xavier, her other half.

"Wonder what the Spider-woman will think of last few day's happenings. Will she still want to teach me? I had a feeling that her spirit was watching over me last night. Odd, even in the daylight, last night feels like a very bad dream, evil was wrapped around Franz like a rotten blanket. I can still sense something hiding just beyond the corners of my eyes when I turn. This is not finished,' she muttered to herself as she stuck out her thumb and focased on car coming towards her.

Those musings kept going through her mind as a car slowed and started to back up. Shit! Only one person, it looked like a man to boot she thought as the car drew closer.

The car backed up until it was beside her, the passenger side window slid slowly down like a mouth opening, a toothless maw. Out of this black maw came a stench so foul it felt like a vicious slap to her sense of smell that sent her mind reeling as she looked into the car. In the driver's seat instead of the face of a man, she saw the face of a demon with pus dripping from cankers all over his face; his eyes were fiery red and glowed while horns grew out of forehead above his bulbous brows, and an axe was embedded in the back of his head.

In a voice that sounded like that of the recently, deceased Franz, the demon said "Hello pretty flower, you killed me so you might as well come and sit beside me, beside I never got to taste that nice looking flesh," as he patted the seat beside him.

Run! Run! A voice in her head yelled as she tripped and almost fell backwards in her panic to get away. Rose managed to turn and flee, but even as she ran down the north embankment she thought she could fell hot rancid breath on her neck and the dark laugh of Franz turned demon. As she reached the mowed grass at the bottom of the hill she heard the squeal of tires and the deep, growl of the engine as the car roared off.

Rose fell to the ground sobbing and shuddering as the memory of that horror kept repeating itself in her head.

Stop! Stop thinking of what just happened, it is only a demon, a wer-sprint sent to terrorize you and thus distract you from your journey, a stern, calm voice enjoined her inside her head. It sounded like the Spider-women's voice; in fact it was of the same tone and timbre that had yelled run.

Try again but use your senses, as you just did, let your understanding of good and evil guide you, the voice of the Spiderwoman urged. You must hurry there are dark spirits that don't want me teaching you. Speed is of the essence as my time on Mother Earth is nearly spent, the voice urged.

Rose stayed on her hands and knees until the Earth stopped swaying and her mind had shut the demon spirit away, she would examine that ugliness later when it did not have the ability to totally unnerve her.

She finally, gingerly stood up when she felt the ground beneath her steady. Rose shivered and zipped up the old, red hoodie she had borrowed from Jimmy. That normal motion seemed to bring everything back into focus. She pushed her hair out of her out of her face and as best she could, and braided it loosely. Rose then climbed back up the embankment she had so recently run down in a panic. When she reached the highway her nose wrinkled at the smell of burnt asphalt. She looked down at the area where the demon car had been and saw the asphalt was melted down to the gravel bed.

So what had happened was not a nightmare, it was reality, she thought as she walked west along the north side of the highway, away from odor.

Rose looked back, occasionally, to see if there were any cars coming. Funny, one of the busiest highways in the province and no cars coming, she thought.

Right as that idea occurred to her, a car appeared in the distance, her stomach twisted with apprehension as she watched it approach.

CHAPTER FOURTEEN

Detective Xavier O'Malley stayed in the shadows away from the old flickering alley light; it was the only one of six that was still working. The others had been broken and replaced so many times that the city had given up on fixing them. Some things were just better done in the dark.

Xavier looked down the alley, known to the druggies that lived in the area and police who worked down here as 'Cocaine Cull-d-sac'. He walked slowly and cautiously down the lane. He didn't want to disturb evidence by stepping on it nor the offal left by the drug and hooker trade in the alley littered with old and broken needles, syringes, dirty pieces of foil and used condoms with a creamy substance leaking out of them and the odd bent spoon.

Further along he could see the large lumpy object covered in a yellow plastic sheet. At least the police tape matched the body-sheet, garish yellow but matching, he thought with a tired sigh. Another body used and abused, laying in the mud like a broken doll. Maybe it had been loved or loved, too late-too late now, death had come and gone leaving naught but the shell. Jeez I'm beginning to sound like Harry, he thought.

Xavier had headed up the integrated Guns and Gang Unit for the last four years and although he still loved the job, life in general had dried into nothingness and blown away since she-he still couldn't say it. His friends could see how exhausted he was. It seemed to them that practically overnight, his thick, black hair had turned silver and his skin had the pallor of lack of sleep and too much work.

Xavier felt nothing except for the emotions brought on by the job and his thoughts of Rose's predicament. If he let his thoughts-emotions drift they would turn traitor and remind him of Rachael's smile, her smell, something of her. His thoughts mostly a bridge of groans across a stream of tears, where had heard that? Oh yeah, someone called Philip Baily, a philosopher perhaps remembered for that sad metaphor. Xavier was barely hanging onto the edge of reason and sanity by his fingertips; only the job gave him the strength to hang on. Things were better when he wasn't alone. When he was on the job he was okay, work filled his mind and he could almost forget her and how they met. Yet thoughts still came unbidden of the beautiful blosom of their life starting together only to be crushed, her's by death, his by a vast empty desert of life without her…lost without her.

* * *

Xavier had been volunteered into give a lecture on gangs as part of a symposium on Criminality and how it affects the Community. When he had found out that because he had shown up late to the Guns And Gangs office everybody had volunteered him. He had begged, threatened and finally resorted to whining, without success. Since he had managed to dodge all the other community crap his fate was sealed, much to the delight of his team. All of his team had been stuck giving speeches or being present while the Police Chief had been talking to community leaders about Guns and Drugs on Xavier's say so.

He had warned his team of dire deeds to come as he reluctantly headed out to give the lecture.

He was about half way through his speech on gangs when the brilliant auburn of her hair caught his attention. He had never seen hair quite that color and the face under all that glorious hair had perfect cheekbones, which emphasized the emerald green, slightly sloe shaped eyes, the cream-colored skin with a smattering of freckles over the nose. Her generous mouth the color of wild strawberries luscious enough to taste.

He suddenly noticed the quiet in the Auditorium and the uncomfortable rustling and coughing. He felt his skin redden because suddenly for the life of him he couldn't remember what the lecture had been about.

"Excuse me sir, but is it really true that all the H.A. - Hells Angels who have the one-percenters patch on their jackets have actually killed someone?" A female voice, with a slight accent, asked. He knew it was her getting him back on track. He looked up with a smile of thanks that took in the audience and then landed back on her.

"I'm, I'm sorry, my mind was drifted back to a case the team is-we are working on and I seemed to have forgotten what I was speaking about. Yes that is the legend that the H.A. and other gangs have put out and in most cases it is probably true." He said somewhat limply and shuffled some papers.

The only way he got through the rest of the speech was by looking at the red exit sign over the opposite door.

She approached the stage after the lecture and had to wait while those in front of her asked their questions. Xavier, was having a hard time answering question from the people around him, it was obvious, to him at least, that his answers were forced and not really on topic. Finally he was talking to her, everybody else had drifted away at his inept, indifferent answers to their questions. They were alone and suddenly his tongue refused to work properly and she suddenly stopped in mid-question, they stood there looking at each other in the now empty lecture hall.

She started to laugh, he joined in and they laughed for a minute as if sharing a secret. He then took her right hand while she smiled at him. He looked at it then turned it over and leaned over it, slowly his warm lips kissed her wrist feeling the pulse racing beneath the soft, fragile skin.

"I, I guess we should go," she said faintly.

"Where shall we go?" he asked still holding her hand.

"I don't know. I don't even know your name," she said

"Xavier is my name, and I think dinner and so much more in this life time."

"My name is Rachel," her right hand still in his, while her left hand had gone to her throat. Her cheeks reddened slightly in a way that complimented her brilliant red hair the color of flames swirling and dancing around her head in contrary curls. She had used hair clips in an attempt to subdue it, without much success. He reached up and removed the clips giving the unruly hair its freedom.

It was the first time ever that he had not thought of the job. All he could think of was how her fiery hair would look spread out on a pillow next to his when he woke up every morning for the rest of his life.

They went to dinner, and talked until the restaurant closed, the waiters and clean up crew waiting in restless boredom for them too leave. Then he walked her home as the magnificent sunrise showed them the way. He knew he had met his other half, not like Rose who felt like his sister in a protective way. He had a feeling Rose would approve.

On the job things were going great, they were busting more and more of 'Jacks' dealers. Things were tense on the street but that was because there were less and less drugs. The balance was shifting at last or so he thought.

CHAPTER FIFTEEN

Xavier took Rachel to meet his family. That, it turned out, had been the biggest mistake he had ever made. I can't believe I was so stupid, he thought as he and Rachel sat there in that frozen, plastic room with a particularly graphic plaster form of a twisted, tortured Jesus on the cross hung above the mantle. Next to the cross, leaning against the mantle a Russian Icon of a gently smiling Madonna with bee's wax candles flickering before her. The candle flames wavered and moved in such a way that to Xavier it seemed that the gentle smile flickered with sorrow at the cold, implacable fanaticism that seemed too lurk in this room. With sadness he also felt that the family of his youth before his father had died, withered away along with the laughter and love. Now there was nothing here but the absolute belief in a religion where there was no laughter, no tenderness, no happiness and worst of all no love. Xavier believed in a God that was capable of laughter, those that loved and compassion. There was none of that in this room. He knew that this was the last time he would be in this room of strident, fanaticism wrapped in plastic.

The room itself had not changed in the years since he left. Plastic covered the couch and chairs. He and Rachel were sitting on the couch that crinkled loudly when they even thought of moving. His mother, who had once been pretty and lively had soured and shriveled into a troll that only knew the bitterness of fanaticism. Mom; no she had always been Mother or Mame. Mother's face looked like she had not laughed, nor smiled since his father had died. Both his mother and his brother, who was now a Monsignor, sat in the chairs on either side of the couch. They were polite but it was like their words would shatter into crystal shards if he or Rachel responded incorrectly.

Rachel sat quietly, while Xavier felt the room closing in on him. His brother and his mother suffocating him, trying too pull him back into the faith they lived for. The unquestioning faith in the room was crushing him. He couldn't take their sanctimonious, unquestioning belief that all else were wrong thinking-sinners but them.

Suddenly he stood up, took Rachel's hand pulling her to her feet and announced that he and Rachel were getting married in the Hebrew faith and then they walked quietly out. Behind him, as he silently closed the front door on his youth and a faith that had become corrupt and perverse in its own self-interest, he could hear his mother screaming out that she was disowning him, while his brother was giving voice too excommunication.

"Stop Xavier," Rachel pleaded as Xavier stormed down the street.

Finally Xavier had worked off his anger and he slowed to a gait she could keep up with.

"I am Jewish, Xavier, and some people will always react that way," Rachel said.

"I was worried you wouldn't want anything to do with me when we first met. I don't care about religion, I just care about you," Xavier returned as he bent over and kissed her. Parents, family problems disappeared and there was just them.

There had come a period when he had wanted time to himself, to be with her, to laugh, talk and sometimes just be together. His faith had always been the 'Job' and then Rachel came into his life and with those two faiths he knew he could be happy.

Rachel's family had always seemed more like the family he should have had. The Goldman's were warm-hearted, there was always laughter and although they were religious in their own way they were not dogmatic about it. They had been delighted when he had started considering joining the Jewish faith. But it was something that they had never pushed him into.

He could do as he wished as long as their Rachel was happy. He and Rachel felt complete when they were together, although she worried about his job. But she was wise enough to know that the job was also part of what made him who he was. They made plans to marry within the Hebrew faith. Xavier, named for a Saint who had instigated an inquisition in medieval times, knew of his namesake's reputation and smiled at the irony, finally a bit of retribution for all the misery that particular Saint had caused.

Rachel worked downtown but had decided to quit and go back to school after she and Xavier were married. On her final day of work some of her friends had taken her to a restaurant in China-Town. The night had been full of fun and giggles for it was also a bridal shower. Finally the night drifted to an end. Rachel stepped out of the restaurant first her arms filled with gifts, a friend almost directly behind her. It was a beautiful night with a clear sky and the fragrance of spring surrounded her.

Suddenly out of the night a dark shadow appeared so quickly that Rachel barely had time to see the movement and the flash of steel. The shadow was gone as quickly as it came. Rachel dropped her packages, stumbled once before falling to the ground. She lay there her long auburn hair spread out about her head, she felt a dull ache in her side and from what seemed like a long distance she heard her friends screaming. Why were they screaming on such a beautiful night when the stars were so close she could almost touch them? "Xavier, see the stars," she said faintly as her life's blood bled away.

CHAPTER SIXTEEN

Xavier was sitting in a surveillance car watching for a dealer, who was one of 'One-Eyed-Jack's' drug dealers to make a meet with the police informant. The informant was buying a Kilo of Coke from the drug dealer. Once the deal was made they would follow both of them back into town and have a marked police cars take them down, that way they wouldn't blow their informant's cover.

Xavier's team would however have the drugs and 'flash' money back plus- big plus- they would have one of 'Jack's' dealers. That would make 'One Eyed Jack' very unhappy.

He looked up and out of the car windshield and noticed how close the stars were tonight; Rachel always loved watching the stars with him.

Suddenly Xavier leaned forward clutching his chest and groaned.

"Jesus, Xav what's wrong, I told you we shouldn't be eating the food at that old Diner," Angus, his partner said as he tried to pat Xavier on the back. Xavier shrugged him off.

Xavier felt like his chest was being crushed in a giant hand, maybe it was a heart attack! It felt like part of his heart had been ripped away! He gave a low moan.

"Xavier! Xav! Christ almighty I'm calling an ambulance!"

"No! Can't blow the operation! I-I'm starting too feel better, maybe too much cat in the food," Xavier returned as he looked at Angus with his mouth twisted into a grimace that he hoped looked like a smile. He looked up at the sky as the pain became almost bearable and noticed that the clouds had blocked the night sky.

"Maybe another car can take me home? I-I just need to lie down for a while."

"Okay-Okay but it sucks you missing this! You gonna miss all the action when we bust one of 'One Eyed Jack's' dealers! It has taken a long time too set up this informant but you're the Boss." Angus said as he looked at Xavier whose skin had taken on a pale, waxy tone.

Xavier looked at Angus as the pain in his chest retreated too a dull roar. He still felt something was very wrong-not wrong with the operational plan but something else. He looked up at where the stars should be and the stars were shrouded-strange; they had been so bright just minutes before. He was missing something, but he would figure it out later besides he could see that the operational plan was going down. 'Jack' was going too know just how good the police were in this city.

"Angus, tell the points that it's going down! 'Jack' how's it feel too have your nuts in a vise?!" Xavier whispered as the image of the dead Linda filled his mind and dulled his intuition. He watched the transaction through his binoculars a grim smile on his lips. The plan was going down without a hitch.

Xavier was half way back to headquarters when the Duty Inspector contacted him and made a meet with him. That was how he learned what had happened to Rachel and finally he understood why the stars were shrouded. He told the Duty Inspector he would call her parents from the morgue and handle that part.

The Duty Inspector, who was a good friend of his, had wanted to meet him at the morgue, to be with him. Xavier shook his head and asked the Duty Inspector to keep watch over his team and make sure they were okay until he himself could tell them the news. Let his team enjoy their victory for now.

He drove his own car over to the coroners, spoke briefly with the Medical Examiner and then went in to be with her, his Rachel.

She was lying naked on steel examination table a white sheet covered her up to just above her breasts. She didn't look dead to him, just in a very quiet sleep, he touched her skin, it was still ever so slightly warm just on the very cusp between warm and cool. He looked at her face and noted that the scattering of freckles across her nose were more noticeable because her skin was leeching from warm cream into death's white. Her wild, willful hair that she was always trying to subdue and he was always tussling, lay about her face in wild curls. Her generous mouth that he had always thought was made for kissing and laughing still retained the natural reddish stain, her lips curved up every so slightly. He leaned over and kissed her like Romeo had kissed his dead Juliet. Her lips melded to his lips and for a moment in his imagination he thought he felt them quiver but it was naught but sorrow's imagination.

Xavier lifted the right side of the sheet where the fatal injury was and gasped at the size of the knife that must have been used. It had been quick though, straight between the ribs and into the heart, she probably didn't even know what had happened.

"But I'll always know, it will be part of me forever or at least until I join you, my sweet Rachel," he muttered to himself. Then he looked at the injury again, there were large bruise's on either side of the knife wound because it had been thrust in with such strength that only the cross guards had prevented it from going in any further.

He called in the Medical Examiner; who went to all death, be they suspicious or natural, and after taking photo's of the body, making notes on position of the body and who initially had attended the scene then had the body moved to the Coroners Office for an Autopsy. He asked her if she had made notes about the wound and were they going to use latex, a type of rubbery latex which is poured into the wound, once the latex dried it is carefully removed and shows exactly the type of knife, ice-pick, screw-driver or other weapon had created the wound. It would also show any chips or tips that had been on the weapon and determine the shape of the weapon. The M.E. indicted that those tests would be done tomorrow. He knew the M.E., Gracie. She put her hand on his arm in sympathy. He gently took it off his arm and shook his head. He just couldn't talk or be around anybody right now.

Despite the grief that had swallowed him, there was a part of his mind that had become razor clear and he knew, without a doubt who was responsible for this death. He also understood the message; he had been getting too close. 'One-Eyed-Jack' was hoping her death would distract him, destroy him.

Xavier went through the motions of notifying the Goldman's of the death of their daughter. Rachel needed to be buried within a certain time. He talked with people, his friends, her friends, her parents and even received a call from his mother who seemed to want to rebuke him for something. He hung up on her. Funny thing though, when the notifications, the funeral, sitting Shiva, it was all over he could barely-vaguely recall that time. The time of death's requirements but not in any definite way, except the wound on Rachel, that was laser clear.

Upper management and H.R. (Human-Resources) wanted him to take some time off to get himself together. Xavier did take the time off for her funeral the day after her death and one other day to sit quietly by himself. To let his mind work through the pain, gather his thoughts back from the haphazard, scattered millions of schemes of bloody revenge and work them into one cohesive plan that could be concealed within the framework of his Guns and Gangs Task-force.

Xavier forced himself to go over the details of Rachael's death until he started to become numb to it-another Homicide. It was not like she had cancer or some other lethal disease where they could have said good-bye. She was dead and he couldn't bring her back. But he could get her killer, maybe that would help bring some color back into his life gone gray and flat. Even the voices of friends or enemies, did not have the same sharp intonation as before but had become dull and spiritless. Of course he told none of this to his friends or H.R. they would have him off the job or flying some desk.

And now for the greatest acting job of my life, yes siree-bob. I have to act like I am in mourning but back to work can't go flying off in six different directions yelling that One-Eyed-Jack killed her. Gotta act normal but start digging around discreetly haveta push that basterd till his sphincter slams shut loud enough for me to hear. He shud never have killed her, shuuda killed me! Shuuda, Cudda, Wudda missed your chance Soul-Slayer or 'One-Eyed-Jack or what ever the fuck your calling your self now. You never got her sweet soul, Xavier thought. He went back to work the next day his plan intact.

The hours bled into the days which blended into the months and finally into a year of flat nothingness. The world kept spinning on its axis but offered a light that seemed dull and in the night he could barely see the stars; they seemed so far away. The job kept him going but the keenest of his pleasure at catching bad-guys had faded by half but he kept working. Slowly at what seemed like a snails crawl, life began to leak into the frozen zombie world he had been residing in. The levity wasn't, as forced and setting up Operational Plans and catching the bad-guys began too feel good again. It was only when he started to think of her that the pleasure dimmed.

"How's it going Xav?" Angus asked as Xavier walked into the office. This had been their first night back after they all had had a few days off. Xavier's facial features, which in the last long year or so had seemed forced-stiff were almost easy going this morning as if a smile lurked close to the surface. Even as Angus watched Xavier the phone rang and Xav picked it up. The almost relaxed expression on Xav's face had disappeared, gone so fast it was like it had never been there.

"Yeah, I'm ok, why?" Xavier asked.

"Oh, nothing, just tired I guess," Angus shrugged.

"That phone call was homicide they have a D.B. still at the scene, figured we might know who it is. You guys, head home get some sleep. I'll go down to the scene and see what they have," Xavier said.

"But Boss, you have had less sleep than any of us," another member of the team said.

"Don't worry about me, I know the Homicide dick, so I'll take a look at the body, talk to the detective, then catch a few Zees," Xavier returned.

CHAPTER SEVENTEEN

Xavier wearily rode the elevator back down to the underground garage to pick up the unmarked vehicle he had just parked twenty minutes ago.

"Only for you mon ami." Xavier muttered to himself as he signed out a non-descript, unmarked car from the dozens of vehicles parked in the police garage.

As he started the vehicle he thought of Vance Le Blanc the homicide detective who had called requesting someone from the Guns and Gang Unit and he smiled. His first honest smile since she had died. It was a relief to think of something else and of late he had found himself actually trying to find ways of working around thoughts of her and yet that made him feel guilty. Still pain didn't seem to fill his days as much. Although his heart was still scared and there were certain places his mind dared not travel to, of late the scar seemed to be growing smaller. He still felt guilt but in some ways she would always be with him, in a way she had helped form what he was now. She had shown him the strength that he possessed.

Xavier had continued his drive out to the homicide site his mind drifted through the flotsam and jetsam of life, his life. He thoughts turned to Vance, that crazy Quebecois, Harry had introduced them back when he was still a rookie and right away, even though he was a rookie, he and Vance hit it off. Many an evening the three of them had sat down at The Gag and Puke as Harry and Vance reminisced about life on the job, the operational plans and the odd plan that management didn't know about. He learned so much from both of them although they were so opposite, Harry was the quintessential family man while Vance had been married three times. Vance would laugh and say he couldn't retire till at least two of his ex-wives had passed on into the sweet-bye-and-bye. The trouble with Vance was that he loved all women and women were attracted to him. Not because he was particularly good looking, he had a barrel- chest that had started to slide down towards his belly. He was not particularly tall for a police officer in fact he was only five-foot-eight. But Vance had more French charm than should be allowed west of Manitoba. He had sparkling blue eyes, brilliant white teeth that flashed in laughter. The laugh lines that age had gradually deepened on either side of his mouth and the corners of his eyes in his olive-brown skin and his brown hair, which had a crisp curl to it, had begun to turn silver, but even with all that he still seemed to attract women like moths to a flame.

Xavier, who was more contemplative than his friends, liked to watch Vance work his magic, he knew that part of Vance's secret was that he actually listened when a women was talking and always treated her respect. Many a 'sword-master' with the looks of an Adonis was deeply surprised when the female he had been 'wooing' all evening ended up with Vance.

Vance also had the intelligence of the curious, many things interested him and he was well read. Xavier remembered the many nights where Harry, Vance and he had had conversations ranging from Catholicism to Buddhism and the Mythology of the 'People' and why humans do what do. Many was the time that the beer-glasses had been dry for hours while they carried on some discussion.

Xavier also remembered how Vance lost most of his voice. He had been working his way down a dark alley one night chasing a suspect for homicide when the suspect had stepped out of doorway and fired off a sawed off shotgun at Vance's head.

The bad-guy was so startled when he heard a roar and two hundred pounds of angry Vance slammed into him and they both crashed to the ground. As they were falling Vance had managed to get one of his muscular arm's around the bad-guy's neck while the other clenched the closed fist on the other side and he snapped his arms in a certain way. There was a large crack like the sound of a big wish-bone being snapped after a turkey dinner, although in this case it was asshole's neck. In fact he nearly ripped the asshole's head off. Vance did it with such force because he was so mad at himself for not sensing the asshole lurking in the doorway. Vance landed on top of the recently deceased and nearly bled to death before his partner finally found him, staunched the flow of blood while yelling for back-up on his radio.

The roar that Vance uttered that night was the last time he spoke in more than a forced whisper for one of the pellets smashed into his voice box and there it stayed because to remove would probably result in a blood clot that would turn his brain into 'Mr. Potato-head'.

Vance accepted his fate and desperately worked at rehabilitating what was left of his voice box and finally worked it to the point where he was understandable although at times, if he was tired, it did sound like a gravel truck dumping a load. But Xavier, Harry and his other friends noticed that the moths flying around Vance's flame had grown expodentially because they had to get in closer and of course there was the sympathy angle.

While Vance was in the hospital his room was never empty, the nurses seem to be always be fluttering around him. His friends, at least two at a time, were always hanging around. Harry and Xavier visited often, the thing that stood out against his tanned skin the most was the large white bandage wrapped around his throat. His usual booming laughter was no larger than whisper and he wrote his comments on a writing pad with a pen. It was only his partner having the presence of mind to stick his finger the gushing hole in his throat and plug it that had saved his life but nothing could save his voice box, which had been almost, but not completely crushed.

Xavier stepped out of the car and walked to this most recent scene looking foreword to seeing Vance Le Blanc.

CHAPTER EIGHTEEN

So here he was walking down Cocaine Cull-d-sac towards another body that could be male or female, an overdose, a homicide or a suicide. Xavier was careful where he walked on the broken old asphalt. He didn't want to disturb the scene nor walk on the debris of broken glass, old needles, bent spoons and rubber's some still with the cream of the quick passionless coupling, leaking from them.

As he drew near the police tape he could see small parts of the body that the sheet did not quite cover, a left foot covered with an old sock, so full of holes it looked like macramé. Dangling from the big toe was a battered old sneaker, spattered with blood. A hand also lay beyond the sheet's protective cover. It was palm up, on top of alley debris, fingers curled slightly. From the size and shape of it and the rest of the body under the sheet, must have been that of a man. Xavier looked at the hand of the deceased, underneath it on the old, broken asphalt lay some of the paraphernalia of what probably had been the victim's life. Xavier could see the mixture of blood and filth smeared on the upturned hand and yet there was a curious gracefulness that had lent to it a kind of vulnerability that perhaps only death can bring.

Xavier ducked under the police tape surrounding the inner crime scene. Just as he did so, a young officer walked out of the shadows where he had been writing in his notebook. With a mild smile, Xavier met the suspicious eyes of the rookie before him. The rookie's cheeks reddened with uncertainty.

"Sir, no one is allowed past the tape. I need some identification please."

The rookie's voice was fairly firm with just the slightest tremor of nervousness.

Rookies were, for the most part, only comfortable around other rookies. Xavier was about to let the young officer off the hook by showing him some I.D. when a raspy voice behind him, called his name. Xavier knew that raw whisper and a grin grew on his face.

"Zav! Quit dancing with the rookie and get over here and I.D. this down and outer for me, will ya." Detective Vance Le Blanc said in his distinctive gravel tinged voice.

Xavier grinned at his old buddy and shook his head. "I only came because I haven't had a chance to see you in a while, Vance Bonne-Chance."

Vance chuckled. He only allowed his closest beer-drinking buddies and friends to call him by that nickname.

Vance smiled at Xavier, the unlit stogie stuck in the corner of his mouth, as he worked his voice, attempting to force it to a level that Xavier could fully understand.

"As always a pleasure, mon-ami. I am sorry…"

Xavier put up his hand and shook his head before saying, "So, 'Bonne Chance', I hear you have a body for me to look at?

"I'm sorry sir, I did not realize who you were," the young officer interceded stiffly as he tried to hide his awe at seeing two legends together. Xavier smiled slightly as he looked at the rookie who looked like he had barely passed through puberty. Then he looked at his old friend.

"Show me, Vance, so I can go home and get some sleep," Xavier said as Vance lifted the sheet. The faint smell of the beginnings of decay coiled up from the corpse and brushed against their noses and a few flies, the vultures of the cold northern citys, began to descend to see if this meat was ripe enough to lay eggs on.

"Jeez, at least this one is reasonably fresh." Xavier said as his thoughts flashed back a couple of years to poor Linda in that shallow grave. "I'm just going to move over to the other side of the D.B. so I can see better." He stepped over the body, which lay on its back and knelt on the other side, as his gaze took in the skinny body clothed in ragged, filthy jeans. Heavy streaks of blood had congealed on the right side of the waistband then had pooled under the victim on the asphalt. He observed some evidence that would be of interest to his Unit.

"Pass me a flashlight, will you, Vance," he said, as he tried to get a better look at the face. The sunlight was still a long way from even casting shadow in the alley.

"Shit! Another local drug dealer, dead," The eyes were still open although the gray fog of death was beginning to creep across the cornea. The area around the nose was slightly pinched; cyanosis was starting to turn the lips and cheekbones a bluish color. He noted the scrapes and partially developed bruises on the cheekbones that were probably Para-mortem. There was a severe laceration and deep dent on the left side of the forehead.

"Can you tell who is Xav" Vance asked?

Xavier sighed. "It is Eduardo Sanchez a.k.a. Sneazy Eddie, a very low level drug dealer, but a most talented drug rip-off artist. Have you called the medical Examiner?"

"Yeah, quite a while ago so she should be here any time," Vance replied.

Xavier decided to hang around until the body was moved, if he could keep awake that was.

"Hey, boys, how the hells it hanging," Martha McAllister laughed as she walked over to join them as they stood by the victim's body.

"To the right, Marty, always to the right," Xavier returned with a smile that exposed his dimples and shaved years off his face.

"Vance, you got an I.D. on that body yet?"

She turned in Vance's direction so Xavier wouldn't see the shock on her face. She hadn't seen Xav since his fiancé had been murdered and the change frightened her.

Women had always been attracted to Xavier because of his kindness and the innate respect they sensed in him. He didn't care who you were as long as you did your job to the best of your ability. He wouldn't tolerate any nonsense from his team either. His outward appearance had changed. He had always been good looking, in a quiet sort of way. Now he looked as if he had some horrible wasting disease that was affecting his body and possibly his mind. His thick, straight thatch of black hair was now mostly silver with the odd streak of black, he had lost weight and the skin seemed pulled too tight for his skull. It almost seemed transparent over his cheekbones and his eyes, those sparkling gray eyes still sparkled but it wasn't with joy but something she couldn't quite identify but it frightened her. There was an aura about him of immense sadness and remoteness although he sounded almost the same but the voice had lost its vibrancy and interest.

Martha listened as Vance and Xavier were talking. Their conversation was the typical, half joking conversation as they we going over some points on the deceased that they wanted Martha, as the M.E., to take special note of. The conversation and the tone of it was normal enough in Vance, but with Xav it was forced, almost as if he were playing the role of the Xavier as he used to be.

Martha and Xavier had a brief, sweet affair long before he had met Rachel. They had realized that the sex between them was good and they both laughed at the same things but they were better as friends than lovers. So they had parted as lovers but stayed together as good friends. They had always called each other when they had troubles or successes. Xavier had called her and told her about meeting Rachel, he never called her about what had happened.

She had tried calling him, left messages but he never called her back. She sensed the emotional wall he had built about himself and they're seemed to be no way over or around it right now. Martha knew, she had tried.

"Ok boys," Martha said, "now that I am gloved up let's go over this guy and see what we can before we move him and take a look at the wound. I see he was a big time needle freak from the looks both arms. See this? The arms are both abscessed and punctured so much they looked like rotting meat. Look at the veins along the sides of his neck. This boy was having trouble finding a vein that hadn't collapsed. I bet when I when I have him on the examination table I'll find that most of his veins are infected or abscessed, probably even the one in the penis. Gives a whole new meaning to a blue veiner."

Vance broke into a silent laugh and Xavier forced a smile.

"Here, help me lift him onto his left side so I can take a look at the wound on the right side. I'll check the injuries on his head when I get him on the table. Make sure you are double gloved, this guy is probably loaded with assorted S.T.D.'s and probably full-blown AIDs. Alrighty, let's move him."

With that the three of them lifted the body so it was resting on the left side. Martha moved the dirty, tattered shirt partially covering the wound. On the ground beneath was a large pool of partially congealed blood.

"Jesus Christ, that was some big, fucking, hunting knife. You can even see the bruising from cross guard through the blood," Vance muttered as they looked at it with their flashlights.

It's him. It's a fresh one, same as…as. Still has the knife, arrogant Son of a Bitch, Xavier thought as he helped hold the body.

"You Ok, Xavier?" Martha asked as she saw his jaws clench suddenly.

"Yes, fine. Are you going to use the liquid latex method to pour into the knife hole to see what kind of knife it was?" Xavier asked in a terse voice.

"Of course I will, Xav. You know our procedures," Martha returned a touch ire in her voice.

Vance gave him an uncomfortable glance and then looked at Martha and shrugged. But the comradely conversation between professionals had ceased as if cut off with a knife and only uncomfortable silence remained.

Martha continued her examination. She gently lifted the left hand and manipulated it. "As you can see Rigor Mortises has not set in yet, indicating that death occurred within the last eight to ten hours." She took photos, measured, numbered and noted in her notebook what she saw of the body at the scene. The scene itself was also was of great importance and once the body was removed, measurements and photos were taken.

"From the looks of things right now," Martha said. "I would say that your bad guy stuck the knife in the victim's right side, he did it with enough force that it broke the rib bone which partially protects the liver, and it sliced the liver open. The victim exsanguinated. Probably took a couple of minutes. I am told that it is painful death, but the blow that dented his forehead may have knocked him unconscious so at least pain wasn't part of his end."

The Alberta Body Removal van rolled to a stop outside the police tape and unloaded a stretcher with the heavy, purple sheets neatly folded on it.

Vance Le Blanc waved them over with a dusty chuckle as he did. "I always get a kick out of that sign. They should put one of those fake bodies on top of the van instead of a fake bug. It should read 'Dirt-bag Removal' course that would be only for dead dirt-bags. I guess they don't eat in many restaurants while driving that meat wagon."

The two body removers sniggered as they rolled the stretcher over beside the body. They spread the purple sheet so that it was draped over the stretcher. They set out a heavy plastic sheet over that and lifted the body onto it. A piece of paper slid out of a shirt pocket and fluttered to the ground.

"Wait, what's that?" Xavier asked as he picked up the paper and opened it. On the inside of the paper was a rough drawing of the Soul-Slayer's Scythe. He wants to show me that he is taking over the underbelly of the city; he knows I understand the message Xavier thought.

As Xavier was looking at the symbol, the men from Alberta Body Removal completed wrapping the body in the plastic, and lifted it onto the stretcher. Then they spread the purple cloth over the bundle on the stretcher and tucked it in so that no errant wind would blow it off and reveal the package on the stretcher.

"So what's on the paper, Xav?" Vance asked as he saw Xavier's face whitened and his body stiffened as he gripped the piece of paper. He handed Vance the piece of paper without a word.

Vance looked at it a moment. "Looks like some type of old time scythe they used to cut grain with. Or maybe one of those things that come with kids Halloween costumes. What do you think is it, Xav?"

"It is the symbol I have found at every drug related homicide I have been to in the last year or so." Xavier replied. "Who knows how many more of these signatures have been missed."

"How can that be? I've been in Homicide for I don't know how long and yes we are short on manpower right now; but this, we can't have missed…" Vance said.

Xavier watched his face go from a blank stunned look, to one where his face was beginning too show the strong ruddiness of annoyance.

Xavier held up his hand to stop Vance's angry outburst. "Before you say anything, you have to know that I have been researching this for a long time or I wouldn't say anything. Most if not all of the homicides I have dug into are druggies that were out and out homicides or in one case a suicide. Initially I got some information from an informant and as with such things once the pattern is pointed out to you suddenly it becomes crystal clear. I started researching some obvious homicides and drug rip-offs. Talking to informants before they became so frightened they refused to even be seen around the police. I have gone through many, many reports and I have all the Case Numbers if you care to read them. Someone or-"

"Or what?" Vance asked as he watched Xav with worry and caution.

"Did I say or? All I'm saying someone, a major dealer in meth and crack seems to be or has taken over the East end. You know heroin, coke, speed and smoke are bad enough but you throw meth, crank and crack into the mix and you've got big trouble. I trust you Vance or I wouldn't say anything."

"I would like to see some of those reports," Vance said as he looked at his friend and although he smiled faintly it was obvious that he was trying to reassure Xav while wondering if Xavier had slipped a gear in his brain.

"I will happy to supply you with the Case Numbers, whatever you need." Xavier sighed to himself as he caught Vance's look, almost blew that one when I started to say 'Or Something' he thought. Xavier had seen this doubting look on too many faces before. But Vance was a friend, maybe; maybe he would check Xavier hoped.

Vance looked Martha's way and saw that she had caught most of the conversation. There was worry in her face before she looked away. Vance suddenly felt tightness in the pit of his stomach (always a warning like something was up); maybe there was something to what Xavier had told him or could be Xav was starting to lose it but Vance doubted it. I just may look into some of those reports he thought.

"Excuse me sir, but the Inspector, Intelligence branch, would like to see you A.S.A.P, his word sir and I am to drive you," a young officer said as he stepped up to where they were standing. "Oh, shit now what!" Xavier responded, and then muttered to himself "It's going to be a long day."

"Promotions, perhaps," Vance said with a smirk.

"Well it won't be mine," Xavier returned with a shrug.

CHAPTER NINETEEN

Xavier managed to get into the front passenger seat of the marked police vehicle although his knees were uncomfortably close to his chest, Vance's last words about being careful what he said still ringing in his ears. He turned his head and looked out of the window in the hopes that his actions would discourage his driver from talking to him. He needed the quiet so he could think things through.

He closed his eyes and the last few years flew by in his brain. A maelstrom of thoughts swirled around two figures. One seemed to help him make sense of his investigative skills, the pattern of his thoughts about the job and what it meant to him, to her, her people and their common enemy. The other figure held his heart, his humor and his sanity; she was giving them back to him with her love. An epiphany washed over him and everything came together. It was time. He understood. Grief over her death was lessening within him.

He was beginning to see the brilliant colors of the sunrise again and when the officer spoke to him it didn't sound flat and muted. It had the proper tonal sounds. He still felt the pain of loss, though it wasn't the tearing, body and mind racking, throbbing agony that he couldn't see or hear through. There was a tender ache that maybe in time would become a beautiful memory. It was possible that he might be able to put the memory of her, of Rachel, away in a place in his mind where he stored special things, like his dad dressed in his uniform and letting him sit in a police car, his dog Tex that got hit by a car but lived long enough to lick his hand. Some of the old loved memories were fading around the edges, faces a bit blurred but still cherished and always loved. Now Rachel was there, sharp and clear with all the times they had had together; not enough time but it would have to be enough.

He would always have her with him and at that thought part of his misery faded and then faded again until the sting of it was almost gone. He almost felt like himself with just a jagged, small piece gone.

"We are here, sir."

"What, oh thank you." Xavier said before he climbed out of the car and stretched for a moment.

He walked up the flagged sidewalk to the big brass doors and reached to open one just as a uniform came out carrying all his gear-shotgun, briefcase and computer for the day on the street. Xavier held the door open for him and then entered the hallowed halls of the puzzle palace a.k.a. Headquarters.

Xavier took the elevator to the eleventh floor. As he moved slowly up, he realized he didn't feel too bad. It was like he just had had a really painful tooth repaired and his tongue kept touching it to make sure the sharply remembered pain was gone. He was tired though. It felt like he and sleep had not been in the same room for a long time. He got out on the eleventh floor and spoke to the receptionist who told him to take a seat. The seat he chose was impossibly comfortable and his eyes closed of their own accord.

"Detective O'Malley! Detective O'Malley!" the receptionist voice kept puncturing his sleep until he opened his eyes.

"What? Oh, Okay sorry," Xavier, muttered as he tried to get himself together and looked up at the receptionist with a crooked smile. She smiled in sympathy and opened the door to a long hallway with office doorways on either side. He went past her desk, walked down the hallway until he reached the right doorway, swore under his breath and then knocked on the door. There was a growl from within. Xavier straightened his shoulders, opened the door and entered.

"Jesus H. Christ, O'Malley!" Inspector Keesic shouted as Xavier finished closing the door to the Inspector's office. "What the fuck, are you doing? You've been burning bridges all over the place! You seem bound and determined too piss off all of upper management although they have made concessions because of, well, you know."

Xavier shrugged and turned to leave, too tired to argue.

"And a sweet hello to you sir," Xavier said over his shoulder as he started to walk out.

Keesic considered the unfocused look of fatigue in Xavier's eyes and the high red fury drained from the inspector's face. "Shit, Xavier," he said as he pushed a chair towards the detective. "Sit down before you fall down. You look like hell."

Xavier slid his lanky body into the offered chair.

"I'm sorry about Rachel…" Keesic started to say.

"Thank you Inspector for your sympathy," Xavier cut in, his exhaustion coming out in his voice. "But I'm sure that is not what you called me down here for?"

"Yes, well I am sure you know you didn't get promoted to Staff Sergeant what with everything going on and the stress you've been under."

"I kinda figured that, but no sense rubbing salt in the wounds," Xavier said as he thought, too tired for this conversation, need to sleep, finally getting my sanity back but too tired to think clearly.

Inspector Keesic looked at Xavier and knew this was probably not the time to be discussing what was happening with a Detective who could barely keep his eyes open. Yet in some curious way O'Malley looked better than he had since Rachel's death, almost as if he had finally accepted her death. Keesic decided that it was best to get this over with now rather than put it off until Xavier was rested. Having too spar with a Xavier, clear-eyed and his brain working on all cylinders, a Xavier, whose team with him in the lead had almost wiped out most of the major dealers in the city?

Trouble was Xav saw the bullshit going on around him like quite a few others, he and some Detectives and Senior Constables were vocal about what they had seen, such as incompetence would get you promoted quicker than being a talented, hard working officer. Xavier was also quick to point out that management trying to force the senior constables into retirement because they were hired when the police department had been advertising for intelligent individual who could make proper decisions quickly. Well management got what they wanted, tough, smart, individuals who wanted to work catching the 'bad-guys'.

Those 'individuals' tended to do things their way while balancing on the thin blue line between justice and criminals and they were very successful at their job. But like most jobs everywhere there were some whose abilities leaned towards staying out of trouble and hiding in office positions where of course they built up relationships with upper-management like a symbiotic relationship that turns eventually into a virus that starts to destroy those who recognize it for what it is.

Keesic was one of those who had recognized what was going on in the Police department. He even knew about what was going on within the ranks of the R.C.M.P. as a result of one at the top of upper management whose picture was beside the word 'medacious' in the dictionary. Keesic and senior supervisors were determined to prevent that from happening in this city. He knew that certain people had to be removed subtly before the rank and file started to take some type of job action. Trouble was Keesic knew that Xavier was right, but that was a fight for another time.

"Look Xavier, you've made some high placed enemies in this department. Your team has been such a success though, that they can't really say or do anything except not to promote anyone from your team."

Xavier was suddenly sitting straight up in the chair and wide-awake. "You mean those assholes would actually punish me by punishing my whole team? I simply have said what I thought about some of the bullshit that was going on around here. The favoritism, and some of the incompetents that got promoted because they were down here with their noses stuck so far up the Deputies and Chief's respective asses that they have a permanent tan around their noses, instead of out doing actual police work like the rest of us."

"You have to realize that the ones that are out to make your life on the job miserable, starting with no promotions are punishing you, not because you are wrong. It's because you're right and the Rank and File know it. You and others who have spoken up know about all the bullshit that is going on. You are right, there are rumblings of strikes and job action again. Unfortunately, sycophants are trying their very best to block the Chief's view of the truth. There are some of us here at the puzzle palace trying to dispose of certain hindrances and clear up the view so to speak.

"Well the Chief better get his site unblocked and soon but it isn't us who have been causing trouble. We have been way to busy between the gang problems and the Homicides rates which have jumped way up as you know," Xavier returned.

"I know, I know. I have tried to shield you and your team but the ravenous hounds of I.A. (Internal Affairs) have been set loose and are looking for blood. I have come up with an idea that might work for the time being."

"Lets hear it."

" I have pulled some strings and did a wee bit of ass-kissing and managed to get you assigned to the Arrest Processing as an Acting Staff Sergeant until the next the next promotion time. If you don't make it then, it will be out of my hands," Keesic said as he watched Xavier's face.

"What!" Xavier sputtered as he jumped out of his chair. "My guys! Who is going to manage the team I built up? Look Sam, I also suspect we have a serial killer on our hands," he added in a ragged voice that teetered on the edge of a shout.

"Calm down. I have arranged for a good guy to take over the team. As for the other, you and I have had this talk before and unless you have more evidence now?"

Xavier shook his head.

"Who knows what information you will find in Arrest Processing Unit?" Keesic said with a slight smile. "Think on this: every arrest goes through there and you have to approve the reports. The guy I want to run your team is also up for promotion to Sergeant and he knows the team inside out and is just as pig-headed and stubborn as you. He has also been your partner for a long time now."

Xavier suddenly realized who Keesic was talking about. "Angus Campbell? You picked him?"

Keesic nodded.

"That's great!" Xavier's voice rose. "You picked a great guy-bit of a Scottish barbarian- but a good man."

"I would say you better have a talk with him about his mouth and what comes out of it for the time being. Now before you go, sit back and let me tell you about Arrest Processing, a totally different world than you are used to."

Xavier only half listened as he tried to think of a way to continue his investigation. Gotta find a way out of that shit hole, he thought.

CHAPTER TWENTY

Night still gripped the city as Xavier walked across the police parking lot the gravel crunching under foot. A slight frown touched his face as he saw that the vehicles belonging to the night shift crew were all still in the lot.

"Must have had a busy last night," low words in a low voice, but still ruptured the silence of the pre-dawn dark. He suddenly regretted that he had broken the stillness.

Xavier continued the rest of the walk in silence, his memories of the last few months his only company. He missed working undercover and his team but this new job as one of the staff-sergeants in Arrest Processing certainly had its moments. As he had learned his new job in Arrest Processing, he found Inspector Keesic had been right. This was the hub of the police department, the crazy hub.

Every thief, predator and piece of human flotsam and jetsam drifted through there. Druggies and drunks constantly filled the cells. Some joked that certain arrestees' gave this as their mailing address because they were in there practically every night. Upper Management tried to avoid Arrest processing in case they saw something they would have to deal with.

Senior police officers with ten years or more on the street were the only ones encouraged and allowed to work in Arrest Processing because of their knowledge of the Criminal Code and the number of arrests they had made over the years. Even then those officers who went into Arrest Processing felt like rookies all over again because of the high, hard learning curve. However once the team, his team, was comfortable with their respective jobs they began to enjoy themselves. The job was tough and intense but along with all the other smells there was always the aroma of adrenalin in the air. The scent actually came up in the prisoner's elevator with the police and their prisoners. Sometimes the adrenalin was so strong it was like a version of crack-cocaine.

The infamous prisoner's elevator was continuously bringing up a mixture of suspects, some of whom were quiet, scared and silent. While others, the regular suspects and drunks or druggies or a combination thereof, who had been in the prisoner's elevator before, decided that was the place to stir up the police and see how much trouble they could cause in the two minutes in the elevator.

Now the elevator had a camera in it to make sure there was no abuse by police, mostly the action it caught were those of the police being abused. It almost seemed at times that the old building had absorbed all the screams of innocence and hate of the guilty. The bricks and concrete had absorbed too much so that it never seemed silent, always there was an echo. All that mixed together and built up into a crescendo. Twelve hours of that on a busy night and those that worked there went home vibrating.

Xavier's thoughts got him to the men's changing room. His brows creased in concern as he looked around the room. No one was there. It was a bit eerie. He didn't think he had ever been in the changing room when it was this quiet. If the night were an ordinary or unusually slow one at about 5:00 a.m. the Staff-Sergeant would start letting staff go home early. He shrugged, but at the same time he hurried changing into his uniform.

As he rode up the elevator he began to hear muffled shouts, screams and banging which grew louder as he drew closer to his floor.

The elevator doors slowly opened onto a scene stolen from some Catholic tome on Hades. There were smears of blood, shit, mucous and mud upon the floors, walls and ceiling of the concrete foyer. Over in the corner of that same foyer two beefy, young police officers were fighting with and trying to subdue a large, squirming, muscled suspect. The suspect was wearing nothing but a bad attitude, tattoos and tight jeans and had managed to get his handcuffed hands around to the front. He was screaming in rage; spittle and frothy blood surrounded his mouth and radiated out across is face. It looked to have been a long fight as both officers' uniform were covered in dirt and the knees of their pants were ripped. Their grim faces were covered in sweat.

Xavier looked over by the processing area and saw a male and a female officer dealing with an emaciated prostitute dressed in a skimpy, dirty dress that bore the stains of her profession. It was obvious from the expression on both officers' faces, that any remnant of compassion had been ripped away by the prostitute's filthy mouth and vicious struggles.

"You fucking pigs! Get your fucking hands off me! Like that, honey?" the prostitute screeched as she tried to thrust her scrawny ass at the female officer, who reddened as she kept trying to remove the handcuffs.

"You gutter-whore, shut the fuck up! If you keep twitching I will drop you to the floor to un-cuff you!" the female officer said in a tone meant only for the prostitute.

"You cunt! You must be a dike cause you like this so much!" the crack induced rage that wrapped the hooker's brain in its grasp said as she made her move and tried to spit. The female officer ducked dropped the prostitute to the floor with a foot sweep and bounced her head off the concrete, then placed her knee in the foul mouthed female's back. The whore kept squirming and the officer grabbed her by hair and bounced her head off the floor again. Apparently this was enough to get the prostitute's attention and she finally settled down except the odd muttered curse word.

Xavier heard another sound that had woven its way above and below the usual sounds of Arrest Processing. A low, hard giggle deepening into a feral, ferocious laugh that kept escalating and worsening at the same time. Like a huge carbuncle filled with crystallized sound that grew and grew until it finally burst into a grotesque howl that seem to send shards of sound through the air. On cue the prisoners in cells and the ones still fighting with the police stopped the fighting, swearing, screaming and were still as if the 'Master' had spoken, or at least that's how it seemed to Xavier.

"What the hell was that?" Xavier shouted just as the howl suddenly stopped leaving him shouting into silence.

"That was and is Reyals, Charles Clarke, or so he told us when he was brought in," said the night shift Staff Sergeant, Frank 'Hardass' Gregor in his usual sour voice. "Came in last night on a minor drug charge. His nickname is 'One Eyed Jack' for reasons you will understand as soon you see his face on the computer. Started a fight with a fight with a prisoner who actually cowed and bowed in the corner. His aggression has stirred the other prisoners to a riot pitch. So he was dragged kicking and screaming to the isolation cell nineteen. Even while in isolation he has been stirring up the other prisoners. You just witnessed the latest one."

He turned to tell Xavier how shitty his night had been because of this goof, but Xavier was already out of his hearing. Frank shrugged his shoulders, the corners of his mouth turned down so far that they could be seen beneath his thick, bushy moustache. With a sigh he started to gather up the leftovers from his lunch and his jacket prior to leaving the unit.

"It's him! I know it's him!" Xavier blurted out as he looked at the photo on the computer.

"What are you talking about?" Frank stepped off the Staff Sergeant dais and walked to the counter.

"He's the asshole I have been looking for, I know it! I have only known him by his nickname 'til now."

"Xav, have you got enough for an arrest warrant?" Frank got his answer from the look of frustration on Xavier's face.

"I have quite a bit of circumstantial evidence."

"Will it hold up in court? Is there a chance of conviction?"

"Not yet but now I know, at least, what he looks like," Xavier said in a flat voice.

"Look Xav, I know you are a good investigator. You certainly don't need my advice, but I have heard through the drums that certain assholes in management are waiting like vultures for you to make a mistake. Xav, those goofs will tear you apart given the chance. You know they have done it to others, so don't let them do it to you. Go after this guy, make it stick, then stick it to them," Frank urged as they both looked at the photo on the computer.

Xavier stared at the photo as if he was trying to engrave it in his mind, which wasn't hard given One-Eyed-Jack's disfigured features. The milky substance that occasionally leaked over the jagged edges of a small dark chamber that had once contained an eye. A purple colored scar that rolled in upon itself like a rope ran from the top of the forehead down across the left side of the face transecting the left eye, then continued down the left side and continued along the left jawbone. The filthy beard around the nasty scar was yellowish gray. Finally, the dirt and ash colored dread locks with dead leaves and twigs twined amongst them. No doubt herds of lice and nits ran free on that long neglected beard and scalp. Abruptly, Xavier shook his head as if coming out of a trance, a strange thought, like someone walking over his grave.

"I'm surprised that this 'One-Eyed-Jack' didn't melt the computer he smelled like something long dead! God, he was foul!" Frank said.

I'm going back to isolation to take a look at him."

"Just be careful, Xavier. The smell back there is enough to put you off your feed and fun for at least a mouth! I saw a rookie stroll back there to take a look. Next thing he rushed by me his hands over his mouth. I'm guessing he was going to the porcelain goddess to make an offering."

Xavier waved in acknowledgement and he walked down the hall between the cells. Suddenly he felt warmth on his forearm, and a hint of a smile warmed his face when he looked at the long slender hand resting on his forearm.

"Need any back up, Xavier?" murmured Sally Murdock.

Xavier gazed quickly and quietly at her. Both sensed there was something growing slowly between them. Both, though, also enjoyed a friendship that they had never pushed beyond, it was the possibility of maybe, that they enjoyed for now.

"Not right now, Sally. I want to talk to this guy myself first," Xavier said as he turned and walked towards the isolation cells. As soon as he turned the corner the smell was that of an ancient abattoir that was still in use. All his senses felt danger and adrenalin surged through his body at the thought of finally facing this Soul-Slayer. He could almost feel the expectation in the silence. It wanted him too turn around and walk away from what caused the smell. The noise that had so stirred up the prisoners had stopped abruptly. The silence was so complete, so cold.

"I knew you would come."

Xavier hesitated momentarily when he had heard the cold, calm voice so different from the sound of the chill shards of screams, gibbering and growling of an idiot he had heard seconds prior.

I sense your, how shall I say it? Your waffling, you're dithering, before you present yourself to me," the voice said with the slightest, gruffness surrounding an almost dainty, bitchy voice.

Xavier smiled slightly to himself when he heard the response to his immediate failure to show himself. He is used to his minions-his followers responding immediately to his commands. His voice is one of his weapons, he thought. With that knowledge tucked safely at the back of his mind, he then stepped briskly into 'One Eyed Jack's line of sight. He noted that the area directly in front cell nineteen had a definite chill.

"Come closer. I wish to get a good look at the 'pig' the street-people-my people, that is, say is interested in little, old, me. Why, pray-- when there is so much pretty prey, especially red headed prey, would you be interested me?"

"Let's just say I am always interested in death," Xavier said in a low, slow voice, ignoring the reference to Rachel. "Be they street-people or others. After all, that is my job."

Xavier looked through the armored, Plexiglas window. If he hadn't seen the photo on the computer, or heard the laughter, screams, squeals and shrieks produced by the creature in the cell—and even with his understanding that he was looking at a Soul-Slayer, he was shocked by the icy yet intelligent sounding voice he had just heard and the creature that had displayed itself before him.

Aside from the smell, which seemed less now. Perhaps because that particularly offensive odor had been beaten down until it lay insensate at the back of his nose. The features were somehow different as if they kept shifting slightly. 'One-Eyed Jack' was supine upon the concrete floor, naked, stretched out with his right elbow supporting his upper body, his left arm lying along the upper part of his body with the left hand, with long, raged nails, relaxed and slightly splayed on the outer left thigh just above the genitals. The skin on the body, where clothing would normally be, was streaked gray while its face and hands were almost blackish brown. His face was half concealed by a dirty yellowish beard with assorted twigs and leaves tangled in it. But Xavier's eyes were drawn to Jack's all-black iris in his right eye and the amusement that bubbled and boiled there.

Probably white under all the years of filth. Gonna hafta clean the cell out real good after he is released. He is big, bigger than the photo makes him seem, Xavier thought.

"Seen enough, pig?"

"So is your name really Charles, Clark Reyals?"

"Perhaps, but I have so many names in so many different places. Jack will do for you and I, don't you think?"

"Or Soul-Slayer?"

There was a clap of thunder and Xavier felt the floor vibrate. Suddenly Jack was at the window. A soundless roar felt but not heard. All of his teeth grown beyond reason, the teeth of an old but lethal lion, strong and yellowed by age. The long canines had holes encrusted with blackish gray at the point of each, with faint hints of blackish smoke issuing from them. His face had turned the red of a lobster thrown into a pot of boiling water and he had the massive horns of a bull on his suddenly bulbous forehead.

"Beware pig or I might have to have a pig roast. I think you would look lovely with an apple in your mouth!" As the Soul-Slayer spoke his body regained its human form as if the morphing had never happened.

I bet that little bit of showy magic never shows on the video playing in this room, Xavier thought, as he stood his ground and smiled. The Soul-Slayer frowned at the lack of reaction from Xavier.

"We shall see who gets roasted by the Creator." He thought he saw just a flicker, a momentary flash of fear in Jack's face, but then it was gone just as quickly, only to be replaced by a sneer.

"Yes we shall see who has the power, for every day I grow stronger with each Soul I consume! Who knows who will be Creator when I am done?"

"Jack, you're a mere Soul-Slayer. The Creator? I think not! The only souls you have slain in the city are those of junkies and degenerates who have spent most of their souls already trying to chase their own Dragons!" With that Xavier started to chuckle, then burst into laughter that so enraged and incensed Jack he actually took a run at Xavier, without morphing into his true form. Head down like a bull with massive horns he had charged into the five-inch solid steel door. Jack managed to knock himself senseless.

Xavier had been shocked but undeniably pleased by what had occurred. It had almost felt like Rose was with him, whispering in his ear telling how to have the Soul-Slayer expose himself. Now the Soul-slayer had a small, infinitesimal crack in his massive ego.

Then it came to Xavier, he knew how it might be possible too defeat the Soul-Slayer.

Xavier heard the sound of feet running as his team came to help. He looked down at Jack and smiled.

CHAPTER TWENTY-ONE

Rose debated whether she should duck back down the embankment or stay where she was and take her chances. She suddenly had a strong feeling that the vehicle coming towards her was safe. Rose reluctantly stuck out her thumb and waited.

The car, an old jeep colored yellow to match the rust, slowed and stopped quite a way down the highway, then after a hesitation backed slowly to where Rose stood, please, please let it be a normal, nice female she thought.

She leaned down and looked through the partially open window, an older woman with long, curly hair, that seemed to have a life of its own, smiled back at her.

"Need a lift, dear? Darkness is coming and you don't want to be caught in the dark," a firm, but pleasant voice said. Rose suddenly felt safe. She climbed into the jeep and sat down.

"Buckle-up dear, I don't worry about my driving but there are others who use this road that are very dangerous," the woman said.

As Rose followed the woman's direction she thought, she has no idea just how right she is about how hazardous it is. A shudder ran down her back at the though of the last car that had stopped for her and invited her in!

"Oh, I have forgotten the amenities, my name is Willow and yours would be?" Willow asked in a voice that was friendly and warm although Rose sensed that her voice could sound very cold when threatened.

Rose turned her head and looked directly into a set of aquamarine colored eyes and said, "My name is Rose."

"Would your secret name be 'Many-Thorns?" Willow asked.

"No one knows that name except..."

"The Spiderwoman told me, and told me too hurry because you're in trouble." Willow said as she turned back to watch the road ahead.

"Yes I was in trouble, but I think that's over now." Rose said as she started to relax in the passenger seat.

"For someone who has managed to survive for so long on your own, given the circumstances you have been through, you are remarkably innocent, or is it stupid!" Willow returned.

Rose would have jumped out of her seat if she had not been buckled in, "Why, you bitch! You have no idea what I have been through!" she yelled as she struggled with the buckle to the seatbelt.

"Relax, Rose, I wanted to make sure you understand that you are far from out of danger until you are with the Spiderwoman and even then you must be cautious. Also one thing you might want to think very clearly about, Rose, there is just as much danger for you from The People as well The White Race. There are some whites that you can trust with your life, like Xavier," Willow responded as she turned and actually smiled at Rose despite the insults that Rose had flung at her.

Rose sat in silence as she thought about what Willow had said. She could feel the essence of Spiderwoman around her, almost as if waiting to see what her response would be. Rose struggled with her feelings, as the jeep drove through the deep purple and faint orange of day's final, faint light before night enveloped them. Hatred, like the fire in the sky at sunset, how it burns me but has never affected the whites except those who tried to do me and mine harm. I worked where I could always stir up the hatred within myself, getting so angry at choices I made for myself. I was filled with hatred for all Whites, but they weren't the ones making the choices, I was. I made the choice to present myself as a 'Ho'. The Whites have done so much damage to The People since they arrived on our shores. What a waste for me to spend my time and energy wrapped in hatred. I could have been helping. What a waste of time even for me, she thought.

"Can I let hatred go?" she whispered to herself as the car drove her further from the city and towards the fading fire of sunset over the western mountains mixing with the dark purple-orange that fore-told of the reign of darkness starting.

Xavier, I have Xavier, my friend, almost my brother. No one can make me laugh like he can. He's a cop, white and named after a Saint, for shit sake! Yet he has watched over me when I have let him. I miss him. Yes I do miss him she thought.

Hatred had begun to feel like a hot, heavy burden that had to be dragged everywhere. Tired, always tired of that feeling always returning the hatred that others feel for me-for The People. Maybe time too let it go, maybe time to be me as I should be and not constantly feeling hate. Time to let go and feel free Rose thought as she stared out the window towards the mountains.

"Maybe your right," Willow echoed. Rose looked at Willow, really looked at her and realized that was something she rarely did with The People. She saw a face that reflected peace and kindness of the soul within. There was a slight smile on her lips. Willow's light, aquamarine blue eyes, which at the moment were checking the side view mirrors, seemed to be capable of reading a persons very thoughts.

"You are right. I'm an Intuitive, one that is a half-n-half, half of The People and half of the Whites-Scottish White. There is only one Intuitive born to The People at a time and we always serve the Spider-woman. I can sense most things about people. I feel the heavy burden you carry and I can tell you that it's time to let it go or you will never look or learn beyond it.

They drove westbound on the Highway for a considerable distance Rose in a thoughtful silence while Willow concentrated on her driving. Willow broke the silence.

"We'll stop at my home for the night, but unfortunately we must be away by first light. We must get too where the Spider-Woman waits by early afternoon." Willow said as she turned north off the highway onto a graveled back road. Although the sun was down and almost completely eaten by the night there was still enough light to see the forests on either side.

"We must be getting close to the Morley area by now? I think I have some relatives in Morley if you rather I stay with them?" Rose asked.

"No, even if we had the time to get you there, which we don't, it would put them in danger over something they know nothing about. Best to stay at my place tonight. There are things in the woods that venture out at night to do harm but don't care for the light," Willow said.

"What things?"

"The Council and the Spiderwoman should have explained more," Willow said with a shake of her head.

"It wasn't really their fault, my mother stole me from the Rez a few days after I saw the Spiderwoman. I was twelve so they had no chance," Rose responded with a shrug.

"Well, I could tell you some of the lore I know. That might help."

"Thank you. At this point I think any information would help me understand," Rose said as she turned towards Willow and gave her a shy smile.

"That must have been hard for you to do?"

"What?" Rose asked.

"Smiling at a half-n-half. I gather you don't smile at any Whites too often or anyone else, for that matter." Willow said.

"Actually I have smiled and laughed with a White person, a cop he is my friend. But your right I don't smile much." Rose returned.

"See some are not all bad." Willow observed with a smile.

"Could be, it is easier to blame others for your troubles," Rose said slowly.

"In a few cases that could be, but in a most of cases where you feel mistrust you are likely right, trust your guts or your senses whatever. They usually won't steer you wrong. But you have to make sure instincts are not clouded by senses like hatred, creatures like the Soul-Slayer gleefully stir up malice, mistrust and scorn. It's like someone or something throwing dirt in your eyes so you are blind and cannot see what is happening." Willow said.

Rose was quiet for a time as she considered Willow's words. She is right, I have been so focused on the dark clouds of what has been done to me and mine that I have very nearly missed what is going on now.

"Your hair is very beautiful." Willow observed as she glanced at Rose.

"What?"

"Your hair is black underneath, but the hair on top is white so it appears like you are wearing a loose white veil. It is very unique," Willow replied

"What, I don't understand?" Rose said as she touched her hair.

"There is a mirror on the other side of the sun-visor, just put the visor down," Willow directed.

Rose did as she was directed and found a small mirror attached there. She looked and sure enough most of her hair was still blue-black but over it was a mantle of pure white hair. The hair grew along the sides of her face and up to the widow's peak on her forehead the hair had turned white, even the hair along center part in her hair had turned white. The white hair shone, even in the darkness of the jeep, and it did indeed look like a veil over her black hair. Rose touched her hair, surprised, she rubbed the white part-no it wasn't some white aberrant dust from the road. It was her hair. She had heard of people being so scared or shocked that all their hair turned white but this?

"Maybe what has happened to you lately has given you a terrible jolt. There must be something, some power within you has refused to let you give in completely to what you saw or felt." Willow said as she saw Rose's reaction.

That was when it dawned on Rose, maybe it was meant to be that her mother stealing her from The People who had loved her was part of the plan, or was it fate. All the danger, the terror, the anger, the hate and the survival skills were part of the training of the being a Spiderwoman?

She sat still saying nothing, letting the revelation wash through her. She understood but the understanding nearly drowned her. I have always looked backwards in the hopes of a better past and nearly fallen over the present and not looked to the future even when both have been presented to me through what has happened. I have been carrying the weight of the past instead of letting it go. The time is now to learn so the future can be better.

Gradually as they drove Rose began too feel better, lighter as her conscious,

subconscious and intuition began to fit together in a type of harmony.

The rest of the journey was done in silence, Willow in understanding. Rose finally seeing and absorbing those lessons already done but not learned 'till now.

It was only when the jeep started to slow that Rose stopped staring inward. She looked about and realized that they were in a barnyard with several yard light that lit up a smallish barn and cottage.

"Well, here we are. Welcome to my home." Willow said.

"It looks lovely, you like your place well lighted." Rose responded.

"As I mentioned before it's best to keep out the worst of the dark and what lurks there. Extend your senses, do you not feel them?" Willow asked.

"Wait, let me try." With that Rose closed her eyes and tried focusing her senses out into the dark. "There, I feel eyes watching, waiting for the lights to go out so they can ravish those that reside within its glow. They are canine in shape but not in thought or heart. They are shadows sent by the Soul-Slayer to do away with or distract us from our plans. They are there and there and there, just beyond the light, waiting," Rose said as she pointed to three different points where the blackness seemed more intense; just beyond the light near the barn and your home."

"Your power and sensing of evil is coming on quickly. Let's go inside, I know you are tired but you need something eat before you go to sleep." Willow said as she walked up the steps and opened the door to let Rose in.

Rose walked in and through the cottage looking around at the comfortable interior and thought it looked just as inviting as the outside of the cottage did. She went into the small kitchen as Willow got a fire going in the wood burning stove and lit another lantern. She sat at the old wooden table and listen as Willow talked as she bustled around. Willow didn't seem to need replies to her chatter but mixed with the sounds of the fire in the stove it was quite pleasant. Rose eyelids grew heavy and she drifted off into a light doze. She only woke when Willow spoke her name as she placed a bowl of soup in front of her.

"I hated to wake you but you should eat something."

Rose managed to eat the soup then Willow showed her to a little guest bedroom and as soon as Rose's head hit the pillow she was asleep.

CHAPTER TWENTY-TWO

It seemed she had just laid her head on the pillow when she felt eyes on her and something large and damp was pushing at her face.

"What the hell...? Rose reluctantly opened her eyes only to look into big golden orbs that were staring back with great intensity. The large damp object that had pushed into her face was the nose of a huge hound whose head was resting on the bed watching her.

"That is Wolf, who is in fact a Wolf-Hound, and has been doing guard duty all night to make sure those that lurk beyond the lights do not get too brave. The big fluffy thing that has been keeping your back warm by curling up on the bed beside you is called Caesar." At which time the massive ball of fur unfurled itself into a cat and stretched, yawed revealing needle sharp teeth and jumped down off the bed.

"We can go now as the sun has touched the top of the mountains so it is safe for us to go. I have made coffee and scones with cheese and fruit so we can eat on the road. We must hurry." Willow urged.

Rose got up and found her clothes clean and folded on the chair beside the bed. She looked up to thank Willow and Willow smiled and shrugged.

"You have time for a very fast shower. I know I always feel better after a shower." Willow said as she handed Rose a towel.

Rose showered quickly, climbed into clean cloths and was out the front door with her hair still damp. She had noted in the mirror in the bathroom that even with a good scrubbing her hair still white in certain places. Well that was something she could ask Spiderwoman about when she had time.

Willow was waiting for her in the Jeep and once Rose was in they drove out of the yard as the sun was just starting to lighten the night sky from black to indigo in the east as the first rays reached beyond the horizon.

"There are warm buttered scones in the canvas bag along with some cheese, just help yourself." Willow said as she handed Rose a thermos of hot coffee.

"Thank you, I needed this. I wish I could have spent more time with Wolf and Caesar." Rose said with a smile then sipped some coffee.

"It's interesting, normally Wolf is very standoffish with strangers. Yet all last night when he wasn't out patrolling, he was by your bed with his head resting on it staring at you. Of course Caesar will sleep up close to anybody, he loves the warmth." Willow said with a laugh.

" I love animals. I always wished I had one with me but as you know my life has not exactly been the kind where I could have one."

"I am still surprised, puzzled and concerned about these new senses. Do you understand all this?" Rose asked as she ate a scone and drank more coffee.

"It is the 'becoming'. To some it comes early and they generally don't survive it. You however, are just about the right age and experience. Do you feel comfortable inside yourself? You showed no alarm when you sensed the creatures in the wood last night. You understood what they were and who had sent them." Willow said in a quiet voice as she drove.

"I do feel right, it feels like a change within me, like something has clicked into place. So many things to think about, to understand." Rose murmured as she leaned her head against the headrest.

The gentle motion of the Jeep lulled Rose into a light sleep where she thought of the spirits last night, of hearing the Spiderwoman's warnings.

"Soon now, very soon, you and I will meet again after such long time." The Spiderwoman whispered in her head.

Willow let Rose sleep as full daylight overcame and banished night completely. They had passed Morley and continued on until Willow found the turn from Highway 1A onto an old logging road that few knew about. The further they climbed the fainter the road got until it faded completely as the forest got thicker. Finally it disappeared completely, only trees ruled here.

"Rose, are you awake, we must walk from here?" Willow said as she got out of the jeep.

"Don't worry I woke up about, oh five potholes ago," Rose laughed as she asked, "is it far away, this meeting place?

"Four or five hours so we can't take many breaks. This time we must get there before early afternoon," Willow said as she pointed out a faint animal trail to the left of where they were standing.

Rose's heart sank as she looked at the steep trail and hoped she wouldn't let Willow or herself down because of all the drug and alcohol she had managed too consumed in the last day and a half.

They started too climb and before long Rose had dearly wanted a to take break. She was sweating profusely but refused to say anything although her lungs and legs were burning. Oddly though, the higher she climbed the more the dregs of her past life of dissipation faded away and the more she felt pulled towards her future. She felt as if she was had been released from the terrible burden that had been her old life.

Now she began to feel many spirits around her. Then she felt she heard a molasses-slow, deep voice welcoming her. The voice was of such a depth it acted like a counter point to the other bright, spirit voices. She wondered who among the spirits had such amazing voice. It had the melodious sound of protection, of safety.

They climbed with no breaks for about four hours and actually beat the Spider-Woman to the Meeting Place, a large flat rock by the side of the path. Both were winded from the climb as they sat on the edge of the rock. Willow pulled a bottle of water and some leftover scones from the knapsack she had been wearing and they feasted on that simple food.

"That was quite the climb." Rose said as she popped the last crumb into her mouth. She sat on the edge of the meeting rock that was slightly under cut so she was kicking her feet back and forth like a small child's. She sat there looking around, admiring the view. Rose had never been this high up. There were white tipped mountains all around her, almost like a crown. Yes that's it, like one of Mother Earth's many crowns, Rose thought.

I feel like I could be an eagle soaring high over the mountains, Rose thought as she shut her eyes and extended her arms until they were at right angles. The crisp mountain air swirled around her and it felt as if she was flying on the currents of air, seeing the world from a different angle. Racing upon the wind watching those who couldn't fly, trudging through their lives. She flew high above the highest peak where the air was light, too light to hold her up and she spiraled down, down until a strong updraft of wind slowed her and pushed under her wings.

"Too soon to fly, first one must learn to walk," a low female voice whispered in her ear.

Willow sat in silence watching Rose with her minds eye', feeling Roses flight within her imagination.

"She belongs up here, a wild creature to long caged that has finally escaped her bonds and now feels freedom, free at last." Willow whispered to herself.

The smell of fresh, high, mountain snow strengthen, the Spider-Woman is here, Rose thought as she brought her arms to her side as she turned to find Spider-Woman standing in the center of The Meeting Place rock.

"Yes I am here and it is time for us to go." The Spider-Woman said before turning to Willow and thanking her for bringing her acolyte to her.

Rose also thanked Willow and hugged her before bidding her farewell.

"Be safe my friend and remember, be off the mountain before dark." The Spider-woman urged as Willow waved and began her long trip back down the mountain.

"Now is our time together, follow me," Spiderwoman said with a slight smile and started up a path that Rose couldn't feel or see.

CHAPTER TWENTY-THREE

Xavier heard the sound of running feet. The first one around the corner was his Sergeant Leighton Brown, followed by Sally and another police officer.

"Sally, grab some restraints, Leighton we need the paramedic with some 'drop and drool' (slang for haldol) quick before this goof wakes up. We don't want to get into a fight with a naked, filthy, crazy man." Xavier said and watched them all scatter. He continued to watch Jack through the window until they arrived back with their tools of the trade.

"Alright Leighton and I are going to cuff him up, while Sally you help the paramedic. We do it now!" Xavier exclaimed as he heard a groan from the floor. Everyone went about His or her job with practiced ease. 'Jack' had just started to moan and move before the drugs hit his system and he was unconscious again.

"Thanks everybody. This cell needs to be cleaned before anybody else uses it.

Everybody, great job, wash up good, Leighton watch the front, and Sally could you check when the ambulance will be here so we can get this goof out of here?" Xavier said as he stood over Jack, while the paramedic checked the pulse of the trussed up bad guy.

"Uh…Staff-Sergeant you might want to get a move on that ambulance, this guy is coming round way too fast. I can give him another shot but that's all the protocols allow," the paramedic warned as he crouched by Jack.

"Have you got more with you?" Xavier asked.

"No, but it will just take me a second to run and grab it."

"Go now!" Xavier said.

The paramedic was out of the cell at a run. Xavier was alone with Jack.

"Alone at last. You know that that drugs don't effect me, don't you?" Jack whispered in an uncanny imitation of Sally.

"Touch any of my team and you'll will be very unhappy, in fact you will be dead. Remember, I know who you are and I am not alone in that knowledge!" Xavier whispered as he listened for the paramedic's footsteps.

Jack made no response as the paramedic came running up and knelt by Jack and gave him another shot of 'drop and drool'. Jack went slack and the paramedic, after checking his pulse, stood up.

"Doesn't do much to him, should get to the hospital though. Oh here are the ambulance guys now."

As soon as the two paramedics got in by the cell they started to complain bitterly about the smell. Then they noticed the more they talked the stronger the smell and the redder the Staff-Sergeant face became and the more pissed off he looked. The paramedic's voices faded away to nothing and they grabbed the guy on the floor, placed him on the strecher and put restraints on record time. They quickly talked with the Duty paramedic before moving the stretcher with Jack in restraints on it.

"This is not over, there are many that follow my lead." Jack whispered.

"That remains to be seen, your time amongst us may be very, very short." Xavier whispered back as he looked down and smiled at Jack. Jack morphed ever so

slightly and gave a short growl. Xavier's smile grew slightly wider. No one else noticed anything as the paramedics rolled Jack into the elevator and the elevator doors slowly closed.

CHAPTER TWENTY-FOUR

"Could someone find the officer who brought in this Reyals, Charles Clark, I would like to talk to him or them."

"I think he has gone home Xav," Sally said as she handed him the package of reports.

"He had better still be in the building." Xav replied as he picked up the phone and dialed the number for the phone in the changing room downstairs. A voice answered.

"I am looking for a Constable J. Whitney."

"You found him, wadda ya want I am on my way home after a long night?"

"This Staff- Sergeant O'Malley, I need you to return to Arrest Processing, so I can talk to you." Xavier said.

"Oh, Um, Yes Sir…be right back up as soon as I change back to my uniform." Constable Whitney returned a slight, wary tremble inhis voice.

"Don't bother changing back as I just need to ask some questions about your last arrest."

Xavier then went over to the property file to check the property report on Reyals, Charles Clark. Once he found it he smirked over the last name being reversed from 'Slayer' to 'Reyals' he took it over to his desk and read it, the more he read the unhappier he became.

"Yes Staff-Sergeant you wanted to see me?" Constable Whitney asked.

Xavier looked up from reading the incident report and looked at Constable Whitney. Whitney wore his newness to the job even without his uniform on. Xavier guessed that he might still be on officer-coach, although there was a hint of cockiness about the way he slouched against the Staff-Sergeant's desk which was mounted on the dias.

Could be a junior officer, for some strange reason, some of them felt once off officer-coach they knew everything he thought.

"I see you are working downtown."

"Yes Sir." Whitney replied.

"You had a partner last night, who searched the prisoner?" Xavier asked.

"Well I gave him a cursory search." Whitney replied.

"Pretty dirty and smelly?"

"Yes sir, I thought I was going to throw up."

"You didn't come across a large hunting knife, did you?" Xavier asked.

"No sir, things would have gone down entirely differently if we had found a weapon. It was kinda odd though."

"In what way?" Xavier asked.

"Well, first off it wasn't a dispatched call. We were driving around down by the Cecil to see if anything was happening. Just as we were slowly driving outside the west side of Ceil when all of a sudden this big tall guy, the accused, out of the blue punched this poor old guy. The punch knocked the old guy over and the accused stood over him yelling about owing for some drug or something like that. Odd though, my partner and I got the feeling that it almost was staged." Constable Whitney said.

"James is your first name? How do you mean staged James?"

"Well as we were drawing up, but still a distance away, they both seemed to be casually leaning against the wall. Soon as we got close enough for them to make sure we were police, driving a police car, they suddenly faced each other and the accused slugs the old guy. Soon as we get out of the car the accused started up yelling. Funny thing, I had my window open as we drove up, he only started yelling when we opened our doors." James looked at Xavier and Xavier could see the uncomfortable, unsure look on his face.

"Thank you, James I appreciate your assessment of the situation. You may very well be right, but we may never know. I see you got the victim's name here, J.T. Kirk with an address at 100 River Rd. N.W.? Xavier asked with a slight smile.

"Yes sir, he refused medical treatment although he had a huge bruise forming on his left cheek."

"Does the name J.T. Kirk, sound somewhat familiar to you? Xavier asked as he looked discreetly to where Leighton was standing with an almost invisible smile on his face.

"Uh yes sir, it kinda did."

"Have you ever seen the 'Star Trek' series or all the movies and other T.V. shows that were spin-offs?"

"Not much of a 'trekkie' fan sir, kinda before my time." Cst. J Whitney said and shrugged.

Xavier could hear the gasp and snort of poorly concealed laughter behind him and sighed to himself. First he would have to explain to this very young constable about Capt. James T. Kirk of the Star-Ship Enterprise. But after he would have to come up with plan to prank Leighton.

"James unfortunately the alleged victim probably scammed you. As a result of my greater number of years I know about 'Trekkies' and 'Star Trek' and the fact that the lead character's name was James T. Kirk which is real close to J.T.Kirk and 100 River Rd N.W. is in the middle of the Bow River." Xavier explained patiently and watched as Constable J. Whitney proud smile slithered down into one of embarrassed unhappiness.

"I wouldn't worry about it, we've had Marilyn Monroe, Buffy the Vampire Slayer and even Paris Hilton plus several other apparently famous people up here, or at least their names were up here. It may be the first time it happened to you but believe me lots of others will try it on you for various reasons. Just look at this as a valuable lesson and move on. We also gained some valuable information from this, thanks to you and your partner, so all was not lost. Go home and get some sleep, in a way you've done good." Xavier said with a sardonic smile.

The more Xavier explained the better the young constable felt and he had a smile on his face when he left Arrest Processing. After he was gone Xavier turned to his traitorous Sergeant, they looked at each other and burst out laughing.

"I expect my Sergeant to back me, not snort and giggle like a little girl behind my back." Xavier said once he stopped laughing.

"I'm sorry Xav, I truly am but it took me back to my first days on the job and the number of times I got suckered, most of them learn fast especially when they get teased enough." Leighton said as he wiped tears of laughter from his eyes.

"Oh, to be young and that cocky again with the wisdom I have now, otherwise I wouldn't want to go through that torture again. Once was enough, thank you very much."

"You hinted that you got some good information out of all the drama this morning?" Leighton asked as he sat down at his desk and started going through reports.

"I did but 'tit for tat' my nemesis got some information on me as well. I will fill you in once I have had time to think it through." Xavier said as he dialed the number for the clean up crew to advise them too make sure they use extra precautions with cell nineteen.

CHAPTER TWENTY-FIVE

Sally Marone had watched the exchange between Xav and Leighton from the background and had laughed with them. Part of her laugh, though, was relief that Xavier seem to be getting his sense of humor back. For the longest time it had seemed like his whimsy and wit were on a back self of his mind, all dusty and dirty from lack of use. He did have a faint smile then that he had used when he felt he had to smile for some reason. It was a pitiful attempt where the corners of his mouth barely turned up, if you weren't watching you missed it. Although he had learned his job quickly and treated his team with respect. His gaze had always seemed to be looking inward, she thought.

Sally was amazed at just how many years an honest smile and laugh shaved off his face. It was like an old film that had been dark, blurry and in a tea colored gray and white had been fixed and now the light shone correctly through it. This was the first time, in what felt like a century, that he was seeing the humor in things. Life up here could almost be called normal in their usual crazy way.

Although time, mostly stayed steady, there were parts that all of a sudden seemed to fly by like joy, a beloved's face or happiness were almost a blur and hard to remember. Then sadness and terrible heartache would wrap itself around the ticking and tocking, of time slowing it down until it seemed like every tortured, throbbing minute felt like an hour. But all of a sudden Xavier's clock seemed like it was back on steady time.

Even his humor, which had deserted him, returned and seemed none the worse for wear.

Xavier was appalled when he realized just how long he had been wrapped in his own misery. Yet his new team had let him come back to himself on his own.

Xavier looked around, saw everybody was busy checking reports, preparing hearings and booking in prisoners. Thing had quieted down considerably since 'One-Eyed-Jack' had been taken out. He had finished checking the reports of several officers and he decided to check on the officers that had been having such a rough time with the arrest they had been struggling with when he had initially walked into the unit. He walked back to the officer's report writing room. He saw the four officers were sitting in a corner finishing up their notes. They all looked tired but they were laughing over the stupid night they had had.

"Quiet night I take it?" Xavier asked.

"Yes sir," the officers all answered at once.

"It's Xavier and I just came back to see if the four of you were all right or if you needed anything?" He asked.

When Xavier introduced himself by his first name the officers loosened up.

"I'll tell you 'Staff' (shortened acceptable name for Staff-Sergeant) I kept checking to make sure it wasn't a full moon on Friday the thirtieth. We've been dealing with shit-heads and goofs all night. We kept trying to tell them to go home and they all insisted they wanted to go to jail."

"You four look like you have had a good time, just have the paramedic check for scratches and clean them up before you go home. Oh and Alice nice leg sweep on the 'Ho', the little ones are the worst." Xavier said with a grin.

The officers laughed and then said they would survive although their uniforms might be beyond reviving. Xavier smiled as he left the room and went back to the actual Arrest Processing office. Before he sat down at his desk he went over to where Sally was entering new prisoners into the computer and removing prisoners that had either been shipped up to 'The Hill' (Spy Hill Remand where prisoners, not released, were housed) or released. He stood beside her looking at the number the prisoners they had right now.

It was comfortable standing beside Sally. She was only two inches shorter than his six foot four inches. The male officers, when she wasn't around, all called her 'Mustang Sally', with a great deal of respect but they were to afraid to say it in her hearing.

Sally was a good-looking woman who wouldn't tolerate any nonsense from either the prisoners or police officers, hence the nickname. She was handsome, rather than pretty with a generous mouth and easy smile. She had long strawberry blonde hair that was pulled back into a severe ponytail then wrapped into a sort of bun. If the day was busy, which it usually was, by the end of the shift there would be tendrils of hair that had defied the severity of her hairdo and escaped to drift down and curl about her face. She looked like a painting by Rafael or Bottocellie, Xavier thought with the loose curling hair and the slightly flushed face. He always felt at ease when she was around and even though their conversations were work based they both laughed at the same odd things that happened up here.

"Shift hadn't even started and we were right into it." Sally said as she continued working on the computer. As she typed away, to anyone else it seemed Xavier was watching the computer, but she sensed he was watching her discreetly. She felt a sudden flush creeping along her high cheekbones as she turned her head slightly away so he wouldn't notice.

"So what's the count on the prisoners we have this morning?" Xavier asked as he noticed the flush and realized she had become disconcerted by his closeness, he gave her a disarming smile before moving to his desk to correct some reports.

The morning went by quickly, first the drunks who were deemed sober enough were given a sandwich of cheese and bread and a juice box then punted out the door. Prisoners going up to the hill had been handcuffed together had been directed out to the prisoner's bus by prison guards. While those going to court that morning had been taken over to court cells, and the ones who were having a hearing with the bail Magistrate were given the same breakfast of bread and cheese sandwich and juice box. It was mid-morning before things quieted down. Sally walked over drinking a coffee and handed Xavier one. Leighton wandered over with his coffee as well.

"Quite a start to the morning. I haven't seen someone that out of control in a while and I haven't seen the paramedic use that many shots of 'drop and drool' to calm someone down." Leighton said with a shake of his head.

"Well he was a huge guy and he was very, very angry, which may have had something to do with it. I heard someone say he was on other drugs as well. Good job on that one, everybody. Nobody hurt, not even the bad-guy, although my sense of smell is going to take time to recover." Xavier said between sips of his coffee.

What tension there had been in the room slid away to be eaten by relief. It had been true that they were a good team. Now that Xavier was back with them, not only in person, but in spirit, it seemed that now it could be a great team. You could almost hear the small intellectual sigh of soothing release, almost as if the thin ice they felt they had been treading on had thickened so it was safe to be themselves.

Anyone checked on that guy in cell 20 (another isolation cell) to see if he has calmed down? I can see him curled up in the corner but he has his back to the camera and I can't see what he is doing?" Xavier asked.

"I'll go back there and check." Rick Rowan said as he took off his glasses, got up from his place at large extended desk where all the Bail Hearing Officers (otherwise known as Crown Prosecutors) worked. By the time he had completely risen from the chair he was six- foot-five inches of amiable muscle.

Rick walked back to cell twenty, open the thick steel door with his cell key and walked in, cautiously, he was just in time to see the prisoner popping a loose baggie of pills into his mouth. Rick grabbed him by the neck and tightened his fingers around his throat so the bad-guy couldn't swallow the pills, (this delicate method is called 'scogging' not a word Internal Affairs was fond of).

"I need some help back here," Rick yelled as he lifted and held the bad-guy against the wall so his toes barely touched the floor.

"Spit em out you fucker! Spit em out or I swear I will squeeze your throat so tight your head will burst like big fucking pimple!" Rick yelled as he watch the bad-guy start to turn a shade of lavender. At which point Xavier, Sally and the paramedic all tried to get through the door at once and were monetarily wedged before Sally popped through followed by the others.

Open your mouth!" Rick yelled and the bad-guy finally complied and open his mouth. Steve could see the baggie at the back of the mouth.

"Ok spit them out! And not on me you dumbass or I will drive your thick head through to the next cell. Reluctantly, with his last gasp of air, the bad-guy spit out the drugs still in the in the baggie. Rick had let him go and head-bone slid down the wall like a thick wad of mucus.

The paramedic grabbed the spit-covered bag and after a quick look at the contents shook his head and swore. "Fuck, morphine tablets! Hey! Buddy! Did you swallow anymore? Shit I gotta call for an ambulance right now, he looks to be 'OD ing'!"

The paramedic rushed out of the room to call for an ambulance while Xavier and Rick tried to keep the bad-guy more or less alert until the ambulance arrived.

The paramedic came back into the cell with his stethoscope and blood pressure cuff.

"Good keep him sitting up and as alert as possible while I check him." The paramedic said. It was getting harder and harder to keep him conscious but just then the paramedics from the ambulance came in pushing the stretcher.

"We have 'Narcan' all ready to go!" one of them said.

"Okay, lets get him on the stretcher and tie him down before we administer the 'Narcan' you know how they come out of the overdose fighting." The Arrest Processing paramedic said. They quickly heaved the now unconscious bad-guy onto the stretcher and restrained him with leather cuffs. They then administered the Narcan. Sure enough suddenly the accused was awake and struggling against the restrains and using every swear word in his vast repertoire.

"Here are the ones from his mouth, we have no idea how many he had already swallowed." Rick said as he handed the baggie filled with capsules over.

The paramedics nodded as they hurried to the prisoner elevator with the bad-guy between them on the stretcher.

"I have a feeling if we hadn't checked on that guy when we did we would be doing all the paperwork for a death in Arrest Processing. Nice job, Rick!" Xavier said as they all walked back to the main office.

"What is our Motto, here in Arrest Processing?" Xavier asked.

"No One Dies On Our Watch!" they all yelled together.

Xavier looked at his watch and found much to his surprise that the day was nearly over and he still had to get his own paperwork done. Everything was just caught up when night shift came in. Xavier passed on pertinent information to Frank Gregor including the two inmates had been sent to the hospital, both spinier than rabid raccoons. Frank had laughed at that, and then looked at Xavier strangely, Xavier caught the look.

"What's wrong Frank?"

"I don't know, somehow you seem different than this morning, happier maybe. Before I always thought you were going after my nickname 'hard-ass' which I have proudly born for these twenty-five years.

"No I would never go after your nickname, that's is something you really worked hard for," Xavier said with a chuckle. "Lets just say I saw my true enemy this morning, not those in the puzzle palace, but my real enemy besides myself. Once I saw him I realized I don't give a shit about promotion, they can promote me or not, whatever. But I have faced my enemy and I understand him finally and I will deal with him. He knows and there was a lightening flash of fear on his face. When all that occurred to me I felt like a dumb ass playing the masculine version of Camille. So yes I am back, all of me, shit-heads watch out!"

CHAPTER TWENTY-SIX

When he finally left Foothills Hospital it was getting dark again. He was utterly consumed by anger and a rage so great that he was having trouble staying in the form of 'One-Eyed-Jack'. He kept partially morphing into his real shape as a 'Soul-Slayer' as he stalked along the sidewalk.

People who were unfortunate enough to walk by and look at him or hear him had their minds suddenly swept back into their childhood; where, with no night-light to hold back the darkness they had lain a bed wrapped in the night's shadows. They knew the Boogieman lurked under the bed or behind the partially opened closet door. The Boogieman waited for little feet to swing down and touch the floor so it could drag them under the bed or pull them into the closet.

There was a magic that existed in the world, called by some 'imagination'. But it was more than that and children saw both the light and dark side of it. As the white children left childhood the magic in life was literally taught out of them and only a few retained their belief in magic. The People, on the other hand, were taught that magic was a part of life that must be protected at all times for what was life without magic and imagination? The people knew that they must take care of Mother Earth's magic in order for her to take care of them.

The People also understood that there were special People among them that did great good and some who, if allowed, would become destroyers.

A Soul-Slayer was concentrated black magic and as he stalked away from the hospital that night some who saw him recognized the boogieman who had lain under the bed or hidden behind the partially closed door to a dark closet when they were young. The gargantuan fear of their childhood returned to them for the briefest moment and they stumble and lost their bearings in the sudden chill of that fear.

Other who saw him for longer and heard the Soul-Slayer's wrath even for the briefest of moments saw not only the darkness of childhood, but also perceived only the lie that there was nothing but bleakness in their lives now. Some people's psyches were so fragile that they were shattered by what had just happened and they walked out in front of a bus or a car.

At the sound of the chaos that followed him he smiled and felt a little better.

He felt the paper in his hand and again his rage started to bubble up, but ripping the Appearance Notice to shreds, stomping on it and then pissing on it made him feel better again. Luckily he had walked into some nearby bushes to do that; the pretty little bush he had pissed on turned brown and formed brambles, which started choking all the other bushes. He felt better now, calmer. The temper-tantrum had dissipated and he was back in human form that would simply cause people to turn away. The display of rage had cost him power that he now needed too replenish and quickly.

"Back to the good ole stomping grounds it is then. Gotta suck on some worthless white souls to regain some power. Shit, in the old days I would trap or trick some 'People's' Warrior' and he would last me the whole winter, fighting me every step of the way 'til nothing was left but the husk. I would honor him by returning him to his People for proper burial." 'Soul-Slayer' muttered.

" What is it about these worthless, pasty-faced whites that causes me so much trouble? The ones that are lured by what they call drugs, are like fruit of the poisonous tree where when you take a bite out of the lovely looking fruit, you realize it is almost rotten to the core. It takes many of them to sustain me for even a short time and the taste of their souls is bitter. I wonder what the soul of that policeman who chases me would be like? He is like the Warriors of old, except for his pasty skin. Too bad I didn't take his mate's soul but there was a light around it and I could not seem to touch it.

Well, we shall see how the policeman's soul tastes, perhaps soon. It is good, in some ways that the old days have passed and with them the Creator, the Spiderwoman and the Turtle have gone the way of 'The People' swallowed by their own magic. So I can make this witless, pale land mine," he whispered to himself as he walked by the riverbank. He always whispered for that was how he thought but in his conceit he didn't realize someone was listening.

CHAPTER TWENTY-SEVEN

Rose watched Willow leave. Willow was the symbol of the last vestiges of her old life and contact with the outside world. She looked towards the Spiderwoman who smiled at her.

"Our time is now, Rose. Can you keep up?" Spiderwoman asked.

"Yes, I believe I can." Rose responded.

The Spiderwoman nodded before starting up a path that only she could see, walking with quick, sure-footed grace. Rose followed her. She had to study the ground ahead of her very carefully before she put her foot down on what appeared to be limestone shale that could slide with one misstep. She did, however, manage to keep up a respectable pace not far behind the Spiderwoman. There were times though when the ground was flat and she could actually see the faint path. At other times she had to cling to roots and then branches of fir trees so she wouldn't fall.

"There, there is where I live." Spiderwoman said as she pointed at a small alpine meadow.

Rose looked where Spiderwoman had pointed and saw a pretty mountain meadow filled with wild flowers of all descriptions, white daisies, bluebells and buffalo beans among the many species that grew there. Butterflies added more touches of color as they flitted from flower to flower.

"Such a beautiful place, the smell of natural mountain grass mixed with the scent of the tousled blossoms; not too sweet but fresh and clean. I could lie here all day watching the clouds, enjoying the scents and the sounds," Rose reflected.

"Perhaps there might be small bits of time here and there, to do that. For the most part I must teach you, in a relatively small amount of time, what usually takes a lifetime to learn," Spiderwoman returned.

"Do we sleep outside? I see no cottage or cabin?" Rose asked as she looked around the meadow.

"Look carefully, Rose, use your eyes, your senses."

Rose raked the meadow with her eyes, as she tentatively let loose her senses to feel the meadow. It was odd yet exhilarating to project her awareness out and about her sharpening her abilities and growing each time she used it. Nothing-no-wait a large mound on the other side of the meadow. Even though it was covered with the same flowers that ran riot throughout the rest of the meadow it seemed out of place somehow.

Rose moved closer, until she was right beside the mound. It was only then that she discovered that the mound was actually three rounded sides and a roof. Because of the way it had been set it looked like a hillock on the edge on the meadow. On the fourth side logs were fitted together to form a wall in which there were two glass windows with a split log door between them. Climbing roses and moss had very nearly covered the logs. The cottage, which was mostly sod, was so well disguised that it was all but invisible.

"Very good Rose, you found our home, a place very few could find. Lets go in and I will get dinner ready," Spiderwoman said with a broad smile.

Rose followed the Spiderwoman into her new home. She was immediately enthralled as she looked around the large room. The smell of sweet-grass surrounded her and she could see sage mixed with mountain grass hanging upside down drying in one of the windows. There were a multitude of selves against the back wall of the one room home. The shelves on the left side were filled with books. The selves on the right side contained old-fashioned, glass medicine bottles with glass-stopper on each of them. Each was filled with different liquids or powders with labels on them. There were some dark unidentifiable objects, perhaps bones of some ancient beast that seemed to move of their own volition. Another shelf had skulls on it, some she could identify and others she could not. In a small alcove there was string woven wooden bed with a thick goose down mattress, woven blankets were folded neatly on it and two fluffy pillows at one side. Another bed made up in similar fashion but it was flush against the opposite wall.

There was a small fire burning brightly in the fireplace with field-stone walls where the smooth river rocks were placed in such a way that they were almost flush with the rest of the walls near the alcove. An ancient armchair covered in some type of woven material was on one side of the fireplace. An old rocking chair containing what looked like a wildcat with large green eyes glared at her his large ears, with black tuffs at the top, flattened as he grumbled and growled. Spider-woman said a word and he resumed his position and his eyes closed to slits. The floor was planked pine and had been cleaned and waxed with bee's wax so many times that it reflected a dull golden glow. There was a small table with two chairs sitting under the right window.

Rose looked up at the ceiling expecting to see dirt and the roots of flowers and grass but instead she saw an intricately worked ceiling of wood. There seemed to be pieces of wood representing all the trees within the forest. Odd but the more she looked at it the more she saw it twisting into a spiral that went on and on endlessly.

"I hope you will find it comfortable here," Spiderwoman said, noting where Rose's eyes were focused.

"Rose?"

Startled, Rose refocused on Spiderwoman.

"That is called a meditation spiral, it can also be handy if you have trouble sleeping."

"This is the most beautiful place I have been in since I was a child," Rose returned.

The Spiderwoman watched her but said nothing. Rose was taken aback when the Spiderwoman said nothing about her past life and met her gaze.

"Don't pity me," Rose said, defiantly.

"I don't pity you, obviously the Creator placed you in a hard positions to see if you were capable of being a Spiderwoman. You seemed to have made the right choices or at least the decisions that would help you survive. Also along the way you helped The People when you could and despite you're hatred for the White Race you have a close friend or what could be called a familiar that is white and a police officer to boot."

Rose was quiet for a moment, the Spiderwoman has taken the wind out of her sails.

"I did make my own choices and some I have had to pay for." Rose said as her voice took on a bitter tone. "Look on the bright side. My mother stole me when I was twelve. Nobody from the Rez even came looking for me. I received no more schooling so the white eye's school has not sullied my brain. The only thing I did learn was how to survive in the ugly underbelly of the city, so I have lots of room in my brain left for knowledge."

The Spiderwoman studied her for a moment and Rose met her gaze for only a moment before she dropped her head as she realized her anger had gotten the best of her tongue again.

" I have heard some of the words or mantra's of a Man known by the name of Buddha. He was a great Shaman and teacher in the east across the oceans long before the whites even thought of religion. I have felt the truth of these words many times. Spiderwoman recited the words with a gentle voice.

"The past is simply the past. 'Life is not a race but a journey to be savored each step of the way. Yesterday is history; today is a gift and tomorrow is a mystery.' You might want to think on that, for if all you do is linger over the past you will never see the future or go forward." Spiderwoman said before she turned to start a fire in the fireplace.

Rose was startled by the Spiderwoman's words and initially was going to respond in kind, but how could she respond without sounding like a foolish child having a temper tantrum? She stepped back outside and walked to an old log where she sat down. The words that had been said were whirling around in her head. This was it. She either made it here or went back to what she had always known.

Rose thought of the brief time she had spent going back to what she used to do, after she got out of jail and how she had felt guilty, even disappointed with herself over that one night of debauchery. She sensed that if she went back to that life she would be dead quickly either by her own hand or The Soul-Slayer would make sure of she left the world after he made her suffer. Then there was Xavier, her friend, her Familiar, she had promised to help him.

Rose thought about the word she had heard, they did make sense... the past was over. Maybe she could help make the future better.

"What can I do to help with dinner?" Rose asked Spiderwoman as she stepped back into the little cottage.

From then on time had no meaning except for learning. Spiderwoman taught her how to read by reciting the words in the ancient books that she and others had obtained over the centuries. Rose even learned Latin from a book so old, she heard small delicate cracks every time she carefully turned a page. The vellum so delicate that it felt like it would crumble into dust. The writing in the book was so faded that she needed Spiderwoman to help her decipher the words. Words of wisdom, the magic that came from understanding and enlightenment from an ancient philosopher Aeschylus: 'That which comes by suffering'.

In many of the other books the ink was so wane that it was nearing the end of its life. Rose always liked to think the eyes of so many Spiderwoman reading the words and understanding their essence somehow faded the words. It was like they were drawing the intent out of the very ink.

The books and their meaning were only a small part of what the Spiderwoman taught her. Rose was like a sponge soaking up all the knowledge. How to dry sweet-grass so it burned fragrant with pure white smoke. There were Native medicines like spider webs could help wounds and prevented infection. There was just so much to learn. Absorbing all that knowledge had literally forced her former life to the very back of her brain. The odd time when she thought of the outside world, it seemed like an old Daguerreotype that had faded and curled at the edges in the back attic of her mind. Oddly the more Rose learned and grew in the strength of the knowledge that Spiderwoman taught her, the more diminished and faded the Spiderwoman became.

Now finally was the time for Rose to take her own vision quest to find out if the Creator, and the Heart of Mother Earth and something called the Universal Turtle would accept her as the new Spiderwoman.

The last words said to her by the Spiderwoman were OM MANI PAD ME HUM, one last thing to understand, to learn.

CHAPTER TWENTY-EIGHT

It was a cool night. A small portion of the velvet darkness was soiled green by a flickering neon sign. The sign matched the building, a tired old brick structure that blended in with the other edifices in the block. The only difference was the flickering neon that advertised 'Liquor', there were bars on the windows and the two figures loitered at the corner just on the outside edge of the light.

There was just enough light for the two figures to complete their conversation and for the taller one to hand the smaller one a small package.

"Be sure ya do this right, you screw this up all the drugs in the world will not help ya, Ratz." The gravelly voice of the taller figure said.

"Don'na worry Boss, ya knowed I will do it, evan da time!" a quavering, whining voice replied.

"Go enjoy your drugs Ratz, but I better hear about something bad happening in jail."

Ok, boss, ya knows Ratz alwus do for ya." the placating voice pleaded.

With that the two figures parted and disappeared into the dark.

Ratz scurried away looking nervously around him to make sure nobody was following or watching him. With his small bent form, large nose and small black eyes that were continually shifting around he did look remarkably like his namesake and had been taunted and tormented about his looks since he could remember. He had become used to it in a way, he sat at the back of the class and daydreamed his days away.

The only thing he learned in school was how to avoid school, people and how to do drugs, specifically opium. Opium was the black, sticky gold that heroin (illegal) and morphine sulfate (legal) were made from. Ratz had always had the money for opium even when he was twelve, he took it from his father's safe and his father, perhaps because he felt guilty, ignored the theft.

Ratz had learned to smoke the black tar opium from an ancient, little man who liked young boys ,even ugly ones.

Since the eighteenth century when the whites had learned of the habit while exploring and exploiting the Asian countries, smoking it had been called Chasing the Dragon.

Even now there were, deep within the confines of China town, opium dens where Ratz would lay upon a bed with the old man beside him doing what he wanted, while Ratz smoked from a long pipe 'Chasing the Dragon' and dreaming of being loved. None, who slipped into these dens were ever questioned and simply lay upon a couch, handing the manager the money required in return for a pipe full of tar.

Ratz was one of those White's who because of their looks, attitude or lack thereof, became invisible. Their looks, speech or mental issues caused discomfort amongst the so-called 'normal folk'. At other times in the history of the White race those had been or looked different were put away or if born in the wrong century charged with witchcraft.

Even Ratz's parents tended to ignore him, mainly because all three of their other children were beautiful. They just couldn't see why he was in their family? He was a mistake and his parent frowned every time they saw him.

Ratz had bought some illegal drugs, acid to be exact, went to his room and took it rather than his usual opium so he could think rather than dream. Alone and high he let his mind wander through several hallucinations and in one he even contemplated killing his parents and their scum-wad kids. But even when hallucination occurred to him it seemed he had a strong sense of survival. He knew in prison his life was worth nothing to anybody except for perhaps the giggles it would supply to some sociopath in watching him die. In the entitled world in which he was born he would always be scorned, not to his face of course but behind his back and he might as well be dead for there would be nothing or nobody for him.

It was his epiphany and when the hallucinations had subsided he packed his packsack with clean socks, underwear and about five thousand dollars from his daddy's safe and left forever.

From that time to the time when he met up with One-Eyed-Jack, some fifteen years of his life had been spent in the lower east side of the city. The people down there actually saw him and immediately called him Ratz and that was OK because some of them were called far worse. He even forgot his real name.

Gradually, over the years, he became known as the facilitator or in the street lingo, the 'go to guy'. If you wanted certain drugs, Ratz could find them for you, with a small commission for himself of course. If someone ripped you off Ratz knew someone that would rough him or her up for you.

Ratz even knew where to find the creatures that would do murder, he took a large commission for that particular deed.

When the SoulSlayer first arrived in the east end, two years prior, he had taken some time to look around to find out who ran the main businesses down here. That's when he discovered Ratz and just how efficient and discreet a businessman he was.

Just because he was ugly and talked dumb didn't mean he was stupid and Ratz was ruthless when it came to business. If anything, his weak spot seemed to be his friendliness with some of the hookers although they paid him a fee for the area they worked.

Now Jack waited patiently at the place had indicated. He sensed Ratz was checking to make sure no one else was around.

"I came alone."

"B-Better s-safe than s-sorry," Ratz responded.

"Quit dancing around out there. Let's talk!"

"Something about you different," Ratz said suspiciously.

"I see you've lost your stutter," Jack said with a chuckle.

"I knew I didn't need it with you. So what do you want with me, or rather what do you need from me?" Ratz asked as he stepped into the dim light in front of Jack.

"First I want your soul!" One-Eyed-Jack said as he took a swift step towards Ratz.

"Can't have what's not there," Ratz said and began to laugh and laugh until he could laugh no more.

"Everything has a soul," he said as he morphed into the Soul-Slayer and grabbed Ratz and pulled him towards him, his open mouth covered Ratz's mouth. Nothing! Just a bitter taste! He roared as he shook Ratz.

"I told you no soul. Shit, you're even uglier than I am. But I think you an I can do business anyway."

The Soul-Slayer looked straight into Ratz's eyes and Ratz returned the look. But the more Ratz looked, the more he began to shake at what he saw in that one eye. Blackness, utter blackness with not even a pinpoint of light in it-he could feel himself getting lost in it, dragged into a black world everything of his lost, his intellect and his understanding of the evil around him. Ratz sniveled as he backed off-for then-as he finally managed to break eye contact with the Soul-Slayer.

'I have shown you what I can do, even without your soul! Understand this! We are not partners and the moment you try to betray me I will know it and you will be lost in my blackness forevermore."

From that moment on Ratz had been his slave, a whipped cur who hated his master far more than he had ever hated anyone in his life, even his family. He never looked in the SoulSlayer's eyes again for he feared that the SoulSlayer would not see dread, but only the hatred with which he really held him. For Ratz knew that where there was only fear there was a slave that would always do your bidding. But hatred or disgust well that was a whole different matter, hate was the reluctant slave who planned how to destroy the Master. For now, Ratz would be his slave and see what this monster, this Soul-Slayer, was up to and then Ratz would know how he could trap and then destroy this thing.

CHAPTER TWENTY-NINE

It had been a busy all day with few chances for a break. Everybody was tired and tended to snap at the police officers bringing up fresh arrests. Nobody was really watching the prisoners that had just been brought in. The officers who had brought them in were standing together and talking. Xavier had a crowd of officers standing around his desk waiting to have their reports approved when suddenly he felt danger, something was going to happen. Something felt wrong, the feeling was so strong that he stood up and walked over to the counter.

The problem was in the foyer beyond the front of the counter. Xavier saw the officer's talking to each other and not watching their prisoners.

"You officers standing there which ones are your prisoners, get control of them!" Xavier said in a loud, firm voice.

The officers froze for a second at the icy look Xavier gave them, before hurriedly started sorting out their prisoners. Sally walked over to where Xavier stood behind the counter watching. There was a sudden blood-curdling scream from a skinny arrest, who had been standing hidden behind some other detainees. He had managed to step through his handcuffed hands and now his hands were in the front, he was charging the front counter. Xavier pushed Sally out of the way as the prisoner leaped at him. Xavier saw a flash of the hypodermic needle in the prisoner's right hand. Xavier ducked under him and grabbed him by his arms and using the prisoner's forward motion to flip him over him his head and smash him to the ground. Sally was there with her nightstick and smashed it into the prisoner's arms.

"Drop it, damn you, drop it or I will break both your fucking arms!"

The prisoner finally dropped the needle but then tried to sit up to bite Xavier. Xavier quickly twisted and booted him in the head. The prisoner dropped unconscious on the floor and two rotted teeth fell on the floor by his mouth.

"Somebody get the paramedic up here now! Are you all right Sally, you didn't get any of this goof's blood on you?"

"I'm furious, but unharmed thank you."

" Xavier take a few deep breaths before you talk to anybody." Sally said quietly.

"Whose prisoner was that?" he asked in a tightly controlled voice looking out over the silent foyer, he could feel Sally's hand on his and that above all else managed to quiet the rage that had started to boil over.

"He was ours sir." Two senior officers stepped forward.

"What was he originally charged with?"

"Just a simple assault and a warrant, sir"

"You will be adding additional charges, I take it?"

"Yes sir!" They both answered at the same time. Both had gone deathly pale.

"See me when you're done. As far as evidence you better call Ident to take photos and samples of his blood, tell them to be careful as no doubt he has A.I.D.S or whatever." Xavier said in a voice gone arctic.

"Yes sir" both senior officers turned and fled, one to check with the paramedic on the condition of their prisoner while the other one went to the Ident Section (Canadian version of CSI) to get one of the technicians.

Sally had never seen Xavier so furious. He turned and walked to his desk, sat down and started writing his notes on the incident.

The area was eerily silent as officers quietly went to Leighton's desk to get their report approved. Usually there was laughter and comments over reports, right now the officers got their report signed and beat a hasty retreat to meet elsewhere to discuss what had just happened. Xavier's face never changed as he finished his notes.

"Leighton will you take over while I check on the prisoner? Sally I know you have pulled up all the information on the suspect, could you bring it and come with me. I will be with the paramedic, Leighton. Please make sure those two officers don't leave." Leighton nodded as he took over Xavier's desk.

No one in the report room wanted to be in the shoes of the two officers. Everybody knew the two could possibly lose their jobs over this mess and everybody vowed to himself or herself that they would be searching their prisoners right down to their skivvies from then on. Those that had seen what had happened had also made notes on it. Nobody went near the two officers who were together at the farthest desks in the report writing room, best to steer clear of those two right now; their bad luck might rub off on others.

Xavier stalked down the corridor that led to the paramedic's office with Sally at his side. Sally looked up at his face and thought he had the look of an ascetic, in fact that was the first time she had seen the resemblance between him and his brother the Monsignor. It frightened her because when she had been introduced once to the Monsignor, she had felt an instance dislike and suspicion of the so-called religious man. Sally was not one to make hasty decisions, but she had felt a shudder of distaste go down her back from the moment she had met him.

Xavier stopped her just short of the paramedic's office.

"Does this guy that decided to come over counter have A.I.D.S. or Hepatitis A.B.C. or flesh-eating disease? Just what has he got that he wants to give to us, so desperately?"

He has most of what you said. In fact, it looks like he won't last more than a few months. Mind you, I've been wrong before," Sally said.

"Never you, Sally. Lets go in and see if this guy is conscious so we can have a little talk with him, what's this goof's name?"

"Jimmy Durban, I think, he has so many alias', but that one seems to be his favorite," Sally replied.

They entered the paramedic's office to find Jimmy Durban trussed up like a chicken on the stretcher with a spit mask over his face. It was apparent that he had tried several times to spit, but it just sprayed back on him. He seemed to bemoaning the loss of two of his rotten teeth. Even through the bloody spit mask Xavier could see the bruise shaped like boot tread that had been left from his attempt to bite Xavier.

"So tell me James, why do you have such a hate on for me and my staff. I don't believe I have ever even seen you before." Xavier turned to Sally and asked if she had seen the accused before.

"No sir."

"Mind you, you have quite a criminal record but from the medical side of it you look to be dying from various and sundry diseases you have managed to pick up along the way. Why bother us? Now wait before you answer that, you have quite a few fresh charges against you including attempted murder with me as the victim."

"Now I can withdraw those charges and you will be punted back out onto the street. The cold, miserable street, left to shiver and die amongst those that told you to do this. Or we lay the charges and you stay in a warm, clean prison ward with nice, legal drugs to keep you comfortable during your final days.

"Shit, I aint no rat!"

"Alright then I am going to withdraw the charges. Now I figure you have a month, two tops, of shivering misery out on the street. Or you may very well be dead within a day of your release because you fucked up and whoever hired you will want to find out what happened. I'm guessing it's going to be a very painful one, your death, that is."

"Lets go constable I believe we are finished here." With that Xavier and Sally turned and made for the door.

"Oh Fuck, wait, WAIT!- All right, I'll take the deal. I guess dying, clean and comfortable, is better than where I've been the last few years."

Sally saw the small smile on Xavier's face that disappeared before he turned and faced Jimmy Durban.

"Do you want me to take the spit masks off, Staff? The paramedic asked. Up to that point he had been silent, as he had listened to the interview. He had heard before about how talented Xavier was at interrogations and he had just seen the Master at work. He couldn't wait to tell his buddies at the firehouse what he had just witnessed.

"No, I think it would be best to leave those on for now, thank you. Now James why don't you tell me what you know."

Jimmy Durban spilled his guts, figuratively, and told them about Ratz. In fact he emphasized how Ratz had always been kind of someone you could go to if you had a problem. Jimmy told them he had lived down in the East side long before this 'One-Eyed-Jack' had come along and started disrupting things and thinking he was boss. Jimmy was glad he had never run into him cause he had heard of the bad things this Jack guy had done.

People were different now, scared and didn't trust nobody and there were some friends of his had turned up dead, like Linda, she might have been a hooker but she had a good heart and Ratz and her had been pretty close and Ratz was supporting Linda's kid. Jimmy, despite his restraints, had tried to lean in closer as his voice sunk to almost a whisper.

"There's one more thing, a secret, something I heard a while back."

"What's that James?"

"Well not even Ratz knows this but one night I was drinking some hooch by the river, right by the shore under some roots of old trees when I heard this awful voice-like bad voo-doo. I don't know why but I always remember that voice, even when I pass out I hear that voice when I come to. Anyways think it was that Jack guy and I think he was talking bout you sarg an ruling the white eyes or some such-it sent a shiver down my back and ruined my plans to get drunk that night cause no matter how much more I drunk couldn't get a buzz on."

"Really? Where on the river-bank were you?"

"Oh, down below the hospital. I like to drink up where the nice homes are sometimes especially if I don't wanna share. The air around there smells nice and hopeful. Yeah know what I mean?"

"Yes I know what you mean James, and in a way I wish I could do more for you." Xavier said as he gave him a sad smile.

Jimmy lifted his eyes and their eyes met through the spit bag, it was a long look and Jimmy's eyes never shifted away, like he was waiting. Xavier continued to look at him as he gave him the slightest nod of acknowledgement. Jimmy sighed and a light smile touched his blood stained lips.

"Ah shit, I made my own choices and now I have to pay for them."

Sally had listen to the conversation and in the end she had felt her eyes start to fill with tears so she looked up and away until they had drained back into her tear ducts.

Xavier's thoughts flashed back to the partially decomposed body of Linda in that scrapped out hole. Hard to believe it had been almost two years since all this had begun thanks to the Soul-Slayer. I wish I could talk to Rose or even just see her he thought.

All of a sudden he smelled snow covered pine trees. He smelled that haunting fragrance for a moment before it was gone, replaced by the usual odors of shit, blood and piss.

"Did you smell that?" Sally asked.

"What?"

"That clean smell of fresh snow in the mountains?"

"No, but it was a nice thought." Xavier said as brief smile touched his lips. She is watching and knows, he thought.

They walked back to the office area.

"Where are they? Xavier asked

"In the report writing room." Leighton replied.

"Would you phone over there and tell them I want to see them now in my office, thanks Leighton."

Xavier went down the corridor to his private office to await the arrival of the two officers. He decided to finish his notes while he waited. All too soon he heard the heavy footsteps.

CHAPTER THIRTY

There was a light knock at the door, almost as if those on the other side were hoping no one would answer. He waited not answering, he could almost sense the two of them looking at each other then shrugging in resignation, time to man up. The next knocking on the door was brisk and hard.

"Come in," his voice was firm and cold.

The door opened and two the police officer came in and stood approximately two feet from Xavier's desk. They could see reports on tonight's incidence on his desk. The room seemed artic cold and yet they were both sweating.

"I-I'm-we are…"

Xavier held up his hand "Sorry, is not going to cut it this time. I am writing you up for negligence and this will be going on your permanent record."

"We were not the only ones, you can't just fucking write us up!" Constable Ryan Baker said in a raised voice. While Constable Steven Houton grabbed his partners arm and shook his head.

"If I were you, I would suggest you follow your partner's advice and be quiet until I am finished. I could have had your job and had any of my people been injured believe me when I say, I would you made sure you were fired. The only job you would get with the city again would be sweeping sidewalks. Of all indifferent, lazy police work I have seen, yours tops it! Two senior constables who have been around the job for a number of years and either do a poor search or no search at all! Then bring this goof up here and don't bother to watch him so he manages to get his hands around front. You two weren't even close enough to him to grab him before he jumped the counter." Xavier said in the same chill, even voice.

Constable Houton's took on an almost whining tone as he said, "But-but we weren't the only ones."

Xavier shook his head in disbelief. These two were just not getting it, he thought.

"If I were you two, I wouldn't be worried about anybody else. I would be more worried about your own futures. I will deal with the others in the way I see fit. I will be talking to both of your sergeants. At least your reports are acceptable. You are dismissed."

Baker whose face had gone from pale, to red, to purple with alarming speed, started to take a step forward. His eyes met Staff Sergeant Xavier O'Mally's steely gaze and composed face and he backed down turned and walked out with Houton.

CHAPTER THIRTY-ONE

Xavier leaned back in his chair and sighed, rubbed his eyes then stared at the ceiling. Thinking about what had just happened and how to deal with it. The two constables that had been negligent had been dealt with. But 'One-Eyed-Jack' was another matter. It might be very interesting to have a discreet discussion with this 'Ratz' character. Xavier sensed, from what Jimmy had told him, that had this been a real attempt he would be dead or injured. It was obvious that this first attempt on him and his team had been a message and a warning, not from the Soul-Slayer, but from his main-man who wanted the Soul-Slayer gone just as much as he did. How to set it up? How to set it up so Ratz wouldn't get burned?

Xavier was still staring at the ceiling when there was a brisk knock at the door. Xavier knew who it was, "Come in Leighton."

Leighton opened door and strolled in, with a made - in- Alberta cowboy walk, he had a dark mustache, that according to regulation's ended above his upper lip but was so thick that it hid his lip. His face was lean with regular features, the only feature that stood out were his dark eyebrows that tended to move according to his mood. Many a constable had watched the eyebrows of the Sergeant as he read through the report, to see if he had missed anything by the way Leighton's brows were cocked. Leighton lowered his tall form into a chair before saying, "Jeez I still see the figurative blood splashed on the wall and the floor is still vibrating.

Xavier smiled at the description. "Yes, I would like to fire them, but hopefully splitting them up and what I said to them today might work. I am writing them up for negligence and I will be talking to their Sergeant and Inspector."

Leighton nodded in agreement before saying, "I believe it's time you told me what is going on?" and this time he didn't have a smile on his face.

Xavier gave him a measured look as he though I know I can trust

Leighton with the regular stuff and maybe even some of the weird stuff. He has a family so I don't want to drag him in to this mess with the Soul-Slayer too far but he might know how to get through to Ratz and I may need him too cover for me.

Xavier ended up telling Leighton about an unsavory character named One-Eyed-Jack who was trying to take over the East End. This character had killed off most of the other pushers, which in one way wasn't a bad thing, but the users had become desperate, so frantic that they would do anything for drugs, including swearing fealty to 'Jack'. It had almost become like the thirties when Capone and other gangster had ruled Chicago. 'Jack' also disposed of some of hookers and others, in partcularly gruesome ways, who had objected to his rules. But this Jimmy Durband who had made the feeble attempt at attacking him today was sent by a guy named Ratz and from what Jimmy had intimated the original order had come from 'One-Eyed-Jack. Ratz had twisted it just enough to send out a warning without giving himself away.

"So now I have to find a way to get Ratz in here so I can talk to him. He may have some ideas about 'Jack' that would help us put a kind of Black-Ops together." Xavier finished.

Xavier gave him a measuring look as he thought, I know I can trust Leighton with the regular stuff but the weird shit, including my relationship with Rose, I best keep to it myself. Hell I have had a hard time believing some of this shit myself; although Leighton might have some ideas about how to contact Ratz.

Xavier told Leighton what had been going on for the last few years and some of the evidence he had collected. He also told him most of the victims had been druggies and those who hung out down around the Cecil and the east end, except for one.

Leighton knew he was talking about Rachel. "The Homicide unit has been working on the killings and disappearances down in that area. Trouble was information and informants have dried up like the Sahara desert because of fear, and everybody was afraid. I think

'One-Eyed-Jack' has made violent examples of some people and the rest are paralyzed with terror. The usual status quo has been disrupted. People don't like chaos and certainly don't like change. Ratz, I think, has sent us a message, extreme I agree, but it was to get my attention. He knows that Jack has promised to hurt me and my team."

Leighton sat silent, twisting a strand of his mustache, while he thought and Xavier went back to staring at the ceiling.

"I think I might have an idea, or at the very least a half baked idea."

"At this point I will consider any idea, half baked or not." Xavier returned as he tilted his chair down and gave his full attention to Leighton.

"When I was up at K-Division for a course I ran into this undercover guy. I swear to you Xavier, I damn near drew down on him outside the boardroom where the class was being held. The 'Horseman' (City Police nick-name for the R.C.M.P.) burst out laughing and introduced him to me as 'Luigi' one of their undercover guys. 'Luigi' was five foot seven, with a sleeve tattoo on one arm, two large diamonds – one in each ear, hadn't shaved in at least five days and magnificent head of real dread-locks that went half way down his back. To top it off he had the voice of a gravel truck with three gears missing and his teeth were like summer – some were here and some were there. I suggest we ask the Mounties if we can borrow him for a short undercover gig before he disappears on into another major operation. I talked to him and he is a pretty good guy and even gave me his number."

"Ok, but how do we get him and Ratz to meet up?"

"Hey, I came up with the undercover guy, now it's your turn to come up with the rest of the plan." Leighton said with a smile as he got up to go phone Luigi.

Xavier went back to contemplating the ceiling. The idea crept into his mind like a cougar creeping up on his prey. A smile came to his face and he continued staring at the ceiling until he had the plan firmly detailed in his mind.

CHAPTER THIRTY-TWO

Finally the time had come for Rose to go on her own vision quest to see if Mother Earth, and the Creator's Universal Turtle would accept her as the Spiderwoman.

"If you come back it will not be as Rose, although you will remember the Rose that you were and the lessons and instincts from that time. I will be gone in the physical sense but I will be a part of you and within you just like all the other Spiderwoman's knowledge down through the ages are within me. There has been a Spiderwoman since the beginning of time. If you do not return that will mean that the Spiderwoman will have gone from Mother Earth and 'The People' will be truly on their own.

Rose felt the pressure of her purpose and a wild laughing thought 'but no pressure right' flashed through her mind before she could pushed it down to where she hid all her odd funny little thoughts.

She looked at the Spiderwoman and caught the faintest up turn of her lips and she could hear a faint voice in her head wishing her luck. Rose nodded turned and started her climb up through the Spirits of Mist Mountain until she could find her place amongst the rocks near the peak.

She wore a simple buckskin sheath with an old trader's blanket about her shoulders and a knife of bone tied to the wrist that clutched the blanket around her and in the other she held a strange small jug that contained a liquid to quench her thirst. The clay jug with odd markings on it that she held with the greatest care for the Spiderwoman had warned her that she must only drink from it when she felt she was absolutely dying from thirst, she would know the right time. When the jug had been given to her Rose had looked up and saw that the Spiderwoman had been crying, was still crying copious tears. Rose had idea what was in the jug and carried it carefully.

It was a long, arduous, climb beyond where the trees grow. Just snow, cold and rocks for company.

But that was not entirely true; there was another who kept her company. Rose sensed something, she or he traveled with her but just beyond her vision and her hearing for now, but it was there for all that.

Of a sudden Rose felt herself humming, then her voice spoke words aloud but again without her understanding the song or the rhyme as she walked along:

The Turtle may seem slow to most.
Unknown to all but three, the Turtle be
The Guardian of the Gate between
Mother Earth and Creator's Universe.
Universal is Turtle whose ancient heart
Beats in harmoney with Earth and Creator.
Nothing does the Turtle miss as he hears
Mother Earth's song and joins in with secrets
Of his own, songs of wisdom and patience
Grow fainter now for this be the place to see all.

Rose stopped singing, looked around and found she was high above the tree line. In fact, she felt she was almost at the very tip of Mother Earth, a place too touch the sky.

Looking around, she discovered she was on a flat rock with the markings of a medicine wheel, some of the markings were timeworn, almost faded beyond recognition and yet she seemed to understand their meaning.

This is where the song and her instincts had lead her. It was a good place she decided and she sat down upon the rock. This was where the spirit mists, the sun, stars and moon would be her company.

When Rose sat upon on what she thought of as a spirit rock she found that she didn't have to squirm around like she did on most hard places. It was almost comfortable here and for some reason the rock wasn't icy like she had though a rock at the peak of the world would be.

She closed her eyes and began to pull her senses in to pray but as she did she began to feel a gentle throbbing like a lover's heart. She didn't open her eyes but put her hand gently on the rock close by where she had placed the small jug.

Yes, a heart pulsated, below her hand deep, deep within the Mother Earth.

With her other hand she reached up and touched the sky and with it the Universe.

She opened her eyes and felt the tears upon her face as she saw the spirits swirling, twirling and twisting about her. Some were rough-raw and tried to lure her into their black, starless world. She uttered a spell that came from her heart and they screamed when it touched them and were sucked back into the corrupted darkness from whence they came.

The spirits that were around her had many voices, some gentle and good, some seemed too smooth covering something that was slithery beneath the smoothness; therein lay trickery. Her mind sorted through them sending some into the abyss and some remained singing like meadowlarks on a spring day. Sweet songs that made her tears flow and touch the rock upon which she sat. Rose looked down and saw her tears did not pool on the rock but were drawn into it.

There was now one sound, one voice that stood out above all others. It was deep, melodious and slow like molasses being poured from an old jug. Rose wondered what kind of creature would speak to her of the magic of the Universe, Mother Earth and her place within it. He-It had such vocal power it seemed to sink into her very soul so that his wisdom became part of her.

She looked around seeking the owner of such a voice and within the mist that swirled about her she saw a faint shape taking form but it was only a very thin outline within the fog, almost beyond the straining of her eyes.

"Look harder, Rose Many-Thorns." The voice urged.

Her sight guided by the deep voice looked deeper into the swirling fog and heavy mist. There, just barely visible was the outline of an oversized Turtle who stood on his two hind legs. His eyes were like diamonds that drilled into her. She felt the pull of eyes looking so deep into her and the eyes found all that she had been and was now and all that she would be. He was the Universal Turtle that the Spiderwoman had spoken of; he was here and she was not afraid.

The Universal Turtle stretched out the thin outline of a paw filled with mist and there was a sudden spark as her a hand touched the vague outline of his paw. She had the feeling they were now welded together with that single touch and she was being lifted up and a boundary broken. She looked down and saw her physical self, sitting on the spirit rock and the carcass that usually held her spirit had not moved. She felt absolutely free as she rose higher and higher her hand held by the Universal Turtle.

"Will we come back to this place?" she asked.

"Do you want to come back Rose?" Turtle asked.

"No. I would like to dance through the universe with you forever. Two tiny bits of debris twisting, swirling throughout this vast, immeasurable universe but I know I must return as Spiderwoman."

"You could stay up here and play among the stars." Turtle replied

She was soaring now. Higher, higher faster than the mighty Thunder Bird until they were at the line where the blue of the atmosphere stopped and black night filled with stars started.

"I know I could but there is much I must do on Mother Earth and for 'The People'. There are responsibilities that I must attend to as my physical self but I will always remember this waltz with you amongst the stars, a secret memory to think of when I have time."

They left the green planet surrounded with the clouds of atmosphere drifting here and there around it. Rose could see other planets, some with many moons around them and the sun, their sun around which they spun, spewing out liquid flame that flared before it splashed back into the sun while here and there within the universe were black tornado like holes with wild blackness swirled around them and stars soaring at the vortex never quite being pulled in.

Rose's spirit saw all but still could barely see the Universal Turtle although his out-line was slightly easier to see while they were touching as they were now.

"I want to see who you are. I need to see who you are." Rose pleaded.

"Patience, my child, I am old, so old that I am becoming new again, new like you. We will be together as always since the very first. But first I must explain why I'm like this."

"All was a black void until The Great Creator spoke the words that caused the explosion that created all the stars, suns, planets and especially Mother Earth the green planet. Everything was in balance or so he thought.

The Creator had thought to use Mother Earth as an experiment, of sorts, and put 'The People' upon the planet to help care for Mother Earth.

Then he created, from his own being, his own soul those few Shamans, Gods, the spirit and heart of Mother Earth, Medicine men and women and one Spiderwoman. They would all help him keep his creation in balance to advise 'The People'. He made the first 'People' to care for the green planet-Mother Earth. The Creator was pleased with his creation until he realized that there were small imperfections, small tears in his universe.

Almost too late he understood where there was matter there was anti-matter. Balance must always be considered. The Universe is vast, so immeasurable that it is beyond imagination but there were holes or tiny rips in the universe even though it is so infinite that the Creator had forgot about 'Balance' that where there is matter there must be anti-matter.

The universe we know is made up of 'matter' but the Creator had not initially perceived that there was another set of planets that were on the opposite side of the universe. There was the possible, potential leak from or into the 'anti-mater universe. Should these two opposite universes ever touch everything that the Creator had made would cease to exist and all would return to the great black void again.

That is when, after a great deal of thought the Creator created me. My skin, my shell in fact all of me is made from what is known as Cosmic String. Cosmic Strings are only two-dimensional. Both mater and anti-mater universes are four-dimensional. So because of what I am I can traverse both the Black-holes and Worm-holes in our universe without upsetting the symmetry. Because I am a Turtle I believe in going slowly so I see all and everything in both universes. I am the Guardian of the Gates to make sure that all remains in Balance and mater and anti-mater do not touch.

Even though I move slowly and my speech may seem longer to some; my brain's connection to the Creator is lightning fast as it is to the Spiderwoman's. There used to be many other High God's, Shamans and Soul-Savers. The light, the life and the magic of life were wondrous in the beginning. You should have seen the light of learning that almost seem to glow around Mother Earth. Wisdom grows in wonder.

Now most of the glory has faded away because some humans came too believe that they were entitled to the magic around them and started to become indifferent to the God-Heads that were there to help. Indifference is just like the torture called death by a thousand cuts and kills with the slow slashes. Some could not take the pain and struggle of staying and faded away, while some few wanted all and felt it was there for them alone. Their Greed gradually destroyed them or changed them into something like the Soul-Slayer.

Some few God-Heads have remained and retained their faith in 'The people'
and the Mother is suffering. 'The Creator' has seen this and is worried that balance is cracking while two that were part of him have turned to the blackness. The one we must deal with immediately is the Soul-Slayer because he has and is causing much trouble and hurting many just for the glee of seeing their pain.

We must return the balance to this world or there is a possibility that life, like a house of cards will come tumbling down. Unfortunately the Soul-Slayer, who at one time was known as the Soul-Saver was one of the best of us and sacrificed much to save the souls of mortals.

His job, his massive duty was to prevent the weakest souls from sliding down the slippery slope into insanity and bringing them back into the light. None had noticed that the Soul-Saver had become weakened and weary. That without thinking he let just a drop of an evil soul enter his being without his usual protection.

Once he had tasted the false sweetness of the darkness. Once one drop had bypassed his protective armour he couldn't stop and more and more he drank of the weak and evil until it changed him into the Soul-Slayer. He has slacked his thirst with the souls of many of 'The People' before he moved onto other humans and now he must be destroyed because he has become so mendacious, so demented, he is the real Boogie-Man that naught can be done with him but to destroy him."

Rose listened to the sad tale of the Soul-Saver and thought to herself, I wonder if he has ever remembered what he once was?

"I often wonder to." The Universal Turtle said reading her thoughts.

"One question I have for you Turtle?"

"Ask it."

"It seems to me that there is no balance between the Whites and 'The People'. Our people have been mistreated since the white have stripped us of our lands and dignity, where is the balance in that?"

The Universal Turtle looked at her before replying, "Balance is a funny thing, take dignity for example. Dignity cannot be stripped from you. You must give it." Rose opened her mouth to give an angry retort but Turtle raised his hand.

"I know your history and it has saddened me. Yet even when you were at your lowest you still strove to help 'The People' and also you were asked many times to go back to the Rez and yet you refused. Maybe the Creator knew that you were needed where you were and the lessons you learned there? As for Mother Earth she has a deep magic and our hope she will overcome what the foolish whites are trying to do to her. She knows 'The People' still care and have the magic to start turning the whites away from their destructive ways. I have seen more and more of 'The People' stand up and say no-no more. So there is the magic of hope and that is where you come in.

It is your time to show 'The People' their magic and their strength to save Mother Earth."

Turtle looked at her and into her before saying, "Still want to dance amongst the stars forever?"

She looked at him and smiled although there was a single tear sparkling in her right eye, "Time to go back to take up the burden that is not burden but a choice."

"We will go back to the green planet. I wanted you to see what I see and it is safer to think and exchange thoughts out here among the stars. There is one more thing you must decide and you may think about it on the way back."

"And what would that be?"

"You must pick a Familiar. It cannot be me as I cannot be close all the time to guide you although our minds are well met. Someone who knows you and perhaps knows something of what is going on. But think on it carefully as it is the final test before becoming a Spiderwoman."

She didn't say anymore to the Turtle but simply smiled and admired the universe that about them as they made there way back to Earth. Soon would come her time to chose and she knew, perhaps she had known from the time when they had been as one many millennia ago; a warrior, strong and fierce now together again only this time to fight side by side.

CHAPTER THIRTY-THREE

Universal Turtle lowered her into her physical body and it was like a hand fitting perfectly into a glove and disengaged his link with her inner spirit. For the briefest moment she felt the loneliness and disappointment almost like a lover leaving her.

As she settled back into her physical self she felt there was more of herself than there ever had been before. She could suddenly see and feel The Creator as he had made her, the first Spiderwoman, many eternal millennia ago and all the time since. Then there was a voice amongst the many voices, one she recognized and she sighed with relief, it was the voice of the Spiderwoman that had taught her.

Suddenly she felt the thirst, a thirst that needed to be slacked or she would turn to dust and blow away, she grabbed the little jug and drank. It tasted like the cool waters of a hidden pool. She drank until thirst was gone and she felt quenched, so full and all the voices that had been disjointed babbling now were bound together into one. Her voice. She offered the Turtle what little was in the jar. She felt a gasp within her and even the Turtle looked stunned as she handed him the jar.

"A Spiderwoman has never offered me the jar of Spiderwoman souls before, never and I am deeply touched but I'm unsure if I have the right to drink?"

"We have danced among the stars together, who has a better right?"

"She heard a fading voice within her mind. You are now the Spider woman and we are here as part of you, your instinct, senses even how you see things we are all part of you. Most of all we are here to help you and be a part of you in your quests to help 'The People' and protect them. Even in this unheard of gesture we agree." Then the voice was gone.

"Drink the little that is left in the jug and let the Spiderwoman's thoughts be a small part of the Universal Turtle's." Spiderwoman thought as she saw him sip the last bit and felt their bond grow even closer she watched him smile as he felt the comfort of a complete bond with the Spiderwoman.

She could feel the 'old' Rose also diminishing and with her went the pain, hatred and the open wound her life had been like since she was twelve. She smiled, and it was a smile at the lightness of being the someone she had yearned to be. She turned and looked to where the Universal Turtle stood faintly outlined in the mist.

"Yes, I'm almost new again as well. One more decision remains that only you can make and that is who is to be your Familiar and then there is much to do but only if you choose well." Turtle said within her head, their bond more complete than it had ever before.

The new Spiderwoman smiled at the Turtle, "I will name him now. Just remember you have given me this decision to make and make it I will. But first I will remind that part of me, my Spiderwoman-mother, teacher of the last thing she said to me before I left on my vision quest. It was a phrase about a man of an eastern religion that was greatly admired for his compassion for others, his kindness, his humor, the terrible sacrifices he had made. His friends and even his enemies admired him. He finally grew weary of life and the loneliness. Life seemed so empty and he felt it was his time to climb the path that would lead him to peace from his pain and suffering. He heard a low moaning behind him and turned to look and there stood many who would miss him and needed him. So instead of ascending the path to peace he turned and went back to those who needed him for he had the jewel of consciousness.

"The Familiar I have chosen is Detective Xavier O'Malley."

She heard and felt the deep intake of breath from Turtle.

"But why Spiderwoman? You've always hated the Whites and not only that he is a police-officer which brings with it other problems!" Turtle asked in a tone far quicker than his usual thoughtful, deep voice.

"Ever since we met many years ago we have been friends, almost like brother and sister even a feeling of twins. Whenever I was re-leased from jail he would sense it and meet with me and tell me what was going on down in the east end of the city. If some of 'The People'

184

were having trouble with someone he would check into it and it was handled. When I came to him distraught because I found out that the Soul-Slayer had entered the city and taken up residence in the east end he started an investigation. Even though that craven beast murdered his beloved and he was near torn in half with the pain of her death he carried on with his investigation."

"Even now he tracks him for me and has made my problems his. I worry about him but he has always watched over me and mine. Now that I'm Spiderwoman I have seen that, in fact, we were in one life a warrior together, one soul and one mind. In another were twins many, many centuries ago. Last but certainly not least, when we talk casually he has always made me laugh something that I had never done before, not since I was twelve". The Spiderwoman said with much passion.

"I can see that this is a man that has served time as one of the "The People" although having a white man as your Familiar is extremely odd but from what you have told me he has certainly earned his way. Perhaps joining of white and Spiderwoman will be good for both races. Do you love this man?"

Spiderwoman knew that this was a pivotal question and honesty was at the root of it.

"Yes I love him but how could I not," she responded. "I love him as my brother or the friend that I never had. I have trusted him and he has never disappointed me as many, many others have. But I, in my heart, have always known that I was meant for something else and Xavier was nearly gutted, his sanity left bleeding and very nearly ripped from him by murder of his fiancé. Now, after a long time, he has healed he has another in his life but still he hunts the beast and awaits word from me."

"Unusual but understandable now that you have explained your reasoning and you are smiling so as Spiderwoman and all that came before are agreeable. Therefore, Hail to the Spiderwoman that was, is now and for the future!

CHAPTER THIRTY-FOUR

It was long past the midnight hour, the warm summer darkness teetered on the cusp of dawn, the darkness fading ever so slightly in the east. The first of the early morning birds were getting in a few practice notes as they waited for dawn to break.

Xavier had been waiting for her when she pulled in and parked her civilian car under the single tree in the large police parking lot. The whole situation of being armed and having a partner when going back and forth from the parking lot to Arrest Processing was a pain in the ass in some ways. In other ways, when it was just the two of them, it was nice. Walking close together, generally talking about the usual business but every once in a while their life outside the job would slip in between the worry and watchfulness. It would seem, just for a moment, like they were a couple with just an ordinary life. Sometimes Xavier would brush her hand, light as an errant breeze. Or give her that quirky smile when she looked at him and he turned to meet her gaze.

"Sally, I think there is someone hiding in the shadows of the doorway. Watch yourself." Xavier said in a low voice, his hand slipping to the butt his gun. He could feel her stiffen beside him as they both stared into the blackness within the doorway. As they drew closer they started to smell stale mouthwash and the shallow wheezing of someone either very old or very sick.

Then a low, sandpapered, nicotine stained voice spoke.

"Don't come no nearer Boss and act natural like. I got two messages. Rose is on her way and Ratz wants to see you. Says he gotta warrant. Be down by Cecil two this afternoon. Tell'em run him down drag em to jail. Now keep moving."

Xavier looked at his shoe as if he had stepped on something, while Sally appeared to lean over to help.

"Thank You." Xavier whispered.

"Did it for my Rose, tell her I tried but the Rez is not in my nature." Jimmy Antelope whispered then faded back into the even darker part of the shadowed doorway.

"Keep walking like we were and don't say anything. These walls have ears." Xavier said so quietly that Sally barely heard him.

Sally and Xavier continued their walk up the back alley with the covered multi-storied police parkade on the left side and an open parking lot for those who worked in the provincial courts, on the right side across the alley way.

Generally they could tell how busy it was by how many police-cars were parked along the left hand side of the alleyway; this morning there was only two police vehicles parked in the back alley. Sally and Xavier reached the door that had a large sign over it stating that it was the 'Prisoner Door'. Xavier reached out with his key unlocked the door, opened it so Sally could walk in first. Instead of going up the elevator they used their keys and went down the stairs to the Men and Ladies changing rooms.

Just before they parted ways at the bottom stairs, Xavier turned to her "I'll explain later." She gave him a small smile before heading to the women's changing rooms.

Xavier was exuberant as he was walking to the changing room and it took a great deal of constraint on his part to keep jubilance from creeping onto his face and his step. He wanted to shout it out but kept quiet because you never knew who was in the shower or would walk in. But he couldn't stop himself from thinking about it, Rose was finally coming back, coming to help him get rid of this thing that had come right out of 'The People's' mythology.

Then there was the other great news, which in its way could be as important. Ratz had set up a meeting, rather than waiting for us. Just as well, because Leighton and I have been running through scenarios on how to get in touch with this Ratz and none of them had seemed very plausible. He pulled open the door and walked into the Men's changing room. He was so engrossed in his own excited thoughts that he ignored several greetings from other police officers. It took a friendly slap on the back to tear him from his thoughts.

"Jeez Xav, whoever she was it must have been great last night? 'Cause your body may be here this morning but your brain sure ain't," Gary, a well known, and prolific 'swordsman' was the one who had given him the slap on the back made the remark. There was general laughter from most of the other officers at the thought of Xavier having sex because he was one of those who never discussed sex or in fact his private life with anyone.

Xavier grinned and shook his head at the joke but inside he was annoyed at Gary and some of the others for their constant discussion of sex and related subjects. He never let on because he didn't want to be considered a prude but that part of his life was private. The other police officers, who were all in some form of dress or undress, including Leighton. Leighton gave him an anxious look and Xavier returned it with a small grin. Leighton finished dressing in a hurry and headed up to Arrest Processing.

Xavier decided to take the rarely used stairs to the third floor so he could have more time to think and plan. He was on the stairs just below the first floor when he smelled the fresh odor of new snow on pine trees. He slowed and would have stopped except a feeling or sense kept him climbing the stairs. Then a thought came to him that he should use Rose's name when he spoke with Ratz and it would best to find out ALL of Ratz's agenda. Then the smell was gone but the thoughts remained.

Sally was of a different mind as she made her way to the Woman's changing room. She had heard of Rose but only in passing and she wondered what part the woman had in Xavier's life.

She began to put on her uniform but found that her breathing always became slightly irregular when she thought of Xavier and she became somewhat tongue-tied like some schoolgirl with her first crush.

"Shit, Shit, Shit! Sally yelled and felt better more like 'Mustang Sally' as she smiled to herself because she knew what the guys called her.

Better to be called Mustang Sally than some of the names other P. W's (Police women) were called she thought. Xavier's business was his and his alone. She heard a snigger behind and whirled to see Lorretta Cramer standing there with a smirk on her face.

Talk of all the swamp-trollops to have heard her swearing, Lorretta 'Ya wanna screw me' Crammer. Sally had no use for Lorretta, who, in her opinion, was a coward and screwed anyone that would help her get off working the streets.

"Jeez Loretta I'm facing ya so you can't slip a knife in my back. I must say fixing reports in a room alone has done nothing for your looks, mind you nothing ever will." Sally said and watched Loretta's face turn an ugly red as she clentched her hands and took a step forward.

"Go for it Lorretta, give me a chance to crush you, I dare you! Mind you, I have the advantage because I'm facing you."

Lorretta actually hissed as she stopped her advance.

Sally looked around before saying "Jeez I do believe you're out of your element because there is no gutter for you to crawl into like the gutter-whore that you are."

"Your time will come, Sally, there are always rumors floating around like pieces of jigsaw puzzles and I love putting them together, you bitch!" with that Lorretta turned around and stalked away.

"Sally watched her as she stormed away and thought to herself, although it's fun tormenting that snake in the grass, I have shouldn't have done it. There are things going on right now that even that fool could throw a monkey wrench in without being aware of it. I better warn Xavier and Leighton. Maybe she should be sent to the artic north of 'C' District until things are settled down here.

Sally was unaware of the fact that she was far more intuitive than most women although others, mainly Xavier, Leighton and Moe were aware of it. Sally was thinking on what was going on and had an idea it had something to do with the East end which would be perfect because she had worked down there so she could help, she thought, as she left the changing room and met up with Leighton by the elevator.

Leighton and Sally took the elevator up together. Both talked of today's shift and prisoners that were likely to be there. They knew the elevator had a camera and a microphone built into it to supposedly help police officers by disproving police brutality. That was the stated reason, but many an officer had forgotten and stated his or hers views on some of the more stupid things management had done, and found themselves transferred to 'Outer Mongolia,' as the outer rim of the large city was called. Nothing much happened there except the rot of many a good police officer.

Every once in a while, when management felt someone was chastised enough they were transferred back in to where the action was. But with some it was like Super-Max prisons, some real tough, wild police officers had been sent to the artic and after a few years of sheer, utter boredom, something in them breaks and they become like a robot. They do the absolute minimum to get their paycheck but don't want to get involved in anything.

Of course there were the few and the mighty. They were the ones hired in eighties, when the Department's stated mission was to hire people, men and women, who could make instant decisions on the street, were independent and would tolerate no nonsense from the 'bums and scum from the east' from eastern Canada. Many of those men and women joined the Police Department and by God that was what they were going to do. They didn't care where the bad guys were; they were there to get the assholes.

These were the men and women who said, "Yes Sir" to upper management and then went out and did exactly what it took to be a police officer. Some of them were crazier than a shit house rat, but turn them loose and get out of the way. Those were the ones that had a nasty habit of pissing off the management of the time, while bringing in more asshole than you could shake a nightstick at. They were the right-brain dominant and came up with some of the most incredible projects to catch bad guys. While the left-brain dominant ones loved order, proper paperwork and proper arrests. You needed them both to have successful operations.

Unfortunately some management, when they got promoted to the puzzle palace, promptly forgot where they came from and it was usually them who had who had the bright ideas about watching the police do their job than how many assholes they caught on the street and their conviction rate. As a result of the fear and paranoia instilled in them during their time in Police Collage, some excellent young officers became Robo-cops unless they were salvaged by some of the older officers who put them through a sort of rehab durng the officer coach phase of rookie training.

Leighton and Sally walked out of the elevator on a relatively quiet scene as the final group of the night's prisoners being readied to send up to remand. The Court Guards were taking morning court prisoners over to court cells to await talks with defense lawyers before they went before a Provincial Judge who would decide their fate; be it be bail, get out jail free, or do not pass go and stay in jail.

CHAPTER THIRTY-FIVE

Once the prisoners had been dispensed to their various destinations, morning shift found themselves with an empty jail. That was the first time that that had happened in a long time. Everybody grabbed a coffee and some began to read the morning paper.

Xavier looked at Leighton and Sally nodded his head, "Ryan would you mind reading your paper up here and sign the odd report that comes in. If it gets busy, buzz my office. Since your armed, stay behind the counter and let the officers do their own searches of prisoners, they're supposed to be doing them anyways."

"Sure thing Boss. Me, my coffee and the paper will be happy to sit just about anywhere." The other two bail officers laughed as they sat down at their desk to take up the same occupation.

Leighton, Sally and Xavier went back to Xav's office and sat down. Leighton took a sip of his coffee before saying, "Well, things certainly seem to be coming together except for the Rose bit."

Both Leighton and Sally looked at Xavier at the mention of Rose's name. Sally was trying to hide her insecurity about Rose and Leighton looked puzzled. Xavier knew that he would have to give up some of Rose's involvement.

He thought about it for a moment before he launched into his explanation.

"I've known Rose since I was a rookie. She has always been a friend and a informant of sorts. She is of 'The People'. The information she has given me over the years has been mostly about those who prey on her people living in and around the east end. That's is how I came to know about 'One-Eyed-Jack'. Rose has been in and out of jail so I haven't seen her that much but each time I do she has had information for me. The message I got from that skinny one of 'The People' this morning told me that Rose was coming back to help because this Jack is known to her, and for that matter so is Ratz."

Xavier could see them both relax and he felt better because he had told them the truth,

in a sort of police and or white kinda way.

Sally felt the honesty in what Xav said and yet knew there was more that they had not

heard, a whole lot more. Something or someone like 'One-Eyed-Jack' who Xavier had seemed obsessed with for at least the last two years even before his fiancé had been murdered. When that had happened Xavier had said that 'One-Eyed-Jack' had been involved, in fact had insisted on it with such passion that an investigation had been done.

Unfortunately, no evidence of 'Jack's' involvement had been found and Xavier had dropped it and went back to The Guns and Gang Unit.

Sally had had one of her flashes of intuition the day Xav had first talked with that 'Jack' creature. As soon as she had seen Jack she had known that he was not human, she couldn't tell why she knew but her feelings were never wrong. She also knew, felt that a battle was coming between good and evil and Xav was somehow involved.

As for this morning, that had something to do with it perhaps on the peripheral, but that was the way with snitches, there were always other things involved when dealing with them. Yet in the back of her mind she sensed this was bigger and far more dangerous than Xav was telling them. Xavier planned to do the dangerous stuff himself maybe with help of this Rose person. Well that was not going to happen, she was going to be there to help! She was just as tough as he was and he was going to need a partner. She also understood the need to make sure Leighton didn't get in too deep because he had a family.

Sally looked up and saw Xavier watching at her and she gave him a small, innocent (she hoped) smile.

Leighton had been sitting foreword listening to Xavier's account of the morning's events and his explanation of Rose. He was more interested in the news about Ratz than any normal informant. He had informants as well and understood how they worked.

"I've already talked to Luigi and he is willing to be here case we need someone who looks like just another prisoner. I'll call him and let him know to be down here round thirteen hours so he gets the info before Ratz is dragged in."

"Who should we send down to the Cecil to pick up Ratz at around two?"

Sally was quiet for a moment before she said thoughtfully, "Personally, I would send the two coppers that are always hanging around the Cecil picking off warrants and busting the small time dealers. Best to give them instructions to be rough but not too rough. We want him to talk to us and he won't if he gets too messed up. I think we should make this as straight forward as possible."

Both Leighton and Xav nodded and Leighton said, "Sally's right we don't want to draw attention to any of this, even if it's a 'cash warrant' and he doesn't have the cash it gets paid out of our Christmas slush fund. But first we stick him in the interview room with Luigi and the two have a little talk."

"We could stick him in the 'special cell' with Luigi and work it that way although I really don't want any other prisoners and as few staff as possible seeing the two of them together. We could stick them in that particular cell but then you have a tape and conversation of the two of them together when that's the last thing we want given that Luigi is deep undercover and Ratz is willing to give us info on 'Jack'. Too many people might put two and two together. Too dangerous for both of them."

"I think we might be over-thinking this. Lets put Ratz through the usual processing and because he says he has money coming we throw him in an interview room. Then we process Luigi except for the wire he will be wearing and put him in there with Ratz. That way we can watch plus we have what was said and no one is the wiser." Leighton said.

"Perfect then we get the info from Ratz, punt him out, warrant paid. We buy Luigi a good dinner, or whatever, and he disappears back into the folds of the Horsemen (Mounties) black-ops with our thanks." Xavier said with a grin that started to fade as he noticed

Leighton's frown.

"What's wrong Leighton?" Xavier said as he thought to himself, here it comes.

"It kinda sounds like we are doing a black-ops ourselves. Are we Xav?"

Xavier met Leighton's look and then looked over at Sally who was wearing a stubborn look and sighed. He had hoped that with everything going on he could kind of slide out without involving his two friends any further.

CHAPTER THIRTY-SIX

"Oh shit! I forgot to mention this before but I had a little set to with Lorreta Cramer this morning so she might be looking for trouble or revenge, pick which ever word you prefer."

"Loretta Cramer-that bitch! How is she suddenly involved?" Leighton asked his filled voice filled with disgust.

Sally's face reddened and she shook her head, "My fault really. I was thinking through some things and not realizing anybody was around, I swore out loud."

"So?" Xavier said with a puzzled frown.

Leighton and Sally looked at each other. Sally shrugged and said, "I'm the one she would like to destroy. Several years ago I was working undercover on a biker operation. I was picked because I was junior and working out in Outer Mongolia for what had seemed like a century."

"It's not likeI had done anything wrong," Sally said in response to Xavier's eyebrow lifting and the query written on his face.

"They were looking for some junior officers that still had some enthusiasm and wouldn't be recognized by the bikers. I was one of the eager juniors chosen. I think it also helped that I had already dug up some shit on the bikers and that worked to my advantage when it came to their choice.

Working undercover was like I'd died and gone to heaven or been given the keys to the city. My partner and I manage to find out about where some bikers houses were. We also figured out which ones were Booze Cans, which ones they were running drugs out of and which ones their whores were working out of. We also found their 'Safe house' that some heavy duty bikers were laying low in while they were 'cooking' ice and meth."

"During surveillance I was taking photos of those going in and coming out of the Booze Can when who should I see but Lorretta going into the Booze Can dressed in plain clothes. I thought at first she might be working on another operational plan. When I checked I found out that she had had nothing to do with the street never mind going undercover. I guess some of the undercover detectives put it all together."

"Whenever Loretta showed up at the biker's place within a day or two one of the operation plans would go for shit. They figured they could get wire (Judge approved audio surveillance) on the place and would have her and take down the safe house. Well the Judge wouldn't approve a warrant. I didn't know any of this til later. So Lorretta couldn't be fired because there wasn't enough evidence. But when they interrogated her she was smart enough not to implicate herself, except that it was a biker house."

"She was bounced from her high-paying job in intelligence and moved to a job correcting old reports before they were put into the computer at a considerable drop in pay. Of course the operational plans after that ran smoothly, they just didn't have enough documentation to fire her ass at the time. For some reason she has always suspected that I was somehow involved and has been looking for chance to get me, she just hasn't found anything."

"You know, now that you mention it, I recall something about that whole mess while I was running the Guns an Gangs Unit. We were working on Asian gangs at the time but the plainclothes units working on the bikers were some choked. So do you think she has found something? Or is she just trying to make you paranoid?" Xavier asked.

"Well, I think it was more of an attempt at mudslinging and she lost, but she has an odd way of somehow getting information."

Leighton had sat there listening while he rubbed his chin. Finally he waded in with his thoughts. "There is a lot of risk here. Maybe we should move her to Outer Mongolia?"

"I understand your concerns, but I think if we suddenly move her she will get suspicious, and as she said, she likes puzzles, so lets not give her one. If she wants to believe Sally has man problems, let her think that," Xavier said with shrug.

Sally nodded in agreement, as she felt a flush coming on, "Yes, I think that would be best."

Leighton laughed and asked, "You don't have any man problems do you Sal?"

The flush that Sally had felt slowly staining her neck was now coming on full bore and she tried to hide it by lifting her cup and swallowing the last mouthful of coffee, while Xavier's cheekbones lost their paleness and turned a healthy color red.

Leighton looked between them and understanding dawned on him, even though his wife had always called him dumb as a post when it came to these kind of things, "Okay we need to decide which car crew is going to pick up Ratz and bring him here for us?" Leighton said hastily to cover the sudden uncomfortable silence.

"I've got the day's schedule." Xavier said almost abruptly as he passed around copies.

By the time they had decided on the car crew and some other details they were all relaxed and laughing.

As they left the office it suddenly dawned on Leighton that Xavier had managed to slide out of who was going to be involved when they went after 'One-Eyed-Jack'.

The whole Sal and Xav situation was, interesting. Did they even know completely or understand yet themselves? His wife would be so proud of him for seeing it before the potential couple did he thought with a wry smile.

That whole Sal and Xavier thing was kinda amusing but it had distracted him from the more important question of who was doing what for this little operational plan and Leighton couldn't shake the feeling that Xavier was planning to do it on his own.

CHAPTER THIRTY-SEVEN

Leighton looked through the schedule and saw the car crew he wanted was working day shift today and smiled, perfect. He phoned dispatch and asked if they could have that car crew attend at Arrest Processing around thirteen hours and ask for the sergeant.

Brad Smyth and his partner Rick Johnson, received the dispatched call on their computer, looked at each other, shrugged and told dispatch that they would wander down now since it 'just ever so busy on the street'.

"I wonder what's up?" Brad said in passing. He had a slight English accent that even fifteen years in cowboy country couldn't stomp out.

"Whatever. At least it keeps us from driving around in circles. Fuck, it is dead out here, if you pardon my expression."

They both sniggered at that just as they pulled into the back ally behind Arrest Processing.

"Who we suppose to see? Brad asked.

"The sergeant who works up here, Leighton Orton, or something," Rick responded. They parked in the back alley and climbed out of their police cruiser.

The two officers got off the elevator at the third floor. "I say someone might want to wash down the elevator as it seems to be more blood and shit encrusted than usual," Brad said in that thick highbrow English accent he did so well as they stepped out of the elevator.

Rick laughed as he listened to his partner and thought, he can make anything sound good with that accent. "We're looking for a Sarg. Orton?"

"That would be me," Leighton responded as he stood up. "Come on, I'll buy you two a coffee while I explain."

Leighton saw Xavier dialing a number and would bet good money that he was calling up the janitors to re-clean the elevator.

Leighton took them down a long hallway to the lunchroom. "Help yourself boys, that's the good stuff," he said pointing to the real coffee roaster. As he watched them pour themselves coffee he discreetly checked his watch and though, twelve-thirty hours, lots of time for them to enjoy their coffee then go scoop Ratz.

Once they were all comfortably ensconced at the lunchroom table and the two constables had had a sip of their coffee Leighton spoke, "Quiet out there?"

"It's dead out there, if you'll pardon the expression, Sergeant," Brad Smyth said with English precision.

"Hey, that's what I said when we were driving down here," Rick said in an offended tone.

"I know, I just cleaned it up a little so the good sergeant knows our position," Brad returned.

Leighton watched the two of them kibitz back and forth and realized this was a pleasant argument that amused them both. "Okay you two, aside from polishing your act and taking it on the road, I do need you two to do something for me."

"Sorry sergeant we sometimes forget. What is it you need sir?" Rick asked.

Leighton had started to lean towards them when he heard when he heard a low cough just outside the slightly open door of the lunchroom. He put his hand up and shook his head as he silently stood up and walked to the door. He stopped and looked down the hallway only to see the backside of Lorretta Cramer turning the corner. Shit! It's a good thing she didn't hear about Ratz, he thought.

The two constables were sitting at the table stunned at Leighton's behavior.

"You'll have to excuse me but I hate eavesdroppers," he said by way of explanation as he firmly shut the door.

Leighton sat down again, "Here is what I need. I have a snitch who tracked down a bad guy named Ratz for me. I've been looking for this shit-head for several months. Apparently, he is going to be around the south side of the Cecil around fourteen hundred hours this afternoon. He will be easy to spot as he bears a remarkable resemblance to his namesake, and he is just a little guy so he shouldn't cause you much trouble-just a lot of yelling. I have a couple of warrants I've been holding on him. Think you're up for it?"

"No problem, we love hanging around the Cecil day and night watching those cockroaches running for cover as we shine our righteous light upon them. Maybe we will catch some others as well as we look for your rat."

"Great, I appreciate this, guys. I have already made up the call and put you on it, so it will be on the computer in your car."

"Enjoy yourself, but don't damage the little guy too much just a jostle or two. I'm sure the dialogue between you two will be torture enough. Just let me know when you are on your way back," Leighton said with a smile.

"Now, we could take offence at your comment about our discussions but we must save our strength for the task at hand," Brad said as they got up from the table.

Both officers headed to their car, chatting in a very in a very amiable way about proper Canadian language as opposed to proper English language.

Leighton grinned as he listened and thought, I bet that argument goes on all the time just to keep each other amused, seems like a good car crew though.

Leighton went and let Xavier know that it was all set up and Ratz should be picked up within the next fifteen minutes.

Both Brad and Rick knew something was up but kept it to themselves.

"Let's pick this clown up and get him down to Arrest Processing. I'm thinking this is something I don't want to be involved in, if you follow my thinking, bud."

Brad looked at his partner then responded, "Yes, quite right, let's pick up the rodent, take him back to them and then depart posthaste but in dignified fashion." They looked at each other and burst out laughing.

" Rodent? You slay me Brad, you really do."

They were both smiling as they turned right, cruised the front of the Cecil and watched all the human cockroaches scurry into the darker shadows.

"There he is! Look at that wee fucker run!"

"Just cut him off Rick, so we don't have to get into a foot chase!"

Just as Rick was going to use the cruiser to cut off their prey, Ratz slipped and fell. Rick slammed on the brakes as Brad jumped from the car and practically landed on the little guy.

"Okay, okay, fuck. Ya don't have don't have ta jump on me! Ratz said in a whinny, tiny voice.

"You wouldn't happen to have a cold, my small friend?" Brad asked as he handcuffed Ratz.

"Naw I talk normal." Ratz said as he looked at Brad as he was doing a cursory search on him.

"You really do look like a rat," Rick said as he looked at Ratz. "Hey man ya donn hav ta insult a guy." Ratz returned.

"You're absolutely right, Mr. Ratz, my partner was positively wrong to do so. Here now, let me assist you into the back of our police car, don't bang your head now."

Ratz was stunned. No one had ever been so polite with him and he got in the cruiser quite easily, then it occurred to him, "Hey wadda I wanted fo?"

"Oh just some old warrants you didn't pay for, apparently," Brad said.

"Aw shit! Good thin I got money anyways."

For the rest of the way back to Arresting Brad and Rick returned to their heated discussion about differences between languages. They even tried dragging Ratz into the discussion when they pointed out that he seemed to be talking a patois of sorts. The more they talked, the more Ratz shrank into the seat. When they reached Arrest Processing and turned Ratz over to the staff.

Once they disposed of what they called the rat problem they wandered over to Leighton's desk.

"What's so funny?" Leighton asked the car crew as Xavier wandered over to Leighton's desk.

"Well let me put it this way, we think that Mr. Ratz will tell you anything you want to hear as long as he never sees us again. Right, Constable Symth?"

"Yes indeed. Mr. Rodent seems to have developed as strong dislike for us, although I can't think why?"

"You guys didn't lay a licking on him, or did a black dog run across the road? Leighton asked with a smile, although he had a pretty good idea about what had happened.

Xavier looked from the car crew to Leighton, "Can someone tell me what the hell is going on?"

"Well number one, it has to be night for a black dog to run across the road. But aside from that, we were simply talking, Rick and I, about the language question. We even tried to include him because he speaks such an interesting patois. It was odd, the more we talked the madder he got." Brad said with only a hint of a smile.

"I must say though that we often get that reaction from the ne'er-do-wells that we pick up on the street. It's not that they want to fight with us they just seem to what us to shut up?" Rick said with a hurt look that twisted into a smirk.

"Yes, we figure all you have to do to make him talk is threaten to have us drive him back down to the Cecil, and he even admit to being on the grassy knoll," Rick said with a big grin.

"If you need anything else just give us a call," Brad said as they sauntered over to the elevator. As they stepped in, they were still chatting to each other.

Leighton shook his head and grinned while Xavier looked after the departing constables with a puzzled look.

"Remind me to tell you about those two when we have more time. In the mean time

I'm putting them on my list of constables that I can trust even though they are shit-house crazy in an odd sort of way. Oh and I had a nasty little surprise when I started to talk to them in the lunchroom.

I thought heard something outside the partially open door. When I checked I, I saw Lorretta Cramer walking briskly around the nearest corner."

"Lorreetta! I wonder how much she heard?"

"Nothing really. I noticed her before we started talking about anything of interest." Leighton responded.

"Oh, I see they have brought Luigi in I'll go help out and take him back to where Mr. Rodent-Gawd they've got me doing it now, is waiting. Luigi is already wearing a wire, so I better be the one that searches him." Leighton walked over to the processing area and did a quick pat down and told the constables that brought him in that it was just an unpaid ticket.

As Leighton walked him down to the interview room where Ratz was waiting he filled him in and Luigi made sure his wire was working.

"So basically you want the tape of me and Ratz talking about a certain individual and once our 'so called' warrants are paid we will be on our way. Ratz's will be paid first and you get the tape from the wire and I get out of here through the back way through the parkade where a car is waiting to whisk me away.

"Yep, in and out, no chance of going to court down the road. This one we will deal with ourselves."

"Geez sounds like some whores I know." Luigi said with a smirk.

"I wouldn't know about that, I'm married."

"I'd like to try that some time, but I've been undercover so long I don't even know what I would look like normally. Right now only sleazebag druggies and Ho's are interested in me" Luigi said with a shrug.

"Maybe it's time?"

"Naw, I'm still having a good time although there have been a few times lately that were so hairy that I checked myself for bullet-holes after. Maybe I'll see after this next gig, who knows."

"Let me go in first," Leighton said as Luigi nodded.

He opened the door to see Ratz sitting on one of the stools, legs crossed one over the other swinging the top leg while he tapped the top of the table in boredom and annoyance.

"Got another guy with a warrant that he is going to pay same as you. So maybe the two of you could talk so neither of you gets bored, get the drift?" Leighton looked directly into Ratz eyes and a barely saw a nod of understand. Leighton move back so Luigi could move passed him and entered the room and sat on the vacant stool.

"Shouldn't be too long."

Luigi looked over at Ratz hunched over on the other stool. He was one of the saddest little creatures he had ever seen.

"Your message that you wanted to see the Staff Sgt. was loud and very clear."

"You ain't the Staff Sgt.." Ratz huffed as he spoke.

"No I'm not, but he did not want to endanger you by being seen with you so he is watching through the hidden camera.

He could almost see Ratz relax slightly before he spoke in a nasally voice, "Youse, and that there Staff Sergeant an I got the same problem, tha bein One-Eyed-Jack an Rose said trust ya."

"So what is your problem with Jack?"

"He cut inta my business then took over, killin, scarin my people an such is bad for business and he is dirty, both ways dirty, nasty. Not human. He don belong up here, tryin to steal souls. He be the Devil's pardner."

"Has he stolen your soul?" Luigi, who had heard many ugly, terrifying things as an undercover officer, felt his stomach clench as he asked the question that might set a trap or some type of ambush for Leighton and the Staff Sergeant.

Ratz hooted and squealed in delight and after wiping the tears from his eyes, said "I ain't got no soul, never had one. That's what my parents used to say' fore I ran away. All Jack tasted was bitterness when he tried to take my soul. He sure din'like me laughen at him, thought he'd choke and nearly turned into what he really is. I got a faded look at was he really looks like and it scart me, scart me bad. I seen plenty in my time but I ani't ever looked into a black eye and seen nothingness jist the blackness of being lost forever. "

Luigi, watching the little fellow, suspected that Ratz did indeed have a soul but it was hidden away in a dark place and carefully guarded. And since Ratz didn't believe he had a soul, then the Monster he talked of might believe it.

"What do you think he really is?" Luigi asked with legitimate curiosity. He had never thought of heaven or hell before and yet here was a little creature who absolutely believed in evil. He thought to himself, I think it might be coming up to the time I go back to normal police life as he felt the cold shudder as death danced along his spine.

"A Demon, Devil's own sent ta stir things up an hunt for souls of the weak."

"Do you think there is a way to destroy him?" Luigi asked in a low voice as he leaned foreword.

"Sure Boss, ya donn think I would risk bein' here unless I figured you'd-that being the Staff Sergeant-had a plan same as me?" Ratz asked with a crooked twist to his mouth.

"What is it?" Luigi asked as he leaned in towards Ratz.

"Well I ain't gonna tell you, don't knowd ya but that there Staff Sergeant he'll

knowed when I say washing machine and water. My warrant should be paid by now 'Jack'

he is watchin, timen me. Gotta go back to being his servant, his snake in the grass.

"Tell him ta watch his self, that Staff Sergeant, cause Jack ain't finished with him an 'Jack' has a mighty high opinion of hissef, thinks he is a Destroyer an mabe is I don knows. Tell ya Boss I'll talk ta him soon.

Ratz stood up and the door opened he walked out. Luigi never saw him again.

CHAPTER THIRTY-EIGHT

It had been Xavier who had opened the door so Ratz could leave. Down the hall just beyond the door to the court room there was a turn in the hallway, that was the only blind spot (no camera's or audio if you spoke quietly) on the prisoner's floor and Xavier stopped Ratz there.

"I figured you was around." Ratz said as he looked up at Xavier. "Ya know he hates ya and wants to destroy you-you and yours."

"I know, and I have a strong feeling he will destroy you once he feels you are of no use to him. It sounds like we have similar plans; his destruction using the washing machine and water.

"Somthin like that but we gotta meet again, the two of us an Rose."

"We are here as well." Both men shook their heads for the sound was in their minds and felt almost like a light tickle. They both looked at each other.

"It isn't me," Xavier said as he looked at Ratz.

"Well, it suras' ell ani't me!"

"Xavier and Ratz, my old friends surely you recognize my voice?"

"Rosie, Rosie is that ya?" Ratz asked out loud while Xavier didn't speak out loud but responded automatically in kind to the voice in his head, surprising himself that he could.

"Say that ain't fair, he can talk back ta ya in his head!"

"You're right Ratz. From now on I will speak to both of you in your mind'. I was Rose and now I'm the Spiderwoman who has risen from the chrysalis who was Rose," she said. "This is my friend the Turtle who has come along with old Rose-new Spiderwoman to help."

"Yes, I am the Universal Turtle spirit and I help guide the Spiderwoman. I also know much of the Soul-Slayer," a gentle low-slow voice said.

"If ya knowed him how come ya let him go?" Ratz asked out loud.

"Yes, that has certainly crossed my mind as well," Xavier added.

"Ratz all you have to do is think and I will understand. I don't want you getting caught or in trouble by speaking out loud." Spiderwoman said in his head.

"The Soul-Slayer started life as a Soul-Saver but alas he became weary from saving so many souls, he became careless and didn't protect himself as well as he usually did. Some part of an evil soul slipped past his protection. It bound him with what he thought was sweetness and he started slacking his thirst on the souls, a little at first, just a taste, but soon he was indifferent to the fact that what he was doing wrong. He began to destroy that which he had spent many millennia saving. All that he left was a hollow husk of those he destroyed.

"The Soul-Slayer was captured by the Creator, Turtle and myself approximately fifty two thousand years ago during the time of the Mayans, just before he could decimated their culture. We bound him by spells and enthralled him by wards that transfixed him in a desolate place where he could harm no one. We thought the spell would hold him forever. Alas, we went on with other things and forgot him. He had fifty-two thousand years to figure out how to escape. From a minute crack not the unlike the crack of the insanity in his brain he worked away at gaining his freedom, you see he had nothing else to think about except escaping. Finally he did escape" Spiderwoman said.

"If Rose had not seen him and recognized him for what he was, we would still not know that he managed gain his freedom.

"The Spiderwoman's voice (firmer but still Rose's) interjected, "This is not the time or place to discuss how he got away, but how to destroy him."

"Ratz and I have compared the knowledge we have on SoulSlayer and discovered that between us we may know how to trap and destroy him," Xavier said.

"If it were only that simple. You do have the beginnings of an excellent plan but it needs both Universal Turtle and myself to say the right words over him at the right time. There is just one problem. We need someone to play the goat."

A silence loomed over all of them.

"Yes, I know and I am it."

It was such a bare, unadorned sentence. Yet the Spiderwoman felt each word as if it were a knife plugging into her heart. She would rather have done it herself but the SoulSlayer would know her for what she was and disappear only to reappear somewhere else to commit his pernicious, perfidious and pervasive, depraved villainy in a place that they may never find.

No not Xavier, not him, anyone else but him but she knew there was no one who could draw out the SoulSlayer. There was nothing else to be done so she said nothing and the silence grew larger.

Turtle finally cut through the dead air " I'm sure SoulSlayer has someone watching to see how long it takes for Ratz to exit so he must leave."

With a nod Xavier took the doorknob in his hand and was about to turn it when both Ratz and he heard Spiderwoman's in both their heads saying, "It is the dark of the moon tonight, so tonight is it. As you have said the plan is simple especially with Turtle and I to complete the plan. It's best done tonight."

"We will meet you at the Boat launch on the south side of the river, just east of the bridge. To leave it any longer is to over-think it, or for time to back out." Xavier nodded as he stepped into view of the cameras and looked down as Ratz nodded with resigned look stared up at Xavier. Xavier opened the door to the court clerk's office.

Leighton watched the video screen as Xavier escort Ratz from the interview room and

lead him to the door leading to the clerk's office. Then they disappeared for couple of minutes into the blind spot. Leighton was about to get up and go check to make sure was all right when Xavier appeared again with Ratz and Ratz looked up at Xavier and nodded just as he exited through the door to the clerk's office.

Xavier then went back and let Luigi out, shook his hand as Luigi said "I am going to get out of the under-cover business, things are getting too weird. You take care of yourself."

Both knew the video was on so they laughed although Xavier could see the worry in Luigi's eyes. Xavier opened the door to the clerk's office and let him out. Leighton who had been watching the video intently had a sudden feeling that something, an agreement perhaps, but something had gone on, he had a bad feeling that plans were moving at hyper-speed and he and Sally were being be left behind.

Within minutes Xavier was back in the offices of Arrest processing. Leighton open his mouth to ask what had gone on, but Xavier only shook his head as he took his seat at his seat at the desk on the dias and picked up some paperwork.

Leighton had questions whirling in his mind, but Xavier had refused to even look at him-merely raised his hand and shook his head.

Xavier sat at his desk for the rest of the day and aside from approving and signing
reports he sat watching the few inebriates in the drunk tank. Sally, after watching him for a while guessed he wasn't really seeing anything around him but staring heavily inwards to his thoughts and by looking at the drunk tanks he didn't have to look in their direction. She to would very much like to know what had gone on in that interview room.

He felt their eyes upon him, burning holes in his back with their unanswered questions. For now he couldn't say anything to anyone for fear that someone or something would hear and decipher what the plan was for One-Eyed-Jack. The thing was, had he told Sally and Leighton what had really gone on in the interview room they may have nodded their heads, but intellectually they would have drawn away from the total weirdness, maddness of the word magic and who Jack really was, none the less they would have gone with him anyway. They had had a hard enough time accepting what little they knew.

Xavier sensed that non-believers were easily killed or even worse drained of the soul that made them the unique individuals they were. It was not for the first time that he was thankful there was no audio in any of the interview rooms and he had taken the wire from Luigi.

And of course the 'Dead Spot' how ironic that simple little phrase; that small space on the prisoner's level where none could watch or hear. Where they had planned the death of evil and perhaps the death of one more.

CHAPTER THIRTY-NINE

Xavier sat there while thoughts whirled and twisted through his head. Sally had to say his name twice before he even noticed that she was speaking to him. He looked up at her.

"Sorry Sally, my mind was elsewhere," he said briefly as he looked into her blue eyes before he dropped his eyes.

"Xavier what's going on? You haven't spoken to Leighton or I since you got back. It's almost as if you have been avoiding us, not even looking our way.

"I've got things on my mind. I will fill you and Leighton in when I can," Xavier responded as he looked so intently at some paperwork almost as if it was going to catch fire at any moment. Sally watched the red stain of red climbing up his neck and then flushing rapidly over his pale face. She turned and stepped down from his desk. She looked over at Leighton and shrugged.

Sally sat down at her desk and put head on her hand so no one would see her cheeks flush with anger. Damn it! I know he is part of some plan! He just doesn't want us to be involved because he thinks we will get hurt or management will go after us. Well Xavier, I'm going you help whether you want me to or not! Wait a minute! I bet something is going on tonight! That's why he won't look us in the face. He knows we will see it there. Well three can play at that game.

Leighton was feeling the same way as Sally. His guts were twisted and he knew something was up and Xavier didn't want them involved because Leighton had a family and Xavier had tender feelings about Sally. Well they were his friends and there was no way he was going to leave him to handle this on his own.

No one noticed Leighton quietly and discreetly use his cell to phone his wife and quietly tell her he had to work late tonight, then called Sally's cell.

When she picked up he quietly "Don't look up or look at me, just act like it's a call from one of the secretary's or a friend. For God sake don't look at Xav and just listen. I think something is happening tonight. I got pretty good at reading lips when I worked undercover and although some of what was being said in the interview room I didn't get; but I did get a lot of what Ratz said about water and a washing-machine. Ratz also said that Jack was out to get Xavier."

"Well we both knew that." Sally retorted quietly.

"Ratz was more of a guess and by golly but Xav also said the same words-water and washing machine. I think they are meeting by the water somewhere."

"But Leighton that could be anywhere on the two rivers that flow through the city." Sally retorted.

"I know so I'm going to tell Xav that one of my kid's got sick and my wife had to take him to the hospital. That gives me time to get an uncover car, take a radio and set up on him as he leaves the police parking lot. That way I can tail him to the meet."

"And leave me behind, I don't think so. I have had the same feeling that something is going down tonight. He won't meet my eyes either. I will stay here 'til Xavier leaves so he doesn't get suspicious. Then I will meet you a block east of the D.I. (Drop-In Center) at that little alley by those rundown houses."

Leighton shook his head slightly before saying in a calm low voice, "No Sally, you would be right in the middle of where those shit-heads live. Next we will be trying to rescue you. I understand your concern, but you can't just thrust yourself in the middle of this without knowing what's going on."

"I think I know more of what's going on. Plus, just who is thrusting themselves in the middle? I'm thinking it's you." Sally retorted.

"I know, I know. Ok sit in your car in the parking lot and wait for my call. If the shit hits the fan you will be close. Make sure you have that nice little shotgun of yours along with your handgun, throw-away piece and lots of ammo."

"What are you going to be doing while I'm twiddling my thumbs in the parking lot?"

"Your going to be listening to me as I track Xavier till we get a fix on him and Ratz. Look Sal, you are positioned right in the middle of this, plus you have all the back-up ammo and extra weapons. If worse comes to worse, you may have too call for more backup."

"There was silence over the phone as Sally thought the plan over then asked "so we will both have spare cells so we are in constant contact?" Hey, wait a minute Leighton, you gotta know this is a black-bag job! This is not a catch the bad guy and take him to court, this is destroy something called a 'One-Eyed-Jack'. We or rather Xav is gonna have a untrustworthy informant with him part of the time. We won't be calling for backup, it's just us, are you sure you want get into this when you have a family? Right now you have complete deniability if something goes wrong. Think on this Leighton because you know all I have is Xavier, yes I caught your look today, You on the other hand have three little boys and one on the way. How are you going to explain this if something or anything goes wrong? You and I know there is a high potential of that happening?"

It seemed like the phone line had gone dead, Sally looked over at Leighton and saw his face had crumpled and his eyes had that disappointed gleam in them which was as close to tears as most men would get.

Sally could almost feel his guilt at wishing he didn't have the kids, that responsibility that held him back from working undercover, T.A.C., or this black-ops with his friends.

"Damn, damn, damn!"

"Shit Leighton, I know!" Sally whispered into the phone. "But ya gotta ask yourself is it worth it and besides you may have to cover for us and since I will have to walk out to the parking lot with Xavier you will have to have the weapons and ammo in your car. I can get away with my glock handgun and ammo in my bag and wear my throw-away but you need to stash the shot-guns and ammo as soon as you see the meet between Xavier and Ratz. Besides I think you are right 'it's going down' real close to here."

"Say I know, I fucking know where it's goin down!"

Leighton looked discreetly in her direction and could almost read her excitement. "Sally calm down, I can read your expression all the way across the room and if

Xav turns around and looks at you the jigs up."

"Listen it's at the weir, you know what the nick name is?"

"The washing-machine!"

"Right all you have to do is stash them under the south side of the bridge, high up right against the steel on the east side. Then you gotta leave Leighton. I'm sorry but we just can't risk you getting hurt, found out or dead. Your family would suffer, and we your Police family can't have that. We will see you tomorrow and I'll tell you everything." Sally whispered into her phone.

"You better!" Leighton returned.

Sally hung up and went back to some judicial paperwork on a bad-guy she was taking in for a hearing. Neither looked at each other as Leighton rose from his desk, approached Xavier and asked if he could have what was left of the day off as it sounded like while playing soccer his one kid had broken or at the very least sprained an ankle. Xavier immediately told him to go. Leighton packed up his bag and left. Sally envied him-at least he was doing something, while she had to play out the day like nothing was wrong.

The rest of the day dragged by; everybody somehow felt uncomfortable like the tingle of an up coming thunderstorm. They were all restless and uneasy. Normally there was laughter and jokes. But today, laughter and smiles were tentative and the quiet was restless. There was almost a collective sigh of relief when the endless day was over.

Xavier greeted the incoming Staff Sergeant in a perfunctory manner then was gone before Sally could gather all of her things. She had to go to the Range Officer room anyway and trying to explain certain things to Xavier might be tricky.

Luckily Sally had thought of some items in the range officers locked room that might be useful. She strode over to the range and weapons room, used her key and then entered and relocked the door. This was not the time to get sloppy she thought as she went over to a lockbox that was partially hidden behind all the racks of shotguns and rifles. She pulled out a small key and unlocked the box and pulled out two silencers for the Glock handguns they both carried. She quickly stashed the silencers under all the ammo she had loaded and threw her black gym jacket over the load before she zipped it up. She unlocked the door and stepped out and turned and locked it turned around and there was Loretta Cramer.

Sally stepped right into her forcing Lorreta back and in a voice dripping sarcasm asked "Why are you watching and besetting me Loretta? Has someone asked you to watch me? I will find out and then I will have your job." Sally said as she continued stepping into Lorretta's space until she had her backed into a corner.

Loretta shrunk into the corner and whined as she muttered, "What were you doing in the range weapons room.

"Well if you bothered to check you, not that it is any of your business, you would find that I'm Range Officer tomorrow at the out door Range. Now get your nearly fired ass out of my way or I will have you gone, gone, gone if I see you lurking around where you don't belong you useless swamp-trollop."

CHAPTER FORTY

Xavier had quickly dispensed with rituals of getting out of work, then hustled through the changing room and out to the parking lot so he didn't have to deal with anyone, especially Sally. Lucky about Leighton having to leave because of a slight, he hoped, injury to his boy.

He was already in his car, battling rush hour traffic before, he thought, before Sally had even changed. He needed time to think on his own and what better place, than in the middle, of gridlocked slow moving traffic. Xavier needed to think the plan through on his own before he met with Rose, or Spiderwoman as she was known now, and the Turtle, with that slow, low voice, whose timbre was soothing as he spoke of something so evil.

Of course, he had to include Ratz within the group, although Ratz motives were certainly more ambiguous than the altruistic motives of the others. But they needed Ratz, and Xavier hoped they would not live-or die-to regret it.

He reviewed the plan several times. Then he would think of a detail and…"Xavier, sometimes going over a plan repeatedly, can be just as bad as not thinking it at all. A plan, a good plan, needs a bit of fluididly in case situations change and with humans there is always that chance." Spiderwoman/Rose's voice said softly. Worrying is not going to help right now and should Ratz start to waver, Turtle and I will take care of him." Xavier's lips formed a twisted smile as he listened to the soft voice.

He watched the road ahead and paid little heed to the road behind or he would have known he was being followed. Spiderwoman and turtle were aware but knew that this must be part of the Creator's plan. The path chosen was of free choice and now must be followed to its end, be it joyous or bitter. The results were not yet revealed.

"When will the actual physical rest of you arrive in the city? Man, I just about jumped out of my skin when I heard your voice in my head when we were in the dead spot by the interview rooms, if anybody had heard the dist-jointed conversation they would have been hauling Ratz and I off to the Looney-bin."

"You set it up very well Xavier, so don't worry, no Looney-bin for you. But I still worry for you my friend. You have suffered enough."

"I was the logical choice since Ratz, who in his own way is smart enough, he just hasn't been in it from the beginning, I have. Plus I think he has a soul and that would be a terrible thing for Ratz to find out as the SoulSlayer ripped it from his body."

"And you don't think it would be a terrible thing for you?" Rose asked him in a soft murmur.

"Yes, it would be to you and a few others." Xavier said with a slight shrug.

"Ahh Xavier, another is beginning too love you," A soft voice said in which he could almost felt a small smile and then he felt an absence. Spiderwoman had left him. With her went the warmth of her life force and he felt only emptiness until he thought of what she had said and then he flushed like a schoolboy.

CHAPTER FORTY-ONE

After he paid his warrant, Ratz was let out the front door. He had been cursing and swearing in his own language that left no doubt what he felt about the police.

"Ya fuckin, black 'earted shit head, I kin tell youse th Ho tha picked an ape from thy zoo cause that be hows I sees ya. Ya big fuckin oaf. Git ya fuckin mitts off me! I is free. Got paper sez so right'ere!" Ratz yelled as he was escorted from the building waving his copy of the paid warrant. His escort's face was beet red, not from fear, but from restraining himself from tearing the little bastard to a billion bits.

Ratz twisted his filthy ball cap so it was on backwards as he strutted down the street. The Police H.Q. was right on the corner of the east end of downtown, so it was an easy distance if a cop walking the beat ended arresting some fool that hadn't heeded the warning: 'Go home or go to jail.'

Everybody he met greeted Ratz and the level of their enthusiasm depended on how much or how little they owed him. Ratz would return their greeting with a breakdown of favors or money owed him and the time left to deal with it.

"Hey Jimmie, how's ya hangin'? Ya gots a week or ya will be hanging. Hey, hey I made a poem." There were some though that tried ducking away so he wouldn't see them but Ratz saw all.

None noticed that the exterior jolliness was hiding a fear that was eating away at him. The further east he went, the darker his world became. Ratz had always believed in the Boogieman and now he was going to meet him again. 'One-Eyed-Jack's' crib was beside the old liquor store, inside the broken basement of the dilapidated, decayed house. The closer he got, the more he could smell the Boss. It was the stench of what hides under ruptured old porches of empty, ancient homes – corpses of little animals and those that feed on such carrion leaving their own rot.

As time had passed, the house absorbed the smell and that added to the feeling of death waiting at the door. The odor of blood had sunk in and dried and had added an ambience inside the old wreck that couldn't be mistaken for anything but what it was. Extinction or terrible termination, both natural and unnatural had taken place here. Old wallpaper still clung to the walls like the dried skin of a huge snake that after so many years begun to fall away from the bones of the house. The local kids, who like most kids loved anything that stank of ghoulishness, ghouls and the walking dead, talked of murder and craziness that clung to the walls like mould, growing in that rotten thing that used to be a home. They would double-dog-dare each other to go in and touch the suspicious stain on the floor and walls. Yet none ever got beyond the first warped step of the poach no matter how many double-dog-dares and hoots of derisions there were. No child, no matter the imagination or even ones with very little between the ears could ever seem to by pass the invisible wall of terror. Mind you over the years there had been tales of children dragged in and eaten joint by joint that only added fascination to the place. Thing was, children could sense magic both good and bad and it was their imagination that had kept out of that very bad place.

CHAPTER FORTY-TWO

Ratz, thinking of how close he was getting to the rot of The Boss's residence began to add up all the favors and money all the rubbies and druggies owed him, anything to get his mind off the hatred he felt for the Boss. Fear, like a poisonous snake began to twist through his bowels, squeezing, pulsating until he wished, not for the first time, there was a can or shitter bout half a block away so at least gas and other things would not leak out in the presence of Him.

Unbidden he thought of Linda's throat cut as two of the Bosses thugs held her so she wouldn't get blood everywhere except in the bowl held under her neck. That last sad look at him before the terror of death took over Linda's face as they slashed her neck open. The Boss laughing-laughing as he drank half her blood and then made everybody who had watched that despicable act drink from the bowl of blood.

'One-Eyed-Jack', The Boss had then asked all of them, including her few friends, "How does it feel to drink the blood of a friend? Remember there are no friends here, you are now all part of a murder."

Ratz felt his gorge rise as he thought of Linda. Hate was below the surface but fear was the thick veneer over it. Especially when he thought of drinking from that bloody bowl.

"Fear darkens all, jist let it hide hate for jist a bit more," he thought. Time was coming when 'One-Eyed-Jack' would get his and then things would go back to the way they was before. Just had to hide his real feelings for a little longer.

The Plan was a good one, he would have too put some pressure on Susie, who owed him big. That shouldn't be a problem; just feed her a little more smack. He liked Susie, just like he had liked Linda, but Linda had been killed in a nasty way and there had been nothing he could do about it. He couldn't even warn her cause it had happened so fast. But this time he figured he could save Susie because they already had a lure and it wasn't her.

Ratz didn't even have to climb down into the basement because Jack was already leaning against the wall, by the hole that was considered a door, cleaning his ragged nailswith a rusty piece of twisted wire while taking in the smell and admiring the cloudy day.

Ratz barely had time to change the look of hatred into one of subservient fear as Jack continued to look up and smiled revealing teeth like summer; som-er are here an som-er ar there. All were rot brown like an old fence that barely held back his tongue. "Been a long time since that little, rodent body of yours was dragged down to the PO-lice H.Q. Watcha been talking about with them pigs?" Jack asked in a playful voice.

Here goes nutting, Ratz thought. "Ah ya knows them fukin pigs says ththers a warrant. Finally got it but wanna talk at me whiles they looks for it. Sommat bout Susie, I didn catch it all. Tha godam 'ho' doin too much smack. I'll deal wit tha bitch."

"No my little friend. Bring her to me and I will deal with her. Things have been getting to lax around here, time for another example."

"Naw tha's ok Boss she a good worker. I can still mak money offa that 'ho.' Hey maybe we get two fer one, that pig with the saint's name interested in her to," Ratz returned, in what he hoped was a relaxed, suck-ass, tone.

"Yes that would be very interesting my little rodent friend. Maybe even more than one." One-Eyed-Jack chuckled as he looked down at Ratz.

This was the one time when he looked up at Jack all he showed was fear, deep unshakeable fear.

Jack looked down at the little creature he owned and all his ego saw was the fear and he began to laugh and laugh and the laugh grew deeper, fouler and more iniquitous.

Finally when he had regained his composure and was only chuckling he said between snickers "In fact why don't you bring the fair Susie down to the bushes behind here where by that cursed river where the water tumbles over the weir and it will be easy to dispose of her."

"That ok with you Ratz? I would certainly hate to take away one of your money-making ventures." Jack looked down at Ratz, watching him and then his one good eye drifted up to meet Ratz's eyes and even in the partial darkness between the decayed houses Ratz could feel that black, dead eye searching his, looking for anything more than fear.

Ratz met his one eye, he was so afraid it was like he had grown carbuncles, worse than any cataract, over both of his eyes so he saw nothing and all Jack saw was an infection of sheer terror had taken over Ratz. He gloried in it for a minute before he released Ratz.

CHAPTER FORTY-THREE

Shit! Shit! Shit! Shit! Shit! Shit! Shit! He knowd, He knowd he thought, his mind firing off like an out of control machinegun."

Finally, after what seemed an hour stretched out like warmed caramel, that was in reality the minute it took for a flea to bite, Ratz had somehow made his excuses. Mainly that he was going to look for Susie for the night's festivities and got the hell out of there.

Strange I thought I saw trust or relief flash in Jack's eyes. Man I ain't ever ever been so scarit. Hey, I gotta think on this. If he sees fear it's good cause then a body is too frightened to do anything else but what the Boss want. Shit! If a body hates more than fears then he will do anything he can against Jack. Fuck he had me so scareered I didna knowd whether I wasa comin or goin. Gotta remembers fear on the outside where Jack kin see it: hate buried deep where no one kin sees it.

Ratz heard in his head, just as he just worked things out for himself a slow gentle voice that agreed with him and told him to find Susie. Time was beginning to run swiftly, working too hastily against them.

They must make haste because they didn't want Susie hurt. The way the voice talked to him made Ratz feel right and good. Ratz, for the first time in his life, felt worthy and adequate two big words that Turtle explained to him. He had never felt true praise before so he rolled it around in his mind for a while then he smiled his secret smile for a flash of a moment, before putting it all back into his secret place in his mind.

Xavier was still fighting his way through rush hour traffic when he heard Rose's voice in his head again.

Xavier, meet me where we used to. You need to hurry though, as time is beginning to speed up, especially for the Turtle.

He could hear the urgency in her voice and without question he began maneuvering his vehicle through traffic like a police on a call.

Unfortunately he wasn't in a marked car or even an unmarked on with lights and sirens. But he certainly knew enough tricks from working undercover to start dodging through traffic with relatively few irate driver's horns honking.

Once he got to where the traffic was lighter, he put the pedal to the metal and within ten minutes was out at their old meeting place. She stepped out from behind some forest bushes and waved at him. For a moment time had trickled past so slowly that it nearly seemed to stand still. She stood there in jeans and a shirt. The only difference was her hair was streaked with white. Xavier stepped quickly from his car, ran to her and spontaneously scooped her up in a bear hug and started to laugh. At first she gave a startled gasp and then joined him in laughing. All of a sudden he realized what he was doing and gently put her down.

"I guess I shouldn't be hugging a Spiderwoman?"

"Nonsense, I haven't had such a good hug in many life-times. We are related, you know. But it was centuries ago. Now is not the time to talk of pleasant things. When the SoulSlayer had been destroyed then there will be time." Rose said as the smile slipped from her face and she took on the Spiderwoman demeanor.

It appears as if the SoulSlayer is becoming wary, perhaps because he can sense himself weakening. He may feel our presence is close, I don't know but I doubt it, he is using all his force just to control those under his power. But something has shifted in the balance; his balance, our balance, we feel it, we must move now."

"Has Ratz found Susie yet?" Xavier asked.

"Not to my knowledge but the Turtle is helping him look in all her usual hiding places," Spiderwoman responded.

"Well I might as well head back downtown and get myself ready to play the Goat (playing the goat means that sometimes a goat was used to lead cattle or sheep into the Abattoir or Slaughter House). Do you need a ride?"

"Oh Xavier, I wish I could get you to stop using that expression. But you are right and there it is, you have called it as you see it. As to the ride, no this is a spiritual battle as well as human and I must dress as what I am, a Spiderwoman. Meet me at the Bow River by the Center Street Bridge. "You remember where?" Rose asked.

"Yes, in the big bunch of bushes by the river, where all the druggies meet to shoot up, hardly a private place to meet," Xavier said.

"No one goes there anymore. The SoulSlayer put a stop to that by gradually taking the souls of the druggies who used to hang out there. Apparently, although their souls were weak, the process of having their souls, or what is left them ripped out, is extremely painful. I'm told that then the soulless creatures must take twice as many drugs to keep the pain from ripping them apart. The SoulSlayer has a deal with the drug dealers, whose souls had left them a long time ago. He gets the extra drugs, so the drug dealers don't lose any money. That way the druggies that he has taken as his own must do his bidding in order to get the drugs to suppress the searing pain they feel.

"What about the drug dealers?"

"As a result of the very nature of what they do they, in their own way, they are soul stealers. The only difference is their power comes from money and drugs, while the SoulSlayer's power comes from ruling others and seeing the terror of what happens if they don't. His cruelty knows no bounds, he glories in the pain of others and gains more power from it."

"What is more, although druggies don't deserve this, he has started looking at the truly innocent such as children of both 'The People' and the White race. Enough of this for right now. I will meet you at the place specified." With that Rose, or rather the Spiderwoman disappeared into the forested area she had come from.

Xavier was left standing alone by his car. He shrugged and got back in his car to drive down to the Center Street Bridge by Second Street S.W. He was unaware that he had a shadow following him.

Ratz in the meantime was getting nervous, even with the Turtle Spirit with him, he hadn't found Susie and he had looked in all the places she normally hid out in. There was only one place left and the chances she was there were so remote as to be almost non-existent.

CHAPTER FORTY-FOUR

"Be calm Ratz, we will find her." The Turtle said in his comforting voice.

"Git outa my fuking 'ead so I kin tink, will ya!"

"Alright, perhaps that might be best at this juncture." The Turtle fell silent.

"Kkay, kay. Think! Where were Leroy's second crib at? Tink, tink. Ha! Mebe that thar ol'building down roun chink town. Ya tha'it. Hey Mr. Turtle, ya still around?"

"What? What! Of course I am still around. I was just being silent as you requested," The Turtle responded although his deep voice sounded somewhat strained like he had been listening to a broken whistle.

"No sense gitten pissed with me, I tink I might knowd where she be! Jist down by the river. Let's go, gotta warn ya, this here Leroy fella might be kinda cranky."

It was starting to get dark on what had been a cloudy day, so the distiction between night and day was only the amount of darkness. Ratz stumbled down an old back alley that had the aroma of rancid grease and other things, possibly food that had turned. Ratz swore he would never eat chink food again. In fact, he was thinking he might never eat again.

Ratz felt and heard Turtle's voice "Come, come Ratz you will eat again and we are just about at the end of the alley."

Ratz, who had just about enough of this Turtle that he couldn't see, just hear, broke out in a ragged whisper, "I tol' ya no speakin. It be bad enough bein down here. Ya gotta be quiet, be quiet or we cud be in trible," he hissed, forgetting that only he could hear Turtle.

The Turtle thought it best not to bring that to Ratz's attention given his mood at the moment.

Ratz made his way to the end of the alley, dodging the flickering light from the old street light while he edged along the rough walls until he felt a doorknob. The knob twisted with a grind and Ratz stopped and held his breath as he watched the street. Once he determined that no one was about, he opened the door slightly and squeezed in. He felt the presence with him and shook his head.

Ratz made his way up some dimly lit, rickety stairs and onto a landing that held the odor of old newspapers. He had lifted his foot in preparation for another step when the heavy sound of a shotgun being racked, practically by ear, froze him with his leg still lifted and even his breath stopped.

"Jeez Ratz, ya gotta find a better perfume, that one smells like shit."

"Leroy, ya fuk 'ead I damn near heard ma 'eart stop! Shit man pud down the shotgun!"

"Ya didn't bring one did ya?" Leroy asked.

"Da ya see one!" Ratz returned.

Leroy pointed the shotgun at the floor, unwilling to give it up just yet. "I thought you was Jack's little butt-fuck?"

"Well ya thought wrong. Susie here?"

The shotgun came up so fast it was a blur and all Ratz was staring at was a very large hole at the wrong end of the shotgun again. Then weird things started to happen. Ratz could have sworn he saw the outline of a Turtle as he heard in his head "Oh, for heavens sake." It looked like Leroy somehow tripped over something, although he hadn't move. The shotgun that so recently had been pointing at Ratz's forehead was now flipping through the air. Both Leroy and Ratz watched mesmerized as the shotgun got closer and closer to the floor. Both knew that fate was going to pick how the gun would go off. The buckshot would either go in Ratz's direction or Leroy's. Both were frozen in place by the possibilities and incapable of moving even to save their own lives.

After what seemed like eons of time, the shotgun hit the floor butt first and both cringed slightly waiting for loud bang of the gun going off.

Leroy suddenly thought of the saying he had heard, "You don't hear the bullet that is meant for you." There was a muted click and the gun fell over and lay on the floor, for all the world looking like a dead python.

There was a huge, pregnant pause and then Ratz completely lost it and jumped up on Leroy and tried to put his strong little hands around Leroy's scrawny neck. Both staggered around, or rather Leroy staggered around with Ratz clinging to his back, rather like a monkey. And even though they were cursing each other out, it was in whispers because the thought of One-Eyed-Jack hearing of this near fiasco was enough to peg down their madness to a whisper.

"For Creator's sake stop this craziness before you kill each other!!" Turtle shouted in Ratz's head. The shout had the effect of cold water being thrown over him and he loosened his hands and slid down off Leroy's back gasping for breath.

"Wha?-wha the 'ell? I...I come to warn Susie an ya, ya, have a shotgun! Ratz barely managed to whisper.

All Leroy managed to do was wave his hand at Ratz as he picked up the shotgun with the other then walked, staggered into another room. Ratz could see the faint, flickering of candlelight as he walked in behind Leroy.

Ratz could see the outline of cheap furniture scattered around the room with an armchair sitting by a fireplace with a small fire in it. Curlded up in the farthest corner of the armchair was Susie.

"Ratz could see, even in the dim light, that she was clean, no heroin had flowed through her veins in a long time. Leroy came and stood beside her, taking her hand in his and she looked up at him. There was an emotion Ratz never seen before in her eyes,

"That is love in her eyes Ratz and in Leroy's. HHHmmm this may change things," Turtle whispered in Ratz's ear.

"People has been looking fa yoz, ya know," was the only thing Ratz could think to say."

"We know Ratz. Believe me we both know. But right now we got no cash and no one to help us get out of town."

"Wwwweeelll, mebe I might be able ta' elp ya,but ya gotta 'elp me first an it involves One-Eyed-Jack." Leroy started to protest.

Ratz put up his hand and said Hol on, hol on, I ain't finished yet' ave I? I will give ya some running money-say five hundred dollars. Ow, Ow, alright right , okay, OK! Ratz said, apparently to the air around him and acted like someone had pricked him.

"All right! All right! Highway robbery it tis but ALL RIGHT! Five thousand dollars an ya never come back,ever!" Ratz muttered as he dodged left and right as if someone was pinching him.

Susie had been watching Ratz and she felt something good about him for a change, oh she knew that deep, deep down there was traces of good but she never let on about what she saw and felt. "What do we have to do and who are we helping?" she asked and some of the roughness of the old Susie's voice had come back.

"Now I'd know ya back, my Susie. Ya gotta help Xavier, me an Rose to get rid of One-Eyed-Jack. Tha's who ya helping."

Susie watched him as she asked, "Really Ratz, you really want to do that?"

Ratz looked at her and let her see all the hatred that he was barely holding inside. She nodded and said," What do we have to do?"

"Well I didn' plan on youse not being a junkie no more nor ya pimp either I'm guessing. But "at's all right, ya can still dress like em and act like 'em?" Susie nodded and Leroy shrugged.

Ratz urged them to hurry and they were dressed and ready to go within ten minutes. Susie had even dirtied her face and using makeup had given herself a shiner that would make a pimp proud. Susie had also been smart enough to cover her arms so no one would take notice of the lack of 'Crystal Meth' scabs.

They went back down the old stairs and through the alley to kind of a T-intersection of alleys that helped them avoid Center St. and all the other streets with bright lights where Jack would have spies.

By the time they reached the bushes by the river Ratz was not the only one who had sworn off Chinese and Vietnamese food, or at the very least going through back alleys behind them. The dark walk through the alleys had also added credence to their appearances as part of the unwashed, indifferent, junkies and pimps that loitered in the area.

Susie smiled secretly before saying to Leroy, "That explains the oddness in Ratz's behavior."

CHAPTER FORTY-FIVE

Sally had seen some weird shit in her life but this beat all. She sense this strange group of people, and the shadow of what seemed to be a very large Turtle had banded together to do something that was right and good – vanquish evil or something like that. She felt like she had read 'Lord Of The Rings' one too many times.

Sally was parked down at the north end of First Street South, approximately half a block from the south end of the Center Street Bridge. Her car was stashed in amongst some ragged, old lilac bushes. She had cringed and cursed every time there was sound of a branch grind or scrape against the side of her relatively new car. She could hear the hollow sound of cars crossing the bridge to her east. Most of the cars were fleeing the downtown core after working all day in hermetically sealed, high-rise offices. The John and Joan's leaving the downtown to those who owned the night.

Sally was glad that today she had just worn a black T-shirt under a black hoodie and dark jeans as she made her way through the tangled bush as low to the ground as she could so she wouldn't break many branches. Trouble was, it would be a lot easier to snake along the ground but this ground was littered with old needles, condoms, bent spoons and other assorted drug paraphernalia. Better to risk a few soft sounds than get some lethal, S.T.D. disease. Sally had forgotten how hard it was to keep quiet when moving slowly and carefully trough rough terrain. This was like training for TAC; keep your breathing shallow, be aware of the branches, what the ground terrain was like, slowly work your way through the branches. It was like a dance of sorts or Tai Chi. It looked easy, slow and graceful but in fact it took a lot of effort blending breath and moving in such a way that for the most part you were supposed to look and feel like a light breeze, well that was a lot of bullshit, light breeze my ass she thought as she wiped some sweat from her brow.

Sally finally found a spot where she had some cover but close enough to hear some of the talk and see who, aside from Xavier, was part of the group. Out of breath, beads of sweat were trickling down her face, and she was having a bit of trouble getting her breath back without making gasping noises.

Once Sally had finally managed to stabilize her breath without passing out, she thought fleetingly; after all this we are definitely destroying something.

Sally watched from her shadowed position in the bush and saw as Xavier arrived first dressed pretty much as she was. Even as shadowy as it was, there was the odd flash of Xavier's silver hair. A female of 'The People' walked gracefully out of the dark and up to where Xavier stood. She was dressed as a Shaman or medicine woman with her long white and black hair braided and the wrapped around her neck. There appeared to be a spider painted on the skirt of her buckskin dress. She stepped up to Xavier and touched his arm in a familiar way. Just then Ratz, along with a slender hooker and her black pimp joined the group from another direction. Suddenly in the midst of the group the white outline of huge Turtle began to appear. Sally was so surprised that she nearly fell over a bush as she tried to get closer.

The Spiderwoman turned to Xavier smiled and in a low voice she asked, "Should we ask your friend in the woods to join us?"

"No, I think he should stay where he is and then make his way back to his car, that will teach him a lesson about following orders, but your right he is my friend." Xavier said in an acerbic voice. "But it is good that he is acting as backup although he has a family and shouldn't be risking his life."

"Xavier it is not a man but a women that hides in the bushes. Could it be the 'Sally' you always think about."

"Sally!" Jesus H. Christ! What the hell are you doing here alone?" he said in said in a stage whisper as he walked towards the clump of shrubs where there was an extra shadow.

"Oh shit! Caught and he looks pissed. To bad I don't have Ring from Lord of The Rings! Should I make a run for it? Oh hell, I might as well face up to him, she thought as she stepped out of the bushes with as much dignity as she could muster. Then she crossed her arms and tapped her foot and managed to put a look of indignation on her face.

Xavier came storming up to where she was standing and when he got a good look at her he hesitated. Before him stood a tall woman dressed in black the butt of her handgun poking slightly out from underneath her hoodie. She was tall, she had a scratch on her cheek and some blonde tendrils were poking out of the hood with dried leaves clinging to them and she looked like a mighty Valkryie with her arms crossed and that look of disdain, by Gawd he had never, ever felt so horny in his entire life! He wanted to grab her and kiss her breathless before she could knee him in his nuts! Xavier heard a slight tittering in his head and the words "you loose." He flushed and blessed the dusk that none could see how red his face was and the lower part of his baggie hoodie that hid another condition as he stepped up and offered his hand to her.

Sally hesitated for a moment before she took his hand and found it warm and her hand fit so easily with his. She looked at him before she said, "You didn't think we were going to leave you alone, did you?"

There was silence for a brief moment as Xavier collected himself and then finally said, "Where is your partner in crime, what tree or bush is he lurking behind?"

"None, I pointed out to him that this was a real black bag op. and there would be no going to court. This was destruction nothing more, nothing less. He needed plausible deniability if things went wrong. I also pointed out to him that he has three boys and one on the way so in one way it was his fault."

Oh, how's that? Xavier asked.

"If his sparky the sperm wasn't so sparky he would be here too."

Xavier's grin said it all, his snicker was only heard by Sally. "I would like to kiss you right now but it will have to wait."

"Don't wait too long." Sally said quietly as they approached the waiting group.

Spiderwoman smiled "Sally? We must talk later. I'm glad we have warrior woman as backup. It is always good to have surprise on our side."

"Ok...kay so what now, what's the plan? Ratz demanded as he jumped from foot to foot and looked around nervously.

The Turtle looked at Ratz and shook his head, "If you don't keep your voice down everybody is going to know what's going on."

Ratz, chastened, stopped talking but continued to look around. Xavier hoped Ratz wouldn't spot Sally with those sharp eyes of his.

Everybody looked to Xavier and the Spiderwoman. Xavier spoke first, "Well, as you all know, there is a reason we are down by the river. You've told Leroy and Susie, right Ratz? Just nod Ratz. We don't know who is around and listening. So now everybody knows the plan?" They all murmured yes or nodded slightly; all except Sally who stayed in Xavier's shadow.

"Okay we meet in forty-five minutes by the fly-over Bridge part of which continued westbound as road while the other section, a small bridge carrying downtown traffic crosses the river. There are no path lights there. That will be when Susie gets tied up and I get handcuffed, in front, with the handcuff key in my hands. Right Ratz? Leroy, you and Ratz can strut along arguing about how much more money Susie can make, while Ratz pushes me along. Now if the SoulSlayer asks why I cam along so easily you know what to say, right Ratz, Leroy?"

Don't worry Xavier, we will both make sure Ratz sticks to the plan. Even though, the Spiderwoman and I are shielded from SoulSlayer we can still make it very uncomfortable for anyone who suddenly decides to switch side.

"Yes and I have a surprise as well." Xavier said and squeezed Sally's hand.

"I don' know'd why youse wud tink I trick ya, I jus' wan my place back! I's not second to nobody! Ya gots my oath!" Ratz said in a forceful, whisper then spit on the ground.

"I'm sorry Ratz, but we have to make sure." Spiderwoman said quietly while the outline of the Turtle patted him on the back, which

Ratz accepted for a little while before he shrugged it off.

"Turtles may be gay, but I ain't." Ratz sniffed and wiped his nose with a sleeve that looked like it had been used for that purpose many times before.

"Time to go. We want to get this party started by the time it's really dark."

They split and took four different ways to the fly-over. They all tried to avoid running into other people, any who might be some of SoulSlayer's soul-less minions or even police friends of Sally's. She knew it would be impossible to explain to any police officer just what she was up to.

When she walked along the sidewalk she walked in a casual manner that suggested she had somewhere to go. When she could, she worked her way towards the river, but that to had its disadvantages, because maybe there might be watchers hiding in the shadows of the woods. Finally, she reached her destination under the small Forth Street Bridge.

CHAPTER FORTY-SIX

"Gawd, I love the smell at the end of Operation." (a police tactical operation against major drug-dealers and gun-runners where only a small well armed tactical force was used after much planning, training and surveillance had been done). Both Xavier and Sally had been involved in some very high profile Operational plans where body-armour was the underwear of the day and everybody involved used balaclava's to disguise their identity while The Staff- Sergeants and Inspector dealt with the media. Sally took a deep smell of the night air, which seemed filled with adrenaline.

She had both Glocks which made a rather large sound when they were fired and that sound attracts police like flies to a corpse."

Sally reminded herself that the silencer cuts the distance you are accurate at so you definitely have to be closer to your target. Leighton left us some shotguns and ammo in a hiding place under the east side of that little bridge by the zoo.

Sally felt the adrenalin surging through her body. Neither saw the two shadows break away from the deep forest and follow her. She could hear the river flowing eastbound swiftly along the deep channel. In the distance she could hear the liquid roar.

Within five minutes she saw Ratz and pushing Xavier in front. Within a few minutes of that, what appeared like Leroy and Susie showed up. They stood in a group not ten feet from where Sally was hidden.

"Ok, time to get this show on the road Ratz shouted to be heard above the roaring of the water. Xavier was already hand-cuffed with the cuffs in front, while the Leroy, who was almost on the edge of looking like a black pimp, tied up the slender hooker, that she had seen earlier. The hooker with a brutal bruise on her face smiled up at the pimp. Sally saw the smile and thought to herself that's the smile a woman gives her lover not her pimp. Not only that, but she is a talented makeup artist, that's not a bruise. What the hell is going on here? Iwish I had more time to talk to Xavier before this all went down.

"We go this way." Ratz pointed south. Till we seed an old flashing liquor sign an some old houses tha'be where we meet him. He be waiting there,a spider in his nest, wit lots of little spiders. Leroy has Susie. Jack he like his women sc ared. Time ta go. Maybe dying time?" Ratz said with a little, nervous snickering, giggle escaped from the fear twisted smile on his face.

Xavier felt a sudden calm come over him as he started walking towards the SoulSlayer's lair. In his mind, his sense of time seemed to have stopped and would not begin again until this was over. He glanced to where the Spiderwoman had been, saw she was gone, and yet felt her warmth. Ratz gave him a push, just enough to look angry, but not enough to make him lose his balance. He looked to where Leroy was dragging Susie along and she caught his fleeting smile with a subtle nod. The Turtle had started to disappear into the shadow of the night but, Xavier could still feel his slow-low voice, "I am with you. this is not the end but the beginning of time; my time, your time. He was sure he saw Sally's face for just a nano second of time.

"Now it begins," Spider-woman whispered in his ear as he was brought to an abrupt stop.

Xavier didn't need words: he could tell by the miasma that had grown stronger as they had gotten closer. It was dark except for the flickering, puke green of the old neon sign in the window. The color turned the skin of Jack and his followers a greenish tinged light gray like the horror film he had watched one night when he couldn't sleep. What was the name? Oh yeah, Night of the living dead.

A sudden pain in his back brought Xavier out of his thoughts and zeroed in on what he had to do. He looked around saw he was surrounded by SoulSlayers acolytes. The SoulSlayer was reaching out for Susie, who had backed into Leroy and they both were surrounded.

Xavier did the only thing he could do, he yelled out, "Yeah fuck you, ya goof. I've seen your type before! Take out the woman first! Well if you're so fucking bad, why don't you try me. When you were in my jail you told me that you were going to take my soul. Well, I see how you have taken all the souls of these useless dopers."

You have probably have forgotten what a real man or woman's soul is like, you are so used to garbage."

The SoulSlayer screamed out in rage as he turned from Susie and Leroy to focus his attention on Xavier. Xavier knew it was time for him to be leaving.

He turned and started ramming his way through the followers. Behind him he could hear the SoulSlayer screaming as he started killing his own acolytes, who stood in his way, just to reach him. What he didn't see was that the SoulSlayer was so outraged that he started to morph into his real self. This so startled his self-described army of followers that they started to focusing on him, rather than Xavier. Xavier,who had been a pretty good quarter back in high-school ducked his head and dodged until he was outside the outer ring and continued zigzagging east toward the howling sound of the river. What he didn't know was Sally was running interference for him shooting those that tried to catch him and she was using a silencer to mask the shots. He could hear in the distance behind him screaming that seemed to be gaining on him. Xavier was working strictly on adrenalin at that point, but he kept going.

Behind him, everybody was still trying to get out of the melee and chaos. Turtle had tripped the SoulSlayer so that he had stumbled into some of his followers, which he immediately tore apart. That sight caused the rest who followed him and had some survival instinct left too ripped, away and as they did they felt like they had left a dark domain, granted they were still attached to drugs but they were free of the SoulSlayer's cruel, edge of death, hold on them.

They were trying every which way to flee. Trouble was, too many drugs and no soul had left them with practically no sense of what to do.

Leroy, who had brought a very large knife with him, cut Susie's bound hands and they made it through the through the chaos and they headed towards the river to see if they could help Xavier.

Ratz, as soon as he realized that the SoulSlayer was coming in his direction, dived out of Xavier's way and curled up in a little ball under followers. Once he figured the coast was clear, he got up and followed the direction of the screams at a discrete distance. He wanted to see Jack destroyed but he didn't want to be involved in any violence.

Xavier made it to the concrete weir, (a water control device that device that caused the water currants on the east side of it to spin in a washing machine fashion) commonly called the drowning-machine or washing machine. He tried to get his breath back as he listened to the rumbling yell get closer and closer.

Then he was there, the SoulSlayer, without his human guise. He stood nearly eight feet tall and was heavily muscled. His skin was a deep, blood red, the red that turned black in the full moon. His eyes were those of a wild boar and concentrated on Xavier. He had heavy horns growing out of his forehead and running down his back he had a ridge of what appeared to be heavy spiked bone that continued onto a tail that swished back and forth in anger. His balls were large and in his rage, which was all consuming, his penis stood out like a jouster's lance. His mouth though, was what drew Xavier's attention. It was open and all his sharp fangs were rounded away from the middle where there was a space where a purple, split tongue flicked in and out as he drew breath. His hands were big and clenched in huge fists.

"So you turn and run human. Ah well, a coward's soul, though somewhat bland is just as good, but not as filling.

"When 'The People ruled this land, I would be lucky to catch a true warrior and he would last the winter before I would have to hunt for more."

Xavier started to laugh as he looked up at the SoulSlayer, "Not too bright are you? I simply wanted you away from your lackeys. Well guess what? We whites rule here now (he hoped he wasn't pissing off those that listened).

"All you seem able to do is catch a few dopers; they can't be too filling to a big ox like you?" He could hear a deep rumble as he took a step closer to the weir. Xavier could hear a warning in his ear from Spiderwoman, which he disregarded.

"You think you're such a hot shot 'cause you come down to the east end where all the failures are and you think you're going to rule the world. Well it doesn't work that way." He took another small step and could feel water wetting his boots while the currant swirled slightly and he could feel the slight pull.

" We have had to deal with goofs like you and your so called plans to rule the world. You're hust not bright enough there, guy; although you are certainly ugly enough. I figure I can can take you in two minutes tops and then I guess I'll have your soul, won't I?"

A huge snarl filled the air as the SoulSlayer leaped at Xavier. While Xavier vaulted up and grabbed him around the chest and that's when time started to slow down and Xavier saw Spiderwoman and The Universal Turtle as they started to speak in unison:

All souls have purity when first they start out.
Love of the Creator is security but weakness in life causes doubt.
The worse the choices the worse the stain,
 deliberate choices to cause pain.
Those that destroy their brothers and sisters must themselves be destroyed.
The stain must be erased. The stain must be washed away.
Time has now come to wash Soul-Slayer away.

Then they were both swept into the drowning machine. The last words that anyone heard from the Soul Slayer was "No! No!" Xavier had managed to take a gasp of air but not even he was prepared for the current; he didn't know which way was up. He felt the Soul-Slayer trying to push him away and then the Soul-Slayer seemed to break apart in the swirling current.

It started to get dark and he felt weary, tired, so tired then there was a light. He would see Rachel again they would be together. He saw her slender, white hand and arm reaching out and he grabbed it and felt himself being lifted up into the light.

CHAPTER FORTY-SEVEN

I tol' ya he was afraid a water, didn' I? I tol' ya!" Ratz exclaimed as he capered around on the riverbank looking faintly like the twenty-first century version of Golum.

"Yes you told us ratz," Leroy said wearily as he and Susie sat on the riverbank. They were anxiously watching Sally and Turtle who were out on the weir doing there best to balance as they tried to pull Xavier out of the drowning machine.

Spiderwoman looked down at Ratz and studied him for a moment," Yes we couldn't have done without you, but don't you forget that it was Xavier who first discovered that SoulSlayer was having trouble holding his human shape because the souls he was feasting on were so frail, and in some cases dying. He saw that when the SoulSlayer became enraged he couldn't hold his shape. Everybody played a part in this and although your part was important we needed everyone."

Ratz toned down his one-man celebration and bowed to the Spiderwoman.

Leroy and stood up suddenly, "They have him! They've got him!" as Sally and Turtle dragged Xavier's lifeless body back to the riverbank and laid him gently on the shore.

Sally felt his for his pulse in his neck, "He hasn't got a pulse! She started CPR on him while turtle stood by. Time seemed to drag by like pulled taffy, and still they worked on him, while Spiderwoman stood over him chanting as she lifted her hands over him in an ancient People ritual. Finally she stood back and touched Sally to stop what she was doing.

"He must decide now whether he wants he wants to stay among us or continue on the road to death." She said as she watched the body before her. Xavier's face was white and his lips were tinted blue. He looked dead.

Sally knelt beside him. A gasping sob escaped her as she whispered to Xavier, "Come back to me, my love, come back." She dropped her head as tears ran down her face and one even touched his face. Suddenly he coughed and water dribbled from his month.

"Turn him on his side so the water can escape from his lungs! Quick!" Sally yelled as they all rolled him on his side and a large amount of water squirted out as he coughed some more.

"What the hell, Rachael, wait!" He muttered and then coughed some more. Leroy helped him sit up and Xavier put his head between his legs as his breathing became more regular, his color started to return and he became aware of his surrounding. "Where is Sally, I thought I saw her?"

Sally had heard his first words and slowly got up. There was a sad, weary slowness to her face and body. Spiderwoman saw her moving away from the group and moved quickly to her before love's pain scarred her forever.

"Sally stop! Listen to me," Spiderwoman said as she saw the sparkle of tears even in the quarter moon's light. "He loves you. Love has grown slowly within him as Rachael's has faded. But he made a choice. He was on the cusp of death's end. He could've chosen to stay with Rachael or come back to you.

"He chose you."

Sally gave her a tentative smile of hope, turned back to help Xavier just in time to hear him ask for her.

The Spiderwoman felt the Turtle beside her.

"Has the Soul-Slayer perished, I saw the cloud of moths above the water where he had become fully submersed. They were so tattered and frail. Did many make it back to those they were stolen from?"

"I helped as many as I could but some were just so frail that they just made it back into their body before the body died."

"Time for us to go before the sun comes up and too many more people see us. Xavier and Sally may have a lot of explaining to do as it is."

"I will say farewell to Xavier before we go," Spiderwoman said as she turned toward the dark silhouette that was still sitting on the ground.

She smiled down at Xavier and Sally. Then she looked to where

Ratz, Leroy and Susie stood.

"We must say our farewells now before the sun paints the clouds in the east. We have cleared your way as much as is possible so there should not be too many questions.

"I suggest that Ratz, Leroy and Susie be on their way, after Ratz gives Leroy five thousand dollars he was promised." Spiderwoman said with a smile at Ratz as he frowned.

"I never break a promise, Spiderwoman. Sure it wasn't Five hundred?"

The Spiderwoman gave Ratz a long look and Ratz turned red and nodded.

"K! K! You're right, it musta slipped my mind."

"As to you two, Leroy and Susie, this town is poison for you. Time for you both to take the money and build a life elsewhere."

"Farewell Xavier, my Familiar, but only for now. Our time will come again."

With that she and Turtle faded away taking the light of their being with them.

CPSIA information can be obtained
at www.ICGtesting.com
Printed in the USA
LVOW01s1437010216
473175LV00021B/896/P

9 780995 007208